I0599384

Winter Rain

Winter Rain

by

Dwight Cathcart

Adriana Books
Boston, Massachusetts
2018

Copyright (c) 2018 Dwight Cathcart
All rights reserved.
ISBN: 978-0-9764043-6-1

Adriana Books
publisher@adrianabooks.com
Boston, Massachusetts
2018

The scanning, uploading, and distribution of this book by the internet or by any other means without the permission of the publishers is illegal and punishable by law. Please purchase only authorized electronic editions, and do not participate in or encourage electronic piracy of copyrighted materials. Your support of the author's rights is appreciated.

Cover image: Hawes Street at Kilby Street, looking toward Congress Street
Boston, Massachusetts
August 18, 2016 at 8:42:02 PM
photographer: Dwight Cathcart

Author photo: Bill Chisholm

Printed from
WR_LULU_20250423.pdf
25355564_cover.pdf

Winter Rain

1

When he came up out of the ground, he hunched his shoulders and ran into the rain (it was all in his face) across the street to a bar.

"A double—." He looked at his watch. He sat on the edge of the stool, more standing than sitting, took two quick sips, looked down the long bar at the row of silent men and at the tv screen hanging from the ceiling showing the head of the President saying something (presidential proposals for dealing with national conditions), the moisture condensing on the inside of the plate glass windows. The drink went down through him; he felt his face flush. He put the glass to his lips again, tossed back his head and took the rest of it, then was out of there, across the street before the tension in him (the noise of the city, the static turned down) began to melt away and to make it possible for him to receive whatever message he was to receive from Amos.

Twenty minutes to get here, ten in the bar, five minutes to the hospital, half an hour with Amos. The gym. Then an evening alone with Michael. This was Alec's life: work, the subway, the hospital, the subway, the gym, the subway, the bar, home. Michael. Stephen. The gang. Amos, Arabella, Gaetano. He ran hard, head down in the rain, taking long jumps with each leg to avoid stepping into the middle of a puddle which concealed a pothole big enough to drown in. He was late forties, heavy set, had once been handsome (the streets had once been cared for). The decay of his looks gave him the aspect of someone permanently tired, of someone suffering from permanent grief, though he told his friends he wasn't and could be

1

found at two in the morning dancing his ass off. The decay which hit every other human being could be kept at bay by an act of will.

Under the awning, he ran past a man whose words ("Sir, can you give me a quarter?"), beginning as he approached him, faded away behind him like ozone after firecrackers, threw open the hospital doors, stepped inside and shook off. He stamped the floor hard, one foot after the other, leaving rain on the bright terrazzo. Upstairs, as he pushed open the door and said, "Amos?" he felt lightheaded from the drink, almost giddy. "Amos? It's me, Alec." Then he held his breath, aware, as a backdrop to this scene, of the black glass of the window, sparkling with the light of the bedside lamp reflected in the drops of rain.

Amos was covered to his neck in a clean, unwrinkled bedspread, his toes, knees, hip bones and shoulders making little sharp hills in the white cloth. Amos's head lay on the small pillow so that his mouth was open. Alec could hear, since he was holding his own breath, Amos's breath in his throat. Amos's flesh had been burned away by his disease, and what was left in the bed was the universal skeleton, hung with skin. This was the classic manifestation of death, the revelation of the skull under the skin, and there was nothing romantic about it, nothing particular (broken bones, loss of blood), nothing of the ego. Alec kissed Amos's forehead. His skin was hot and dry. "Amos?" It was a tentative call into a dark house.

He turned away, found a chair, pulled it up, sat down. "It's me. Alec." The only sound was Amos's breath in his throat. He felt the drink fully now, everywhere in his body. Now he felt alive after the hours at work, now here with Amos; now he could handle trauma. This is what he had run across the city for, through the rain, to be in this silent hospital room with Amos, who was dying, Alec's brain making direct contact with the energy around the sick man's body.

He put his hand on Amos's thigh, but nothing stirred. For the next 20 minutes, half an hour, the silent room was filled with noises, his own breath, which, though he heaved his chest, seemed now to be zephyr-like in comparison to the hot dry winds coming from Amos's throat, the rain hitting the window beginning to freeze, the honk and roar of traffic from four floors below, all the noise of a great city dying at night. Out the window, Alec could see, far below, far away, the expressway to the communities on the South Shore, the red lights of the cars in the close traffic leaving the city transcribing slow arcs against the black. Twice, he said, "Amos? It's me, Alec," moved his palm up and down Amos's thigh, felt the hot flesh through the sheet and spread.

There must be someone there if Amos awoke. Alec came every day after work, but his life pulled him, Michael pulled him. He stood up to go. Amos and he had closed bars together, had seen the sun come up red and hot through the window of a taxi home after an afterhours party. Alec had felt this man's cock against his throat. Now it was clear, for the bedspread had no wrinkles, that he had not moved since the nurse had covered him. Even running hard, Alec would not be able to keep up with this still figure, slipping away from him. Like the greatest events—the explosions of stars—and all spiritual discoveries, Amos's dying was happening in silence. Alec touched Amos's forehead with his fingers, leaned over and kissed him in his hair, and left. The great drama was gathering, but it wasn't going to start right now.

At first, he covered his head when he went back out into the icy rain, then he threw his head back and took it full in the face. It was not worth going back underground. He ran, his head up against the rain, two blocks down, one block over to the gym, through the wet streets flashing with the headlights and red brakelights of the cars whose tires sibilated on the wet pavement.

"Hey, Buddy. Got a quarter?" Hand out, eyes on Alec moist, pleading.

Alec ducked the rain, pulled change from his pocket, turned away and put the coins in the outstretched hand. The hand was dry, hard. Then he ran.

He was in the street alone again, the moving cars' lights shining off every wet surface.

Inside the gym, he pulled off his clothes in front of his locker, into his shorts and tee, into the weight room.

"Hiya—" He spoke to the men already there. Men nodded, "Hiya —," and returned to their weights. There were large windows, all black now, near the ceiling, equipment and mirrors around the walls underneath the windows, racks of dumbbells, lines of benches, pulleys, black chipped iron.

"Back today," he said and began the furious labor that consumed the next hour and a half. First bent-over rows, using a barbell with 150 lbs, bent-over dumbbell rows, with 75 lbs, cable rows, cable pulldowns, pullups in front, pullups in back, the military drill that convinced him he was alive and healthy and wasn't like Amos. As he worked, he and the other men sometimes made eye contact. They knew each other by their

3

bodies. They nodded, returned their attention to the weights. He performed 16 repetitions of each exercise in each set, 3 sets of repetitions, resting 60 seconds between sets, two minutes between exercises. His back and shoulder and upper arm muscles—trapezius, latissimus dorsi, spinal erector, deltoid, triceps and biceps—grew heavy and hot and tight as he worked. He re-introduced himself, part by part, to his body. His hair, which had been wet from the rain, now was wet with sweat. His breath came from deep in his lungs; his chest expanded for oxygen. The air in the weight room was muggy, acrid with the smell of bodies.

He found an unoccupied bench. He was lying on it, ready to lift the dumbbells.

"Alec—."

Gaetano.

"What'ya doin' later?"

Alec sat up. Shrugged. "Why?"

"Paradise?"

"Sure."

"How's Amos?"

"Dying."

"I knew that. What's happ'nin'?"

"Blind, lesions in the brain, 68-70 pounds—"

Gaetano stared at Alec, expressionless. Gaetano was ten years younger than Alec, somewhere in his late thirties. He was Italian, hairy, had a body that made him one of the stars of the early evening shift in the weight room——thick heavy pectoral muscles, big, clearly defined trapezius and deltoids, truly big arms.

"—you should go visit him."

"He wouldn't know me."

Alec put himself back on the bench, reached for the dumbbells. "No. He wouldn't."

As he lifted the dumbbells (fifty pounds each), sucking in a lungful of breath, he heard the sounds of the weight room, the clank of iron, the heavy thump of weights falling on the matting, the grunts, the occasional scream as a man pushed or pulled against a bar that was too heavy to lift.

"Tell him I asked about him." Alec had the door open in his hand; Gaetano had stopped him.

"Tell him yourself. It's only good if you say that yourself."

Winter Rain

"Ah—" Gaetano, this big hunky Italian stallion, was embarrassed. "I been busy."

Twenty yards down the hall, Alec stood at the bank of telephones. Gaetano, Amos, the beggars were like pots on a stove. He had one too many for the burners, and he shuffled them around. He had the phone to his ear, listening to the message:

"Look: I can't stand it any more. I'll go crazy if I don't get away. I'm coming into the city for some fun, and I want to do it with you. Let me take you to dinner, honey, someplace cool, hear? You choose it. I'll be at your place at eight?" Her voice had the cloudy, rich, tart quality of a margarita.

Alec checked his watch: seven. There was no way to reach her. She would already be on the road, the jumping wiper clearing the windshield for a moment, showing the black slick highway whose shiny surface reflected back blinding smears of red and white. Alec, who felt the important things seemed always to be postponed, pressed the button, dropped in the coin, punched the keys hard, fast: 8! 5! 9! 0! 8! 1! 5!, heard the soft sound of the ring in his apartment.

"Yo."

"Michael. There's a fuckup. Arabella is on her way in right now. She left a message on my machine—"

"Shit."

"She wants to go to dinner. Will you join us?"

Michael didn't answer. "That wasn't what I had in mind."

"Me neither. Will you?"

"Well, sure. Damn it. I wanted to talk."

"How are you?"

"How is Amos?"

"I'll tell you later."

"Wait. We have to talk. Do you have to work tomorrow?"

"If I want to eat."

"Let me put it another way. Do you have a job for tomorrow?"

"No."

"Good. We'll talk then."

Alec stood on the steps of the gym, turned his head into the rain and ran down the steps, down behind the museum, along the road at the edge of the fens, avoiding the puddles. He turned into the fens — there was ice under the water on the walkways—running from tree to tree, wet, cold, his breath coming heavy now and deep in his chest. During the summer, Alec ran on a loop around the fens; he had run these paths with Amos, the wind in their hair, until Amos got too sick a year ago. Sometimes Michael ran with him now. There was a spot over in a bend in the stream where a willow hung over the water; Alec came sometimes in good weather to play his flute, long lines of somber melody that he made up as he played.

Alec lived on the other side of the fens.

"You have ice in your hair." Michael's manner was ironic without a smile. Michael lived in Brookline, shared his apartment with a man who had answered an advertisement, and he had no allegiances of any kind.

Alec dropped his coat over the bike in the hall. He kicked off his boots. He pulled off his sweatshirt, shirt, tee shirt, his pants, until he was standing naked. "I'm lucky I'mot dead." He turned to Michael. "I'm home."

Michael, from the sofa in the living room, appraised Alec's body, as if it were for rent.

"Drink?"

"I've got one. Come in here, I want to talk."

Alec threw ice cubes in the glass and splashed in the whiskey. He was cold, wet, hungry. He raised the drink to his lips and swallowed, standing naked at the kitchen counter, aware of the number of things that must be thought about, tried to order them in his mind.

"Stephen called."

"What'd he say?"

"Just he'd called."

Alec went into the living room and stood at the chest, aware of Michael's eyes. Stephen lived with Alec, but he was twenty-one, and sometimes he went to his girl's place, or to a buddy's, and Alec didn't hear from him for a couple of days.

"Come sit down."

The tv was on without sound. The President's head was talking (presidential proposals for dealing with national, international contingencies). He punched the buttons and listened to the messages.

"Mr. Argento, I thought you'd like to know—." Alec was making a list in his head, Arabella, Stephen, this new one. "—Amos has come out of it and talked. He's sleeping now. He asked for you. He will be discharged tomorrow at eleven. Could you come by?"

"Holy shit!"

Another click.

"Mr. Argento, this is Karen at the Skill Bureau. Would you call when you get in?" The job: he would have to have a job. He wrote down on the list he was making in his head: Get a job.

Another click.

"Alec, this is your father. Would you call me? I have stupendous news." Any news at all from Alec's father was stupendous. He was old enough (82) to be dead and had done nothing during his lifetime to make anyone wish that it would be prolonged.

Alec put the papers chronicling the ongoing decay (headlines: "War Imminent," "Recession Deepens," "Blue Cross/Blue Shield Lays Off 100," "State Closes Home for Mentally Retarded") on the coffee table and sat down on the sofa next to Michael, his arm along Michael's shoulders. He saw the President's head, moral, earnest, fastidious, self-excusing. "OK. What's up?"

"They're discharging Amos—"

"I heard."

"What'll we do?"

"Cope—"

Michael appraised him. "Arabella's coming. Get some clothes on. You're wet. You'll scare her. I want to talk."

Alec grinned. "Not Arabella. Get me a drink. Then we'll talk."

When Michael came back, Alec threw his leg along Michael's lap. He rested his head back against the arm of the sofa and closed his eyes.

"Are you going to call that woman, or not? Your father wants you to call him. He has stupendous news."

"I thought you wanted to talk." He watched the tv screen, the President's earnest head speaking of the New World Order.

Alec reached around behind him and found the phone. He left a message at the temp agency that he wanted whatever job she had for him in the morning. "Call me at seven." He looked at Michael. "That OK?"

"Will you really take anything she has?"

"No."

"You're arrogant."

"I do what pleases me." Alec stared into the drink. "What's he saying?"

"Who?"

"Him." He nodded at the tv screen.

"We're going to war at noon tomorrow if they don't give us what we want."

"How long has this been going on?"

"Since noon today. Give him what he wants. Don't you want to know what his stupendous news is?"

7

Alec stood up and went toward the door.

"Alec, come back. I want to talk."

Alec was aware that his rump was churning as he left the room. He yelled back at Michael. "Get some cheese and stuff. I'm hungry."

"Your father!" A few minutes later, Michael was sitting on the john watching Alec shower. "I've got some news."

Alec soaped himself and didn't seem to pay attention. In the continuous replacement of one thing by another, each successive thing presented for Alec's attention, there was a quality of transience. Nothing arrived and stayed. If his life had been a novel, Alec considered the question how he might have described what it was about. Each succeeding chapter introduced a new principal theme.

"It's hard."

Alec turned to Michael. "Get me a drink, would you? Then tell me about it."

"You drink too much. You can be a shit." Michael expected that Alec would hurt him. When he came back, he sat down on the john again. The little room was hot and steamy.

"So talk." Alec didn't want to hear. He wanted to get drunk, have sex, go to eat, dance.

"I've been to the doctor."

Alec spoke with only a barely perceptible pause. "Well?"

"I'm positive."

At that moment, so, *this is the moment*, the bell rang, and Michael left to answer it, left Alec thinking, *this is the moment*. Alec heard Michael shouting into the speaker. This was what he didn't want to hear, that the lottery had thrown up their number. The odds of being struck by lightning.

"Hey! Don't leave me! Come back!"

He got out of the shower, wrapped himself in a towel and was in the hall going toward his room, toward Michael. He was about to say, Why did you tell me now? when Michael opened the door, and there was Arabella.

"Beautiful!" She looked him up and down.

The fact that Michael was positive was now like a small pebble in his mouth. While he could walk and talk and think and grin, those things had to be done around the small hard slick round thing in his mouth that he could neither spit out nor swallow.

"You've always known I only married your brother because I wanted your body!" She threw her arms around him (he dropped his towel and returned her hug) and kissed him. She slapped him on his butt. "Get some clothes on, we're going out to party. If we're not going to do that—" She turned away from him, from his pebble! toward the living room, searching already in her bag for her cigarettes. "—could I use your bedroom for a minute? I want to kill myself. Alec. Your brother is a monster. Michael, honey—" She turned around, searching as if Michael were small and the hall were immense. "—get me a drink, would you dear?"

"Michael, come in here for a minute." But Michael went to get Arabella's drink.

Alec went to his room with his drink and his pebble to dress. He had heard the words often enough. Everyone he knew had heard the words, on the street, in bars, in a letter. At first, it was from men, or about men, he barely knew. Then it was men he knew only by sight. Do you remember that man at Charlie's that Christmas? The dragon tattoo? Him. Then it was men he knew well, had known for years, had slept with or worked with. It was possible to forget all the men who had been infected for years and never developed symptoms and to remember only the men who wasted away, lost flesh, turned gaunt, went blind, lost their minds and died. It was easy to think of Michael already dead.

They were in the living room. Alec stood behind Michael's chair. "Life is hell." She lit a cigarette, crossed her long beautiful legs at the knee, tucked them back under her, looked around her. "Why do I feel you've just moved in?" She took in the whole room—the posters, photographs, stacks of books, dumbbells.

"It's the books still in boxes."

"How long has it been?"

"He's been here six years."

"Alec. For God's sake. When are you going to admit you're going to be here for a while!"

"He doesn't like to commit." Alec looked down on his skull. When Michael was dead, there would be spaces in his life whose size he could not calculate.

She leaned her head back. "I couldn't have stood it another minute. Your brother's home, drunk, and he's vicious. He hit me last night. Can I spend the night with you! I want to laugh. You're allowed to laugh at me. Your brother's a monster, and for some reason I want to kill myself. Would one of you tell me to kill him?" She surveyed the room, including the silent tv set with the head of the President. "And now we have a war on our hands." She lifted her glass. "To war!" She turned to the two men. Alec was knead ing

9

Michael's shoulder. "What's the matter with you two? The gloom is so thick here I want to turn on the light." She looked from Alec to Michael and back. "What's up?" Then, "Have you heard from your father?"

Arabella had been married to Alec's brother, Horace, for 17 years. Two or three times a year she called, as today, and came into the city from the suburbs to spend an evening with Alec. "I'm an actress in a drama. This is like being able to have a cigarette in the wings before I go back on sta ge." Sitting in dark smoky bars in the Back Bay, late at night, she had told them the story of her marriage.

Now she looked back and forth at the two men and waited. She had known Michael almost as long as Alec had known him. "I'm not a baby, guys."

Michael took a sip of his drink and put it on the floor beside him, his anger showing in the squint of his eyes. "I wanted to talk to Alec before you came. He was an asshole, Arabella —"

Alec felt this scene develop from a distance. He left Michael and sat on the other end of the sofa from Arabella.

"It must run in his family."

Someday he would visit Michael in the hospital, slide his hand along his hot thigh, saying, Michael, *it's me, Alec.* "Michael, don't do this—"

"What did you want to talk to him about? Do it now. Don't mind me." She picked up her drink. "I'll go in the bedroom —" She searched for her purse.

"I'm positive. I just told him. You don't need to go anywhere."

"Oh, Michael, that's devastating!" The rush of emotion out of her, unforced, untempered, raised envy in Alec. "What a blow! What a horrible blow." She reached out, her fingers open, inviting. Michael responded, reaching toward her. Just at the tips of their fingers, they almost touched across the open space between them. "What did Alec say?"

"He hasn't said anything, yet."

"Nothing!" She turned on Alec, hitting his shoulder with her fist. "You pig! Say something!"

"What's there to say? I need a drink."

"Great. Just great. A drink he needs!"

"You gang up on me. I don't know what to say. I hate it." When Alec came back, he stood behind Michael's chair, kneading his shoulders. "I love you."

Michael clenched his teeth.

"I'm sorry you're positive."

There were tears in Michael's eyes.

"I'm sorry I was a shit" Alec searched for words, what should he say? what feel? and stammered, Arabella watching. "How do you feel?" It seemed pointless, weak, silly.

Michael laughed, tears wet on his face. "I feel fine."

"Fine!" Arabella recrossed her legs. She covered her eyes. "Men!"

"No, truly, I feel fine."

Then they talked, these three friends, about Michael's health, what had made him go to the doctor —"Do you have symptoms?"— how long he thought he had been infected. After a while, they moved from their chairs to the sofa, with Alec on one end, his back against the arm, Michael between his legs, his back against Alec's chest, and Arabella at the other end, their legs and fingers entwined. The sympathy among them softened the hurt they felt and the corrosive sense of their failures. As they talked, their eyes rested occasionally on the picture on the silent tv screen, where men's and women's heads, talking, were substituted for the President's head, talking, and for pictures of the troops dug into trenches in a barren, flat country who would fight the impending war.

Eventually, the phone rang. Alec reached behind him. It was Stephen.

The young man's voice was rich, low, and tentative: "Dad?" He was a young version of Alec's own father.

Alec told him he had gotten his message. "How are you?" Michael and Arabella watched him.

Stephen was "fine."

"What's up?"

"Who's there, Dad?"

"Your aunt Arabella. And Michael. We're going out to eat shortly."

Alec walked his way through the conversation, pulling his attention away from Horace and Arabella, from silent and still Amos, from Michael (the enemy sat on his pillow, waiting for him to go to sleep), waiting for its point to be revealed. Often, with Stephen, it was difficult to tell. In that way he was like Alec's father, assuming you knew what was going on and then getting angry when you didn't. Stephen worked in the city as a bike messenger.

"Have you heard from Granddad?"

"No. What's happening?"

"He has stupendous news."

"So I've heard—"

Stephen laughed. "He's gotten married, Dad."

Alec had heard this before. "He should have told us he'd died."

"So you're happy to have a new mom, Dad?"

"Happy to see Medusa."

Stephen laughed. He asked his father to call him back "— when —" The pause was a symptom of the failure. "—when you are by yourself."

"Sure." Stephen needed privacy to talk. It would be of some catastrophe.

"Goodnight, Dad."

"Wait—" He didn't want the connection to be broken. "—How are you?" Tell me.

"I'm fine. Call me tomorrow night, OK?" Then the click.

I don't know where you are. He told them what Stephen had said.

Arabella pointed to the bedroom. "Go in there and call him back. Talk to that boy."

"I don't know where he is. He said, 'Call me tomorrow,' which must mean he isn't coming back here tonight, but he didn't say where he was going to be."

"His girl's?"

"I don't know which one he's going with now—" Stephen would call back tomorrow. Tomorrow he would get off work, visit Amos, lift (chest, legs), come home, eat, play the flute. When things were quiet, he would find Stephen and they would talk. He would call his father, 82 and newly married.

"I am not worried about myself. It's us, I'm worried about. What is this going to do to us?"

Arabella held Michael's hand.

Alec listened, thinking of the mechanics of sex. Semen was a lotion, and with their fingers they spread it liberally over belly and chest.

"It will change things. Alec won't want to have sex with me anymore. After a while, he'll decide he wants someone safe to have sex with. It is the everyday undertaking of risk. A risk you are willing to undertake for a day becomes impossible if you have to undertake it every day. I'll get sick, and he won't want to have a sick lover. I don't know."

Arabella held her eyes steady on his face and lips as he talked.

"He won't want to have to deal with all the shit you have to deal with."

Michael was nestled down between Alec's knees, Alec's arms around him. As he talked, he rested his head back in the crook of Alec's shoulder. "Maybe I'll come to hate him." Arabella rubbed his hand as he talked.

Alec interrupted. "You're assuming I'm negative. I'm positive too." It was probable, and, under the circumstances, even something to be desired.

So far these were just words. While it seemed huge, the dimensions of what they faced were unclear, and there was no way to experience beforehand how it would feel.

"Do you have insurance?"

Michael nodded.

"What does your doctor say?"

"Further tests. T-cell count. Next week."

She turned to him. "Will you see a doctor, Alec?"

Eventually, after nine, they got up, put down their empty glasses, left the apartment, going down the long hall past the piles of plastic sacks of garbage left out by other tenants, out into the rain and a cab downtown to Chinatown for dinner.

"We're not driving?"

"A cab is better in the rain."

"Alec wakes up the next morning and has to ask, What happened to the car!"

It was an odd sensation, which he had had often in the last ten years, of being somewhere late at night, a bar, a disco, checking out his senses, feeling the music, seeing the smoke in the air, touching Michael's arm, thinking, I know everything that is happening, the sweating crowd of men pulsing up and down to the music reflected through the smoke in the hard bright distorting mirrors, their bodies smooth with sweat shining in the light, the lasers a giant bright spider's web above their heads, knowing that tomorrow morning he would know nothing of any of this.

The cab pulled out into traffic, its fogged windows lighting up with smeared lights, red, green, orange, steady or flashing. They knew where they were because they were familiar with the city and sensed where they were, but they couldn't see where they were going.

"Stephen says Dad's married."

"The old goat—"

"That's his stupendous news."

13

"Well, I'm not stupefied. How many is this, Alec, three? four?"
"Fourth. There was Mother, Helena, Jennette, and this one."
"What's her name?"
"Bernice."
"Old fool. Alec's whole family is bizarre, Michael. They create their own reality." Michael was in the center, cradled against Alec's chest, Arabella next to the window, holding Michael's hand, the lurid lights transforming the interior of the car. "They never notice a crisis until it's too late. Then they blame it on somebody else." She talked, celebrating her powers of observation by gesticulating with long, manicured fingers, her rings flashing in the odd light, the cigarette she held between two fingers a baton by which she orchestrated her words. She turned to Alec and Michael. "When is the bombing supposed to start? They haven't stopped talking about it since noon today. It's supposed to start tomorrow. Armageddon, brought into your home live, as Armageddon is supposed to be, so there's no escaping it! Do you know Horace is in trouble?" She watched as they registered surprise. "Last week. Auditors visited his office. I don't know what happened. Before it was over, he hired a lawyer!" She stared into a luminous chrome yellow window. "Oh, do let's have fun! He comes home, Alec, disappointed and angry, and suddenly I am in a fight with him—" She put out her hand again on Michael's knee. "—a real fight. He hit me last night. What makes him think hitting me is going to make him feel better?"

"Horace is a bastard."

Alec held onto Michael, his fingers gripping Michael's chest.

"How is Amos? You haven't said."

How is Stephen? He wouldn't say. Alec's eyes, prevented from seeing outside, focussed on the cabbie's license picture, indistinguishable from the picture of a criminal. Stephen and he had lived together since Stephen was 14. They had not learned how to use the phone, use this electronic instrument as a means of being close to one another, and when they were together, while they said the right things—*How are you? I love you*—they were prevented from speaking openly with one another. The failure embarrassed both men. It was as if they couldn't speak for fear of admitting to failures far worse than the inability to speak.

"Apparently he's survived this one. If the doctors let him go home, kick him out, tomorrow morning there's no place for him to go. He has no money left. Three weeks ago when we took him to the hospital, we put his things in storage and closed his apartment. It's

14

been rented again. He still owes his landlord for two months' rent. I
don't know what he is going to do. What we're going to do."

"He has no money and no family—"

"The hospital won't keep him—"

"He's not dying yet, so the hospice is out —"

"A friend has to take him in—"

"—or else he is on the street—"

Later, in the restaurant (dim, candles in brass sticks, white linen,
smiling Maitre d', rich, deep vermilion carpet everywhere underfoot),
Arabella and Michael sat on one side of a booth, Alec on the other.
Waiters went quickly back and forth with a minimum of gesture.
Music played everywhere on a hidden and powerful sound system.

"Of course that won't happen. Some one of us will do something.
Amos has too many friends to die on the street."

She lit a cigarette. "There are people like him who have no
friends."

"Any of us could end up on the street. All it takes is one big
illness and the loss of a job." Michael looked from Arabella to Alec
and back. "There's nothing to separate me from those people except
that I have my health right now and a job."

The waiter, smiling, solicitous, brought their drinks and took their
orders. The alcohol had settled in on Alec. The feelings which had
been sharp, harsh, even choppy, earlier had smoothed out, had
become more mellow, deeper, even more pleasurable. The grief
caused by Amos's illness had become something to savor. Alec looked
across at Michael, who, at thirty-eight had lost none of the beauty of
his twenties, whose face, in the golden light of the candle, showed an
absolute delight in himself and in his life. Everything beyond his
golden head fell, deep red, into shadows. He was talking, charming
Arabella with a funny story. He was something to love, and grief
could be postponed. Alec tongued his pebble.

"Oh, but I've got another. There's a friend of ours —" Michael
nodded across the table at Alec. "—we've known for years.
Southern, soft voice, large eyes, always looking at you from the side,
as if mocking you or inviting you to something, you never knew. He
was small, and when Alec and I met him, he was always in jeans and
a white tee shirt, stripped down, plain. I asked him one night what he
did. He grinned. Seems he got dressed up—"

Arabella's eyes played over Michael's face as he talked (he used
his hands), nodding, her eyes widening or narrowing with surprise or
disapproval, a half-smile playing around her lips.

15

"—in a dress, went down to a couple of bars in the combat zone. Did I tell you he had shoulder-length golden brown hair which hung down in big curls?"

Arabella frowned, shook her head.

"This was all four years ago. Sometime one of us would say, 'Wonder what's happened to Sandy!' But nobody had seen him, and during those years when we weren't seeing him, we were thinking about Sandy, his long loose curls, tight dress, spike heels, and a cigarette—"

Alec, laughing, because he knew what was coming, put his drink down and leaned across the table. "Come on, tell her!"

"What?" She leaned back in her seat, away from Michael. "What are you two boys telling me?"

"Tell her, Alec." Michael leaned back in the booth against the red leather cushion to listen, his job done. "Tell her."

"I saw Sandy three weeks ago—"

"Wait." She wasn't laughing. "Is this an unhappy story? I don't want to hear it if it's unhappy. If he's not OK, don't go any further—"

"I didn't recognize him! We were on the street. He was wearing a suit, and there was something different—"

"This better not be sad—"

"He'd gotten fat. Tragic, Arabella. I couldn't forewarn you. Lost all his looks. Looked forty. I said, 'What're ya doin' with ya'self nowadays, Sandy m'boy—'"

Michael was laughing, helplessly.

"You boys—"

Alec leaned his head back against the cushion, closed his eyes. "He's become a stockbroker!"

"A stockbroker!" She hit Michael's arm with her fist.

"He's a stockbroker! That's what he does!"

"You're lying! You made all this up!"

"Swear to God. He wears a suit, has gotten fat, cut his hair, and sells fucking stocks! The most successful, the most beautiful transvestite prostitute north of the East River! It is, Arabella—" Here he reached across the table to touch her arm. "—a very sad story."

"I could kill you."

Michael laughed till tears ran down his cheeks.

Suddenly Alec wasn't laughing. "The light had gone out of his eyes."

"I hate that story."

Winter Rain

They ate like that, telling stories, three friends, laughing, while they ate their clams with black bean sauce, Lung Har Guy Poo Lo Mein, Fu Yung Three Treasure, hearing the soft hum and clatter of a large restaurant around them.

"You have no idea what it's like, living with Horace. I never know what he is going to be when he comes home. He can be a monster, screaming at me over anything I do, or he can be perfectly docile, absent even, just not there, ignoring everything in the house around him. The way he looks at me suggests I am responsible for everything that makes him angry. He hates me. When we have sex, it's like being raped. And your father, Alec, thinks I'm a bitch. He worships him. What is it I am causing? I can't figure it out. He's angry, but he won't tell me what he is angry at. I get angry. I told him last night he has no real feelings except whatever you feel when you experience triumph or defeat. He likes ordering me around. He likes it that he makes so much money, which gives him power. He can say, *No*, and close the checkbook. Your whole family is like that. Your father! That poor woman! They use money as a weapon—"

Money. At a table near them, a couple stood up to go. The man helped her into her coat, a full-length black mink, and for a second, she settled it on her shoulders until it was comfortable. She smiled at him; he put his hand on her back below her neck, and she looked at him affectionately. His fingers were lost in the glossy fur.

Alec watched their backs as they left, this elegant couple in their expensive clothes, her long black mink swaying gently from side to side as she walked.

"I love you, Michael." He leaned across the table toward Michael. "I love you now, and I will love you always, and I will never change."

Michael and Arabella were startled.

"Hey, what's with you!"

Arabella extended her hand across the table. "Are you all right?"

"No! No! I am not all right! I am angry as hell! And no matter what happens—" He choked. "—everything happens. Everything's changing."

"Calm down."

"I won't stop loving you!" He was shouting. Alec stood up, and his chair fell over behind him.

"Alec!"

Arabella was rising. At the same time the Maitre d', smiling, restrained, elegant, impervious as polished steel, could be seen

17

moving among the guests toward their table, seeming almost to come out of a wall behind him covered with crimson velvet and a huge golden dragon, mouth open and breathing fire, leaping into your face.

"Oh forget him, Michael, look after Alec."

"Sir, can I help you?" The menacing smile.

"No! You can't help me!"

Then the rain, which had turned to sleet, and another cab. "I don't know what to say to him. I search and search for words —"

"Are you worried about being positive your self?" Arabella, reaching across Michael, touched his forearm, but he searched the fogged red window, didn't hear, strung the hot words together on his tongue.

"—I want a drink. The problem is not my words. I think of whole books to say to him. I have no trouble telling him about poverty, about the origins of American intervention in the Middle East, how the Constitutional Convention defined some of us as two-thirds human, the effect of divorce on the mind. But everything is blocked inside me, waiting for him to speak, and the only words which would free me, he doesn't say—"

"What words?"

What words! "I forgive you!"

"He forgives you, Alec." She said this in the flat, matter-of-fact tone of someone saying, *It's too late to bet*.

In the unhindered fall through the cold air of Alec's last five years, out of the comfortable thick pieties of the middle-class suburban world, the voice which he heard most distinctly was his son's saying, *Dad*. It had come down to him like a voice in a dream, echoing from everywhere all around him, and while the voices of Stephen's mother and of Alec's father had become indistinct, blurry and difficult to decipher even if they could be heard, Stephen's voice pulled him back, made him strain to hear, fight for understanding. It carried with it messages, values, meanings which seemed important even while everything else had become inhuman, electronic, thin, falsely, hollowly amplified, like a voice from a television set. It was a younger version of his father's voice, before cigarettes and despair had done their distortions. The voice carried hope, they could always reestablish something, couldn't they? and despair, if they didn't, or couldn't, lost this opportunity, something irreplaceable would be lost forever.

"I should have called him back." I should not have gotten drunk when she was dying.

"Why didn't you? I told you to."

"Alec is afraid of failing."

Arabella wiped the window and looked out. They were passing under a highway. There against the concrete pilings was a shadowy group, five or six people in dark blankets (they appeared from this distance to be draped like togas) staring into the bright lights. The vision lasted only a second as the cab tore on down the Avenue. They had stood motionless, sepulchral, rising up out of the mist and sinking back down into it. Sometimes Alec's mother appeared to him, a face looking out of a subway train window, gliding fast through a station, gone before she was recognized, leaving an afterimage which lingered like the taste of milk gone sour.

The rain made everything surreal.

Then they were inside, enveloped by the music, shaking the water from them, shivering against the cold now they were in the warmth.

Arabella shouted something in Alec's ear.

"I can't hear you."

"I want a drink!"

"So do I."

He made his way to the bar through the crowd of men. How had he and Michael had sex? What had they exchanged? He was positive also. Years of having sex together would have done it. Michael, infected, passed it on to him. He, infected, had given it to Michael. They had both been infected by other people before they met. Memory was like car headlights, sweeping a landscape, bringing this object, that tableau, into brilliant light for a moment, allowing it to fade, unable to illuminate at all whole scenes, whole plots and subplots, characters and walk-ons.

"Why didn't I marry you?" Arabella took her drink, put her arm around his neck, touching the back of his neck with the back of her hand. "You're nicer than your brother. He has ambition."

He kissed her. "I'm already taken, beautiful. Besides —" He smiled. "—I have ambition."

"Oh don't. Ambition corrupts people."

They stood on the edge of the dance floor and watched the men who were wet with perspiration, their faces flushed with exertion as they danced, lasers shooting hard sharp beams of light across the room above their heads, ricocheting off the mirrors until the space above their heads was a cat's cradle of sharp light.

19

Winter Rain

All evening long, Michael had drifted away, borne on his thoughts, only to come back. Now the three of them went out onto the dance floor. They drifted away into their own thoughts, occasionally making eye contact and smiling, touching finger to finger, sliding a hand down a moist back, crinkling their noses at one another, laughing, exchanging something before they drifted away into solitude.

They had another round of drinks. Michael bought this time, and then another which Arabella bought. The alcohol smoothed everything out, plowed through the rocky terrain of their emotions and turned up smooth dark soil. At one point, taking a break, her hand in the crook of Michael's arm, Arabella told them about life in the suburbs. "People wear yellow ribbons tied in bows to suggest their devotion to the soldiers. They are happy about the war." She laughed. "They hate that dictator almost as much as they hate taxes. I don't know how it happened that I ended up there. What am I doing —" She put her hand on Alec's arm. "—living in a place where people think they're ok? But I don't care, finally. I used to care. I don't now. I don't know where these people come from—" She was staring into the mass of men dancing but she was not seeing. "—that the poll takers talk to. 78%! 83%! 91%! 91% of Americans interviewed approved. Of what? In a healthy country, you couldn't get 91% of the citizens to agree on suffering."

Michael had moved to Alec's side while Arabella talked, his fingers searching for Alec's. Alec kissed him.

"Get me a drink, would you?"

"Are you OK?" Alec ran his hand down Michael's spine. "How do you feel?"

"I feel fine. I don't want you to start being solicitous. It doesn't suit you. Or me."

"We have no racial memory. We are selective in what we put down, and we color it any way we want. We've forgotten—"

Alec, going to the bar and hearing Arabella's voice receding in the din, wondered if he were drunk yet. He felt in absolute control of his faculties. Everything was pin-prick sharp, the magenta lights, the dark red lasers, the yellow neon over the bar, and the hard breathtaking music throbbing from all over the club.

"I don't know what this means. The virus can stay dormant for ten years. The time you're symptomatic keeps getting longer. Some people have been positive for ten years and still are not symptomatic. Nobody knows. A new level of uncertainty, an unknown factor, to

live with. I can do that. Nobody knows when he is going to die. I
can accept not knowing. I don't want you and Alec—" Alec had
walked up just as Michael began. "—to start acting as if I were
condemned to something. I'm thirty-eight. I don't know when I was
infected. Maybe just yesterday—" He looked at the dance floor, not
at Alec. "—and if that's the case, I've got ten years before a symptom
appears. Forty-eight. That's not too young to die. Medicine gets
better all the time. A fatal disease is turning into a chronic disease. I
may die of heart failure at 73—" He turned to Alec, put his hand
behind Alec's neck and pulled him toward him. "Kiss me."

"Hi, guys." Alec turned from Michael to face Gaetano.
Gaetano moved to Arabella's side. "You're way ahead of me."
"Then catch up."
He showed them his drink, raising it up in front of his eyes,
smiling. Arabella put her hand on Gaetano's arm. "Let's dance."

Alec watched them on the floor. Conversation proceeded in fits
and starts, under or over the music, drowned out in the middle of a
sentence, suddenly at the level of a shout in a momentarily quiet
club. Much of their friendship had been played out here at the
Paradise, where much of the social life of the community of which
they were a part took place.

Now Michael said, "How do you feel?"
"I want to get very drunk."
"I think you are."
Alec frowned. "Not yet. Not yet. About what?"
"About me?"
"You?"
Michael nodded, staring out into the dancers, his arms crossed on
his chest. "About me."

"The same as always. Different now. I love you. I'm going to be
there for you." They saw Arabella and Gaetano on the dance floor,
their bodies thrusting at each other to the music. "That's a promise."

Then Michael and Alec were on the danc e floor too, thrusting
their bodies at each other, working up a sweat, barely aware of all the
other wet bodies around them. Alec's eyes searched for himself in
the mass of men in the mirrors but couldn't find himself.

No matter what happened, Alec would not abandon Michael.
Neither would he throw him out of his bed or his life, and while he
danced, the alcohol settling down over him like a hot late summer
afternoon until he could not differentiate any of his senses, he

21

thought of all the ways he would be "there" for Michael, when there was a need.

He thought, too, of Arabella, and of Horace. He would have to talk to Horace. Amos lay in the hospital, sleeping, and Stephen now lay sleeping—somewhere in the city. He would call him tomorrow night, when he found out where he was. And he would have to call his father. Congratulate the old shit. Self-centered selfish egotistical bastard. Rich bastard.

They danced. Finally, it was like going to sleep. The heavy pulse of the music, which surrounded them like sand in a desert storm, the inability to speak and be heard, the deadening effect of the alcohol, the rhythmic movement of his body and of the six hundred other bodies in the hot room, the random piercing lasers in the web above their heads, all these brought to an end the speculations, even the feelings, of the long evening. He gave himself up to it, closed his eyes, and danced.

Later, when he and Michael were in bed (Arabella was on the sleepsofa in the living room with Gaetano), they fumbled with each other, brought each other to erection and climax, sought with confused, uncomprehending fingers to contain the semen, failed, gave up in a cascade of choked, uneasy laughter and finally went to sleep, facing one another, arms around each other, in a d eep, troubled, dreamless stupor.

2

Alec, who woke up at eight thinking of Michael being positive, had to turn to the more immediate question of what to do with Amos after he was discharged in three hours. Sudden transformations like these were characteristic of the disease and led to anxiety, frustration and uncertainty in those who were affected by it.

Among their friends, Alec chose the bar or the restaurant, decided the time, said, "Let's go home." His mind was always racing fast, what has to be done? He gathered people around him, and he, always, had pursued the other man. He would have laughed if it had been Michael who had first come across the bar to him and said, "I think you're hot," the order of things being so reversed. It was in the natural order therefore that Amos's friends let Alec go to the hospital this morning and take the lead in finding Amos a place to die.

Outside, it was still raining, but even colder than the night before, and the tears in Alec's eyes, caused by the cold, ran down his cheeks. At the hospital Alec, his mind working fast (the discharge papers, final consultation with nurse and doctor, Amos's personal things, the flower vase that belonged to Michael), made arrangements for a wheelchair and a taxi, then called Michael at work to tell him how things were falling out. He had a handful of dimes, and between calls to Amos's friends, his last lover Wayne and his best friend from work, Gus, hearing the dial tone and the soft ringing, waiting for an answer, squeegeeing the water in his shoes, his eyes on nurses and doctors hurrying down the hall, Alec calculated his money. He had enough in his pocket to get through Friday (the taxi would reduce that). Today was Wednesday. If he worked tomorrow and Friday, he would have enough to get to next Friday. This would not get him enough to pay rent, and if he were working, someone must be found to stay with Amos, if Amos were to stay. Margaret could help. Food would cost more with him there. There were also the medications, and Alec knew nothing about those and had to remember to ask. He wrote down in his datebook: *weekly cost of medications.* He had called the temp agency and told them he couldn't work today.

He would bring Amos home with him (there was nowhere else), get him settled in the bed, then he would think about the rest of it—the money, someone to stay with Amos while Alec was working, his headache, how long all this was to last—while Amos slept. Alec would have a drink, dissolve the sharp rocks in his head, savor the pebble under his tongue. He would call Stephen to find out what he wanted. And his father. The newspapers and all the television channels said the United States was to begin bombing Iraq at noon. First, the taxi.

Amos's head lolled back against the back of the wheelchair, his eyes half open. There was no recognition when they passed over Alec. The movement of the chair down the long corridors of the hospital caused his body to lurch, and Alec slowed their progress to a stroll. He had to lift Amos into the cab under the awning, which protected them and a beggar from the rain. He was as light as an adolescent, this forty-year old man who used to be a hunk. Amos settled back against the door as if he were descending into a bed for a sleep after a long day. Rain made the windows translucent, and on the journey through the city streets Alec held Amos's fingers (dry, without response) in his hand. In front of his apartment, he went around the car, leaned over and eased Amos from the seat, one arm under his legs, the other around his back, his hand holding Amos's head against his neck, into the wheelchair for the quick trip through the rain into the building. The driver turned around and watched.

Sitting on his sofa, rain on the window, the telephone by his hand, a piece of paper on his lap on which he had written columns of figures—IN OUT—his money and where it was going, a drink partly consumed sitting on the cushion beside him, the television showing the first silent pictures of the bombing in the middle of the night on the other side of the globe, Amos asleep in the bedroom, Alec was baffled when the phone rang, and he heard his father say, "You're going to be delighted to hear my news."

His voice, gravelly and shaky, was suburban upperclass. He didn't care about the old man.

"None of us have seen you since Christmas, and there you are in the city all alone."

"I am not alone, Dad. A friend is here." The old man had it fixed in his mind, since Alec had divorced his wife, that he lived "alone," was "alone."

"That's it. It's good to be with friends." His voice said he didn't believe Alec had friends.

"How are you, Dad?"

The old man toyed with him, told him his health, complained of the doctors, scorned his friends who were less fit, ran on, knowing he had Alec trapped.

The doorbell rang.

It was Michael, sweeping into the room with solutions. "I've brought sheets. How is he?" Michael's face didn't waste energy on smiles and frowns and perplexed looks. His face framed seriously, economically around the words, an appropriate setting for dealing with facts. "How much has he eaten today?"

Alec fixed Michael's drink and another for himself, thoughtlessly, like someone running his fingers through his hair, the telephone with its connection to his father and his father's v oice wedged between his ear and his shoulder. He saw his father irregularly ("You're looking fit") and called him once a week. They talked about the funerals of his father's friends. There were more of them than weddings of their grandchildren. Alec's father found Alec's home, the stainless steel flatwear, the makeshift furniture, the books in cardboard boxes, pictures stuck on the walls with thumbtacks, to be transitory, tentative, and suggesting something insubstantial, as if he were always packing to move. The voice in Alec's ear went on animatedly, its pitch and volume varying widely, out of control, in the manner of very old men, speaking of philosophy, how wrong it was for men to live alone, how companionship was the balm of a sore life.

"Have you got money?" Alec spoke with his hand over the receiver.

"It's all I've got." Michael counted out bills on the coffee table.

Alec picked them up and counted. "This'll help." Then, into the phone, "What's your big news, Dad?"

Michael walked around the apartment, his chin down, his arms folded across his chest, staring but not seeing. "But he can't stay here." He turned to Alec. "How is he?" Michael had no antecedents.

27

Winter Rain

He had come to adulthood already having shed his parents in some dark way. Alec understood not to ask. He lived in the present tense, which seemed rigid to Alec and lacked resonance.

"You'll be astonished to hear that Bernice and I were married three days ago, on Sunday. The chapel of St Bartholomew's church— "

Alec held the glass to his lips and sipped the drink. He could do what he had to do with the help of the money Michael had brought, put Amos in his bed, find food for a meal. "That was sudden—"

"What else?" Michael was trying to cover all bases.

"Oh no. We are both mature persons and know our own minds and have no reason to doubt—" Alec's father went on, describing the run-up to the wedding, the passion, the design of the bride's dress and the honeymoon, which they were at the beginning of now. While he talked, Alec, his hand over the receiver, went on with his conversation with Michael.

"Look, he's going to stay here tonight—"

"Can you handle that?"

"Nothing to it."

"What about tomorrow?"

"Let him stay here—"

"Permanently?"

Alec shrugged. "Until we can't handle it."

"That'll happen soon enough—"

"I'm going to need help with sitting—"

"We should find someone on unemployment to come sit with him. Who do we know who has given up looking for a job? Gaetano is coming when he gets off I think."

His father was referring to the new bride. "—her name is Bernice. She is little more than a child. Your age, I should say, but of course considerably more mature. She has learned to handle herself with distinctly more responsibility—"

Alec laughed. He put up his hand to stop the conversation with Michael while he dealt with his father: "You old goat. Are you trying to pick a fight?"

"I don't have to, Alec. You usually do that for me."

The conversation ended, having turned sour. Before hanging up, Alec's father left Alec with the threat that he would bring his new mother to visit soon.

"I look forward to that—" The empty social words fell out of his mouth before he could stop them and made him feel dirty and silly.

Winter Rain

When he put down the phone, the part convention played in his love for Michael being unexplored, he was able to put out his arm and pull Michael down the length of the sofa to him. "How are you? What does the doctor say?"

Michael struggled with him, pulled back, looked him directly in the face. "I don't want you to ask." Alec released him. "OK?" He kissed Alec lightly.

"No. That is not OK. I love you. Have you been to the doctor?"

"I'm not going to tell you. I know you do. That's my business. I just found out yesterday. I haven't been to the doctor today." He pointed at the silent tv screen. "It's started."

They watched for a few moments, the dark screen flashing with lights like lightning behind clouds, showing a dark skyline.

"He told 'em he'd do it, and now he has."

"I'm gonna beat the shit outta you."

Then he was gone, to a client.

Every half hour Alec checked on Amos asleep in his bedroom. The money Michael had brought would make it possible to keep Amos here two days. He had to reach Gaetano. He fixed a drink and kept it with him, whether he was by Amos's bed or in the living room, and when it needed replenishing, he fixed himself another, thinking about the drama going on in his head. He got very drunk, alone in the apartment with Amos.

During that evening, Alec, coming into the living room, discovered a message from Stephen on the answering machine: "Dad, you can reach me at 783-5962. I'll be staying here for a couple of days." Sitting on the sofa, watching the silent pictures of the bombing, sipping his drink, he called the number every half hour and let the phone ring. Stephen wanted something. He was staying away. He called Gaetano. Gaetano was docile and could be led. They must talk Thursday. Stephen could not be reached at this number (783-5962) and there was no answering machine. Alec didn't know whose number it was.

In the morning, Alec called the temp agency. They had a job for him with the telephone company, but he couldn't find someone to stay with Amos, so he turned it down. He had worked for them before: single rooms occupying entire floors of large downtown office buildings, windows on all four sides, elevator bank in the middle, long rows of desks, "OUT" box and "IN" box, someone coming by every half hour dropping papers in the "IN" box to be processed

29

through the computer and deposited in the "OUT" box, to be collected every half hour by someone traveling by.

He thought the money would take care of itself. During the first days after Amos came home from the hospital, while he went back and forth from the living room to the bedroom to check on Amos, he returned to the choices he had made which had placed him here, his decision, among others, that he wouldn't be confined any longer by something known as a "career." This—he raised his drink glass and waved it vaguely toward the bedroom where Amos lay—is what is important, not the temp agency, and not work. He sat on the sofa, listening to Amos breathing in the next room, dialing over and over one of several numbers—Stephen (783-5962), Gaetano, and Arabella.

The gang dropped by sporadically. Some stayed away. Gaetano came at Alec's specific invitation. Arabella, Gus, Wayne. Since Michael was there most of the time anyway, you couldn't say he was visiting. Some men stood at the foot of the bed and watched with out saying anything. Others talked. Men had different styles when faced with Amos dying. Some wanted to domesticate it by arranging pillows, and others seemed to want to celebrate the mystery of it. The men stayed with Amos for short periods, allowing Alec to go to the grocery store or the pharmacy for supplies. Sometimes Margaret, the super, who lived in the basement, came up for a minute and sat while he took the car and double-parked, running in through the rain and getting what he needed and racing home again.

Alec read the newspapers—lottery winners, children killed by stray bullets, news of the recession—and watched the pictures of the bombing, of a truck crossing a bridge and achieving safety moments before the bridge was blown up. He became accustomed to the mounting count of sorties flown, thousands in the first night and increasing exponentially every night thereafter. The media kept track of the total tonnage of bombs dropped each day and each week and "so far in this war" and compared it to the number of tons dropped on Tokyo or Coventry or Dresden during the Second World War or the number of tons dropped on Cambodia —previous instances of automated destruction on a vast scale. This violence sometimes made it seem that civilization was endangered.

The visiting nurse started coming the second morning after Amos's arrival. She came each day, arriving about eight -thirty and bustling about Amos's room. She checked the IV apparatus hooked to the permanent aperture in Amos's chest and inspected the medications being given him. She took his temperature and asked him how he was feeling. Alec asked her how it was, visiting houses where the patients did not recover. She shrugged. "You know you can't change anything. What's going to happen is going to happen. But between now and then, drugs need to be administered and sheets changed. They need to be paid attention to, given respect." She waited a moment for him to respond, but Alec could think of nothing to say.

Just when Alec was beginning t o believe that the only reason for his not reaching Stephen was Stephen's refusal to answer, the phone rang, and there was Stephen.

"I don't understand, Dad."

"What don't you understand?"

"Why you called."

"I called because you called, and I told you Michael and Arabella were here, and we decided that I should call you the next night. Then I didn't have your number, and once I got it, I've been trying to reach you ever since. You're never there. Where are you?"

"Dad we talked last night."

Last night. Alec remembered nothing of last night. He had brought Amos home from the hospital. Michael had brought sheets. There had been several nights. Days. He had tried to reach Stephen. Gaetano. He didn't know what day it was.

He felt his face flush and his head go light. He was not naive. He knew what this meant, but he wouldn't admit to Stephen that he knew what it meant. He had to think of something to say. "Amos is —." He heard himself slur his words. "You know Amos is here. I got him from the hospital."

"You're drunk, Dad." His voice was weary and angry.

"Stephen." Quick give me something to say, but his mind worked as if it were filled with tar. "I didn't tell you about Michael."

"What I said last night was I don't want to live with you, Dad." Then Stephen hung up on him. What night had it been that Amos had come home from the hospital? He looked about him at his apartment. He could see what was there, but he had forgotten what he had known last night, or the night before. The feeling was so tight in his throat he felt he was choking. He could not take a deep breath. He heard Amos from the other room. He went in to check on the inert body under the unwrinkled covers.

"Bring me some water, please."

Until Amos spoke, you didn't know if he were awake or asleep.
Alec held the water to his lips. Amos swallowed. Some ran down his
cheeks onto his neck. He swallowed again. Alec wiped it up with
the bedspread. He swallowed a third time, then he turned his head
slightly.

"No."

He suffered. Did he know where he was? Did he know that it
was Alec sitting on the side of the bed? What did he know of what
was happening to him? There was nothing here which pricked Alec's
memory, and it was difficult to have feelings about this moment,
except fear. The man, this thing lying in his bed, who barely was
able to say no, had in Alec's own memory carried on a loud colloquy
with a desicated Cardinal in the sanctuary of a cathedral in front of
3500 shocked Christians.

Down to the last moment, Alec's mother had still been herself.
She had about her head and face the sense of well bred dissatisfaction,
as she lay dying, with which she had moved among her husband's
family at a Sunday picnic on the lawn. The sigh she gave minutes
before a final convulsion was the same sigh Alec remembered all his
life. The emotional warfare which had characterized their love
continued during the last days, even down to the last minutes, no
truce offered. Stephen had lived with him since he was 14, and of all
of the attributes of his life of which he was proud, he was most proud
that his son wanted to live with him. Now he was gone.

He returned to the living room, the screen showing pictures of
bombs falling away underneath planes, clean, silent, passionless, and
made telephone calls, searching out across the city, punching the
numbers in hard and fast, sitting on one thigh and resting his hand on
the other as he waited for the ringing to stop. He would walk into the
kitchen and, as he cleared the door, reach for the phone.

"Gaetano. I need help. Call me."

He poured a drink with one hand, punching the numbers with the
other, in a panic.

His apartment was dominated by the sound of Amos's breathing in
the other room, the labored, irreducible effort, which demonstrated
inescapably the difference between living (walking, reading, dancing,
feeling, hating, crying, lifting, suffering, passionately rejecting the
dogma of Cardinals) and the mere maintenance of body functions
(breathing, shitting). The visiting nurse, who had come every day

since Amos arrived, had given him no indication of where Amos was in his illness.

"There is no way of knowing."

"Should we be preparing for his funeral?"

"Of course!—" It was scorn for a child being stupid again. "—you should have taken care of everything." She was putting on her coat at the door. "He can't stay here. Find a small apartment for him in case he gets better."

While Alec was capable of organizing anything and was willing to be the one who would do it, sometimes the feelings he was aware of, underneath his confidence, suggested apprehension that he might not be able to do it, or that others might think he was less capable than he himself felt. This apprehension might sometimes, for a fleeting moment, have been an anxiety, and then sometimes, at moments of crisis, the apprehension, the anxiety manifested themselves in a stronger emotion—fear, which came on him with the suddenness of a thunderclap, and was gone as suddenly. Coming back into the living room, Alec felt terror for a second, the sudden sense of the dark and of the unexplainable, the sudden fear for his life, and then, by the time he was back on the sofa, it was gone, leaving the air in the room smelling clean. He felt light-headed. But he didn't know he had been afraid. And he didn't know what he had been afraid of.

A postcard arrived from his father and Bernice. They were in Czechoslovakia. "You cannot imagine my inexpressible happiness at being given the gift of Bernice. After all these years of searching. Prague is not at all what Kafka said it was." The breakup of the old Soviet Empire. Why had they gone there? The newspapers referred to the US as the last superpower.

When Alec's mother died, Alec's father had called from Pennsylvania the night Alec got home from the funeral. He seemed lost, and, to Alec, bewildered and pitiful, without his wife of fifty years. He had called every night. He didn't know how to fill up his time. He was seventy, and he didn't know what to do with his day, once he had had breakfast. He called Alec sometimes three and four times a day and came to visit him every several weeks. When he was not visiting Alec, he was traveling, visiting friends he called it, even in cities where he had no friends. And from all these cities, domestic and foreign, he called Alec.

Alec's father had begun dating a woman seven weeks after Alec's mother was buried. Six months after she died, he was married to a woman younger than Alec. At this time, the calls stopped and the visits stopped, and the only thing that continued was the postcards from Marseilles, Naples, Singapore, Agra, Sidney, Pago Pago, as he made his way around the world with his new young wife. Then, in a year, the marriage was over, the woman gone. She was richer and he was poorer. The phone calls started again—and the visits.

He had married, and divorced, again, before this current wife, the period between marriages characterized by daily calls from around the world and monthly visits, filled with tears an d weeping, bitterness and loneliness. Alec's father didn't often visit him during a marriage. But he did come soon after a ceremony, to show off his new young wife to his sons. During these visits, his desperate calls and profound loneliness were never mentioned.

Alec's father was carefully groomed and dressed (distinguished looking, it was said), and his manner was studied and polite. He always wore a suit and rarely attended any event where it would be appropriate to wear more casual clothing. He wor e his suits like armor—they protected him from casual contact and increased the likelihood that everyone around him would adjust to the formality of his ways. Before Alec's own divorce, the old man used to stay with him with his new young wife. Now, however, he stayed at the Ritz and dealt with Alec across a gulf of class and money and attitude, using the house phone to set up dates at restaurants on Newbury Street.

Alec found a temp job with a construction firm, writing specifications, his first job in ten days, making twice the minimum wage and half what he needed to live, if he were only to work three days a week. He had to find someone to stay with Amos.

"—only three days. And only until five. I get off at 4:30 and can be back by five. That means you can get to work only half an hour late—"

He was walking around the living room, circling Gaetano in the sling chair, who was staring at his fingernails.

"I can't be late at the restaurant every day, even half an hour"

"Bullshit. This is Amos we're talking about. And it's only three—"

"Three days. I don't do this kind of thing. You do this better than me—"

"What kind of thing—"

"Look after people. Weirds me out, sick people —"

"You could learn."
Gaetano was silent. Alec was looking down at him.
"Just this week. We'll talk about next week next week."
This would be harder if he worked a full week.
"Look, OK. I'll get Gus and Wayne to come too. We'll get enough to cover." Gus and Wayne would be there so that Gaetano would not be alone with what was happening in the bedroom. As Gaetano was leaving, he stopped in the doorway. "Makes everything weird if you have to think about dying, don't it? Screws everything up."

It was unlikely Alec would be asked to work a full week. All over the city, buildings already built were called "transparent buildings" because, with no tenants, there was nothing to stop you from seeing through them from one side to the other. At noon from the temp job, Alec left the office and ran down to a pharmacy where he filled two of Amos's prescriptions (cost: enough to buy food for them both for a week, or a one-way flight for one of them to New York, or a case of gin), running back by the sandwich shop for a sandwich he could eat at his desk. The job, taking notes and turning them into a polished draft of specifications for a highway building project, did not occupy his mind, which was on Gaetano, who at the moment was sitting with Amos, and on Amos, who had experienced a rally after five that morning and seemed to be able to talk (he said, looking at the picture of a field of flowers, "That picture is a mean picture.") and on Stephen. Having Stephen living with him gave an anchor to his life which Alec had found steadying. He enjoyed having to consider Stephen's needs. Without him he felt weightless, unanchored.
Leaving the sandwich shop, he had to pass a bar before he got to his corner. He ducked in. It was twenty-three minutes past the hour. He had seven minutes. "Double, please—" throwing the bills on the counter, reducing by one meal the amount of money he had to keep Amos, money which came from Michael. He put the glass to his lips, tasted the bitter whiskey in his nose, and swallowed. He had called Stephen (783-5962), but there was no answer. He didn' t know whose number Stephen had given him. Alec resisted the idea that Stephen knew something he didn't know. He was afraid that Stephen felt the same about his childhood that Alec felt about his. The thought came across his synapses like a hair on an eye lash.

Winter Rain

Margaret came in at four to clean the halls and take out the trash. She walked with a limp, her shoes were heavy, brokendown-on-the-side oxfords, and it apparently caused her pain to walk. She dragged one foot and pushed the large barrel on wheels in front of her. Her gray hair was dyed black and pulled back in a bun. He saw her in the halls as she was finishing.

"See you tomorrow."

"God willing." She spoke grimly, with such pessimism that Alec was certain she didn't believe she would ever see him again.

A letter came from Stephen. "I told you I was going to move out, but that I was going to come to see you and when I was going to come. Now, twenty-four hours later, you can't remember you had the conversation."

Stephen was nine when Alec divorced Gloria, Stephen's mother. "Dad only cares about himself" was his judgment on the last seven years. Arabella, who had watched this rupture develop between father and son and had heard both sides in long, painful outpourings from her brother-in-law and nephew, told Alec, "Everybody suffers. Some better than others."

Stephen wrote, "I'm sick of being jerked around. I'm sick of you. You're domineering, unstable, overbearing, unreliable. I want you to pay attention to me, and you don't—"

"What have I done to him that's so awful?" They were on the phone.

Arabella laughed that broken laugh of hers. "The worst thing imaginable"

The worst thing imaginable would be murder.

"You left him when he was nine. There isn't anything worse for a kid. It's unforgivable. He'll remember that even if he thinks he has forgiven it."

His efforts to reach Stephen became insistent, obsessive. He came home from work and dialed him (783 -5962) before getting out of his rain gear. Then he dialed again every hour until midnight, when he went to bed. What had Stephen wanted to talk about? Whose number was it that they were using? The image Alec carried around in his head was of himself, sitting at a bar, and Stephen, 21 now, sitting next to him, both of them with thei r heads inclined slightly, eyes on their drinks, fingers gently moving their glasses occasionally to make new rings on the rosewood, talking. They'd sit a while, staring at their drinks, making wet circles in the rosewood, the people around them coming in and going out of range, like extras in a movie, walking on a slant, hair slicked back, laden with jewels.

"Dad?" Stephen's eyes didn't squint yet, hadn't learned to protect themselves.

"What?"

"Did you love me when you left Mom?"

"Yes. You know I did."

"Michael's cool."

"I think so too."

It never happened. Did Stephen know he did? Had Alec, anyway? Arabella was wrong. What did Stephen know? Alec thought of himself as a perfect father, but he couldn't be perfect if he didn't have a perfect son. The boy smoldered, with a resentment so old it had grown cold, and Alec's hurt at being cut off from him was overwhelmed by his anger that the boy was showing him up.

The television screen was dark blue, almost black, and lit up with explosive flashes, showing in outline, a skyline, a horizon. Tracer bullets cut jagged paths of light upwards, the light they made lingering for a moment on the screen, a forest of golden birch trees against the blue sky. The camera captured a rocket streaking upward, exploding and destroying Iraqi missile toward the top of the screen. Silent, without commentary, the pictures were mesmerizing. Watched so far from the sound the explosions made, they seemed harmless and beautiful.

Prior to this war, in Alec's memory, the United States had fought a war every five or six years, found one or another of its enemies intolerable, went into a seizure and attacked some small backward country. The goal of the bombing was always to create a "preindustrial society" at the end of a post-industrial century, to "bomb them back into the Stone Age." Alec had his own seizures, when he was overwhelmed with the stupendous sensation that he was about to die, when the inability to know what was unknowable brought such fear to his surface that he reached out with his fist to hit at something, to hurt something before it could hurt him. He had hit men this way and had later asked himself what it was that had so terrified him—and couldn't remember. He had hit Gloria, too, and the terror there was clearer. Most of the time, it was that she belittled him ("men!"), made him feel it, and he hated feeling small. His instinct was to hit her and show her how big he was. But sometimes, a few times, it was something else. It usually had to do

with children, and she said something so mystifying, something so
foreign, that Alec was terrified of it, and struck out at her to get at it.
It had to do with being the mother of Stephen, with the mysterious
connection with him which a mother has and a father doesn't. Alec,
in his cups, didn't like it, didn't understand it, was afraid of it, and
struck out at it.

He sat by the bed, holding Amos's hand.

At length, Amos spoke. "What's that light?"

"The tv is on. It's at the end of the bed."

Amos was still.

"I'm watching the bombing." He waited and listened. "Would you
like to see it?"

The silence from the bed was profound.

Stephen was draft age. Alec watched the bombs and thought of
them exploding on Stephen's soft body. He lurched up out of his
reverie, his fingers hitting the buttons (783 -5962).

Then Alec was on the phone with Arabella.

"I'm short of money—" It was a way of getting at how he was.

"How much are you spending on Amos?"

"Somebody—"

"—has to do it. Alec—!" Her voice suggested her rich emotions,
something many-layered, love and irony together.

He heard her light a cigarette.

"Look, I want to come into town tonight. Can I stay with you —"

It was late for her to call.

"I know, dear, but I thought I could count on you."

He was her port (he was both his brother and distinctly not his
brother). Alec glanced around the room, at the furniture and the
stacks of books, searching for the space to pull out the sofa bed
without a reorganization of the furniture. He sensed the
impermanence of things; his home was a stage set, a hotel room
suitable for any drama by any paying guest. Alec was all of them.
Sure she could come. Let the whole earth come. He felt expansive.
Let them come two-by-two in their variety. His chest swelled.

An hour later, Alec was moving furniture when the phone rang
again.

"Look, Alec—" It was Horace. "I know you and Arabella have
this thing, and you think I don't know, well I do, and she's not here,
and naturally the first thing I thought of—" Horace's goal in life
was to be secure, financially, and more secure than everybody else he

knew. He had a career, but he trusted nothing, suspected everyone he knew of seeking to do him in. It was this fear —together with greed —which made capitalism work. Alec heard Amos stir in the bedroom, a deep, long sigh. Arabella would not want Horace to
know she was coming to the city and would not want him to know where she was.

"No. I haven't heard from her. What's up?"

"I'm getting fucked over—"

He was also being audited by the feds. "Wait a minute. Let me check on Amos."

"Don't keep me waiting. I'm not in a mood —"

Amos lay immobile in the bed, eyes closed, head back, and mouth open.

"You OK?"

Eventually, Amos spoke. "Come sit with me."

"In a minute."

On the way back, he detoured by the refrigerator: ice, a glass, whiskey. "Now." He seated himself in the corner of the sofa. "What's up?"

"Is she with you?"

"Arabella? No. What's up, Horace?"

"She's got my car. She coulda taken her own, but she took mine. I don't think she's coming back. Why do I think she's with you?"

"Search me, Horace. What's happening?" Alec partly enjoyed Horace's anger and partly was bored by it. "Start at the beginning."

"She says I think with my dick. What does that mean, think with my dick? Look, tell her—I know what she's going to tell you."

"What, Horace?"

"I came home late and we got in a fight. We were standing in the kitchen, and she said I didn't have balls. My right hand was right by the kitchen counter, by the drawer, which was open a little bit. There was this knife, and when she said, 'You don't have balls,' I picked up the knife. I don't know what I was thinking of. I just picked it up and waved it at her and—"

The doorbell rang. This bell, which was rung from the vestibule at the main front door, was used by Michael as a way of announcing his arrival (the bell would be almost immediately followed by a knock at the apartment door and the sound of keys in the lock). Now Arabella, who had her own keys, was entering the same way.

She came into the room, saw he was on the phone, went into the kitchen to fix herself a drink.

Alec put his hand over the receiver. "Check on Amos. He needs something—" He sipped his drink and tried to remember Horace.

"You don't know what they want. Who're you talking to?"

Arabella was back in the living room. She watched him while he talked. How was Amos? He mouthed the words and pointed toward the bedroom. Arabella nodded: OK.

"—women! They eat you alive—"

Alec, listening, imagined their marriage from Horace's point of view, stood by his side and looked over his shoulder at Arabella eating him alive. Alec considered what he could do for Amos with Horace's money. But in front of him was Arabella. Horace thought money was interesting; he thought money was an adequate goal in life, and, even though Alec had watched Arabella open wounds in Horace's skin, she was no threat to him.

"Is Arabella there? Are you fucking me over?"

"No—" Alec was laughing. He considered asking him about the audit.

"I don't believe you. I think she's there. What does she have to say to you? What do you say to each other? You talk about men, don't you—"

"Horace—"

"—my faggot brother, and my fucking wife—"

Arabella knew who he was speaking to. She was amused at both of them.

When he hung up and turned to her, she said, "He doesn't know what's happening. He'll come after me one day and find me here. He'll flay us alive."

"And Dad will believe him."

"Drink?"

Alec nodded. In his memories of the last ten years, through the drugs and alcohol and sex, as he himself burned bridge after bridge behind him leading back to middleclass piety, he could hear his father's cultured voice telling him of Horace's life —his move, step by step, up the ladder of financial success as he bought a second home in the mountains and then a third on the shore, educated four children, worked hard his father said. Alec wrote down on the pad by the phone: Call Stephen (783-5962). He had to get through to him.

He found Amos, his eyes open, the room energized, as if rich in oxygen.

"Where am I?"

40

Winter Rain

Alec sat down on the bed, gently, slowly, so as not to disturb him. "My place." He nodded at the room. "This is my bedroom."
Amos' face showed confusion. "Have I ever been in this room?"
"Lots of times. I've made love to you in this bed."
"I don't think I have ever been in this room before."
Alec sought out Amos's hand. "Maybe it's been changed since last time you saw it."
"That must be it. I'm sure I never saw this room before."
He was silent and drifted away again. With Horace's money he wouldn't have to work. He could spend more time in a cool, dark bar where his own thoughts were the only company he needed, or, after the party and after everyone else had gone home, Stephen and he could fix a drink and settle back into the easy chairs and laugh and, with lowered voices, talk about what really mattered: of course, things hurt.
He was back in the living room.
Arabella was just snapping her purse shut. She dropped a postcard on the coffee table. "This is not the way it was supposed to be. He's sorry he ever married me. He says I suck him dry. I discover things about myself that I didn't know about. Gaetano!"
"Have you seen him since then?"
"No. Gaetano is not part of my life. But your brother would kill me if he found out. That's every one of his nightmares come true. That's what I mean, Alec. How did that happen?"
"I wondered too the next morning. I couldn't figure—" He was laughing.
"I know. You didn't remember introducing us, but that is what I mean. I haven't slept with any one but Horace since we were married. I wake up thinking, how has this happened? I seem unable to stop myself. I am becoming something—There is nothing in my past, in my education and training, to explain what is happening to me. I had thought, I suppose, except that if the truth were admitted, I don't think I ever thought about any of it, I had thought that I would be presented with choices: You may do this or you may do that. Clear choices. I have never had difficulty seeing my professional life as a sequence of clear choices. I had thought that if a choice about Horace ever arose, I would already be so ready to leave him (if I could even consider the choice, I must no longer be in love with him) that the immediate question would be *When do I leave him?* How did I get here, where this difference (is this the word?) could be so casual? What have I done? Why do I feel the way I do?"

"I thought Gaetano was gay. I didn't know he had ever been with a woman. What did you do to him?"

"Do you remember your story about the transvestite prostitute? the one who became a stockbroker? I can't stop thinking about him. Do you ever see him now?"

Alec was shaking his head.

"How does he feel? And I didn't do anything to him. He did it all himself." She laughed. "Although it was a surprise." She was crying. "I want to kill him. I want to hurt him. I can't remember how I got this way. What am I like, Alec? Nothing explains itself any more. He's such a shit. He is so proud of himself when he's defeated somebody—he comes home, his chest out, his neck thick, strutting. It always happens when he's drinking. No matter how the night starts, when he's drinking, when it ends, he's after me. Did he tell you about the knife? He chased me—he got this knife out of the drawer, you know?—and came at me, brandishing it, yelling he was going to cut me up. You know, he drinks a lot. Hell, we all drink a lot. Everybody in your family drinks too much. He's got his neck thick, and he can't think of anybody else in the room. He's just like your father. Such a shit—"

Alec picked up the postcard. The picture was of a terrace of white stone above a blue sea beyond. On the other side, Alec's father's handwriting—strong, emphatic—read, "It is a great pleasure to be enjoying the fruits of my labors these many years —" Alec's father was a heavy man, his face pulled tight into an expression of sharp, insistent pain, his eyelids lowered as if gazing on stupidity. Done in marble, it would have been a Head of the Chief of the Secret Police in a totalitarian country. His words, which Alec remembered most often, were, *That was stupid.* He went bankrupt two years before Alec's mother died, though Alec's mother used the words lost his business. Then, six months after her death, he made a killing mysteriously in the stock market and was rich again. For Alec, his father was distilled down to the one image—the persistent, steady gaze of disapproval through narrowed lids, as if staring through smoke. Alec's mother had tiptoed around the house, her heels barely touching the hardwood floors.

"He's gotten married again." She wiped her eyes. "That poor dumb woman. Even if she did it for the old bastard's money, she'll pay—" She stood up and began to circle the room, going to the door and leaning on the doorjamb, coming back in and walking to the windows, passing by the coffee table, and on her way back, passing by the stereo against the wall. "I had ideas of being a good mother! I used to have a sense of myself—I know who I am, I have no difficulty being effective professionally, and I know how the world works—and children need that in their parents. Something solid. Now, I find I am afraid of what I don't know. It's paralyzing. I not only can't say any more to them, *Go to bed.* Or *Use a condom.* I can't say anything. I think I drink too much. Only it's not all my fault. It's not just me. Alec, it's not just me whose going crazy, is it?"

There was another postcard from Alec's father, this time from Pest. His father had been rich, poor, was rich again, was alternately proud and arrogant and whiny and self-pitying. Each time now that a message came to Alec in one or the other of his father's modes, Alec suspected it, sensing the other. This postcard carried the words, "If you would live your life as I do, you would experience the satisfaction which I feel at this moment."

Several weeks after Amos was brought to Alec's apartment, his friends gathered to discuss the future. Michael sat in the chair at the end of the sofa. Gaetano was on the sofa. Alec sat on the floor.

"Well, he can't stay here."

"It's my place, Michael, and I am the one to decide that —"

"—gotta stay someplace. We're his friends—"

"You don't have any money, you don't have a job —"

"—we asking how to do this, or whether we have to do this? What?"

"You can't handle this forever—"

"So? All we have to do is be more organized about giving him some relief—"

"Relief!"

"—make a list. Seven nights a week, seven days. Each of us sign up for one—that's me, you, Alec, Arabella, we'll get some others — and each of us handle food for one twenty-four hour period. What about drugs—" Gaetano saw no problem.

"It's important that we assume one of us is going to do this, right?" Alec looked around. "Are we agreed on that?"

Gaetano stood with Alec in seeing the thing as essentially simple. "I can give you three hours a week—"

"Is that all?"

"—say, seven to ten."

43

"Longer. I need more time off than that. Make it six to twelve."
"I can't get in gym time before work—"
"But that's what I need."
"This week. Next week my schedule is different at the
restaurant—"
There were complications. "Some people can give some money
but don't have the time to come over here and babysit —"
"It's not babysitting, guys—"
"Well, we all should make an equal contribution, either time or
money—."
"—hey, hey, this ain't charity, guys, this is us —"
"We have unequal abilities, resources—"
"Michael—"
"It's unfair."
"Yeah, you bet your ass—"
So, people gave time and money in unequal amounts. Somewhere
it was agreed on, though it wasn't ever said very clearly, that Amos
would die at home, at one of their homes, unless his medical situation
called for something more technologically sophisticated. It was as if
they hadn't wanted to look in the face the size of the commitment
they were making. Another thing that never got very clearly
articulated was the nature of the commitment. Charity for a sick and
needy friend? or were they establishing guidelines by which each of
them would be cared for in turn? In any case, a system was
established by which Alec's life simplified itself. He was to
command the forces taking care of Amos. These forces, which
amounted to a gift of time and money, allowed him to pay attention
to the pebble under his tongue.

Michael had allowed him to inspect his skin, to see if there were
lesions. Alec spent half an hour, crouching beside him, who was on
his stomach on the floor, going over his back with a minute scrutiny.
He tried to fix in his mind the topography of his lover's back, with
attention to each blemish, so that tomorrow and next week, he could
see the progress of the disease.
One Friday night late in February, Alec left Amos in Gaetano's
care. He had tried Stephen (783-5962) before he left, but there was
no answer. He went out into the rain wearing foulweather gear over a
hooded sweatshirt. He started at a bar on outer Boylston (smells:
beer, alcohol, cigarettes, salt), and drank down two doubles, then
moved in a methodical way down the street, the smear of bright

lights reflecting off the pavement, running in out of the rain at each bar he passed, like moving from steam baths to pool. The disease progressed, but Amos's health deteriorated. Language took them in two directions at once.

Gaetano was at home looking after Amos. Someday, Alec would be at home looking after Michael. When would it be that someone would be looking after him? Michael had asked him when he was going to have it done, anonymous tests whose results were so freighted that they wouldn't give the results without talking to you for an hour, but there was no point in having it done since there was nothing they could do. Even with the new medications prolonging life, there was nothing they could do. What had settled down around him was hopelessness. It had settled so lightly on him—like acid rain—that he hardly noticed it and wasn't made unhappy by it. It was merely there. Without being despondent, he was becoming without hope.

He called Stephen regularly (783-5962), who had hung up on him. Sometimes the phone was answered by an answering machine. He would leave messages: "Stephen, this is your Dad. Would you call me?" "Stephen, call me buddy. I want to talk." "Stephen, I haven't heard from you for a while, and I thought I'd call. Give me a call back, will you? This is your Dad." He tried to keep the sound of pleading out of his voice, and there were messages in his head (*Stephen, don't be a shit. Stephen, you've got to love me. Stephen, I'm not like my Dad. Stephen, we can love one another*) which he never left on Stephen's machine. Going down Boylston in the rain, from bar to bar, he held a conversation in his mind with Stephen: *You wouldn't hate me if you knew.*

But it never got very far. Alec, looking into the mirror over the bar, was always ashamed of the pleading sound in his voice, which he heard in his mind, and allowed his voice to fall silent. It was important not to be like his father. His anger against his father was justifiable only if he were not causing Stephen the same pain his father caused him. *Hate me for what? What have I done?*

With each drink, the register of pain in his heart lowered. It was as if the playback of his emotions were at high speed, and nothing was recognizable, all was tense and gibberish. What was needed was to slow everything down. With each drink, his feelings slid into lower registers, down to where they began to resonate, to cau se a deep vibrato. As he became drunk, his feelings became more recognizable, more definable. Out of the hundred thousand feelings he might have had during the day—impatience with Amos's long time dying, relief at the swallow of his first drink at eleven , murderous rage at Horace—now they resolved themselves, sorted themselves out, into two, or three: grief, shame, desire.

The rain on his face (he held his head up high, facing into it) ran down his neck. Alec would come out into the street, hunch his shoulders against the rain and cold and walk close to the building down the street to the next bar, passing parking valets and beggars jostling one another in the streets. After two or three of these bars, he came to Copley Square, and now he was drunk enough not to feel the need to stay next to the protection of the building side. He went out into the street and across it into the square, the rain on his face, oblivious to the cold. The rain, turned white in the light of the street lamps, swirled around above the square, caught in the downdrafts from the buildings and then in the updrafts so that it seemed that the only drops of rain which reached the street were thrown inadvertently out of the maelstrom above his head. The lights seemed suspended above the square, their poles lost in the dark.

The scene matched his feeling—dark, stormy, drenched—and above it loomed the great church, Romanesque, heavy stone, monumental, imponderable, oppressive. Michael had the virus, Alec had given it to him. Alec crossed the square to the court in front and held out his arms in the rain, facing up to the spires. It was only in its architecture that the church still had something to say.

Alec's father had stood in the rain, arms out. When Alec thought of him he smelt alcohol. He smelt of alcohol, and he had a short, brush cut, dark skin and large veins. He had entered a succession of sanatoriums after Alec had reached puberty. He went back in to dry out, as one takes a bath and dries off. Standing in front of the church, his arms out, aware of both his father and his son, Alec felt his hands being taken, and, without looking, knew what it was. People were clasping his hands. There was someone on each side of him holding his hands. He began to smile. It would be his father— and Stephen. They would have come to take his hands and to walk with him here in the rain in the square.

When he was drinking, as he sat at a bar and watched himself in the mirror behind the glasses, he would draw Stephen and his father closer to him, carry on conversations with them in his heart, remind them of Stephen's childhood or of his own—and even of what he knew of his father's—remember what it was like when he, or Stephen, was small and reached up to hold the large hand and trotted

46

along beside the large feet. With the drink in his hand, it was possible to move back beyond the anguish to a time when his father had been a large, warm, vibrant presence, even to a time which he couldn't place, when he rode on his father's shoulders in a creek, pulling a shrimp sein, while he held Stephen, an infant, on his shoulder, Stephen's head resting in the hollow of his neck.

He sought a way to get beyond the things that got in the way (the answering machine that would not take messages), to get beyond, escape from, the walls of his own apartment, the pictures, prints, paintings, books, the letters, the ordinary shape of his bathroom, each of which had already done its work on him, beyond the crowd of his friends, Michael's grim assurance, Gaetano's placid confidence, the photographs in frames of his friends smiling, beyond the sameness of the city, of the fountains in the park. These things trapped him, smothered his feelings with familiar sameness, and in the rain in the winter in the sixth week of another war, what he sought by this movement in and out of the bars (steam bath cold shower) was to open up his heart the way it might have opened up his pores. If he drank enough, toured enough bars, the familiar confinements in his heart would break down, wash away in the flood of rain and alcohol and he would be able to feel.

But he pulled back from that. When he drank, he remembered —or imagined—conversations he had had with Stephen. They were the best of his memories, and if he knew it was true that these "memories" had never happened, the feelings they gave rise to, of well-being, were real.

"Dad, what do I need to know?"

"Come with me." He would be proud to be asked, proud that he had an answer. "Let's find some place better to sit." They 'd leave the stools and wander back past the bar in search of privacy, past the cigarette machines, the pinball machines, the men's room door, the neon beer sign, to the booths, to a corner booth, where they'd slide in away from the noise and the neon, Stephen leaning back expectantly against the seat while Alec, his elbows on the formica, leaned forward, thinking, eager, proud, about to roam over the whole range of his philosophy: "There are only one or two things you can count on in this life—" while Stephen, his eyes half-closed, would nod and declare, *yeah yeah.*

While he stood on the pavement in front of the church, a policeman walked up to the steps of the porch. The rain was coming down in waves on gusts of wind. The policeman climbed the steps and entered the dark shadows under the porch roof. There was a heap of rags there in the dark, which the policeman spoke to. The heap moved, shuddered and moved. The policeman spoke more sharply to the heap, and slowly it rose up against the rusticated stone of the church. Alec watched as an old man's hands rose up and searched out a handhold on the stone. He pulled himself up. But he fell. Alec watched as the process began again, the hand searching across the face of the stone for a hold, then the feet seeking a firm ground, and the body gradually rising, propped against the stone. He fell again.

The cop waited patiently. Immovably. Finally, the old man made it to a standing position. In a few moments, Alec could see him again standing near the steps, in the light. The old man appeared under the eaves, wrapped in a blanket, his face showing the righteous anger of age. The cop gestured toward the square, and the old man stumbled down the steps into the rain. Alec watched all this, watched while the old man came toward him, his face screwed up into a bitterly condemnatory frown, and then passed him, dropping the blanket in the water on the pavement as he passed.

He felt around him his father's enveloping presence. He was a child, sitting between his father's legs, digging in sand. Alec felt his father's chest behind his shoulders—he was enveloped in his father's arms—as his father talked to someone else. He smelt the salt, his father's cigarettes and aftershave, his hair tonic, the odor of gin on his breath as he talked.

The scene that actually took place happened thirteen years ago. Alec woke up to find Stephen, at eight, sitting on the floor staring at him. Alec was lying on his stomach on the bed, his arm hanging down onto the floor, his face partly hidden in the pillow. He sensed someone's presence, so he opened the one eye which was not directly in the pillow.

"You wouldn't wake up, Dad."

"I'm awake."

"You wouldn't wake up. Mom's left."

"Wha—?"

"Mom said she was leaving—"

Alec rose up from the bed.

"—she's not coming back. I tried to wake you up but I couldn't."
The jagged, wrenching intake of breath broke up the words and made them almost unrecognizable as speech.

48

Winter Rain

With a stride, Alec was there, over him, and leaned down and wrapped the boy in his arms—"Stephen"—about to stroke him.

The boy was screaming, beating on Alec's back. "I hate you! I hate you! I hate you!" struggling against Alec's grip around his legs.

The raw glare of the lights swirled around his head. The boy's fists beat harmlessly on his back and then around his forehead and temples. "I didn't want Mom to leave me with you!"

"Stephen!"

Alec had the ability not to remember this memory, when he was remembering Stephen's childhood, and when he was thinking of himself as the father of his boy. *I hate you* didn't spring to mind when he came to wonder how it had been. In fact, he was able to go for years without remembering Stephen on the floor of the bedroom that morning. It was another memory so packed in alcohol that it wasn't normally available to him, when he looked for it, and so, for years at a time, he forgot to look. Much of Alec's life was like this, whole events blacked out by alcohol, by the oddly selective way drunkenness treats the past—blotting out memories so saturated in blood that they would otherwise have stained every other image of the past, and, at the same time, latching on to apparently benign memories and turning them inside out so that the chance memory of a late summer's afternoon at the lake darkened to fit the memory of a feeling, grew purple with rage.

So selective was Alec's memory that his past was like three-thousand year old scrolls found in jars—half, three-quarters of the text was missing. His method of reconstruction was simple, although he could not have described it if you had asked. He had a feeling, and he sought for memories to sustain it. His anger and his self-pity now, in his middle age, were like money. They transformed everything, caused him to blot out whole years of his life, to twist out of all recognition the significance of great events, and even, though he would have been unable to admit to this, to create the past. He could now, at forty-eight, because he was angry, tell you why he was angry, give you events and remarks, scenes and sound effects, with himself at various ages and sizes surrounded by a changing cast. He had used his feelings, which had their own coherence, to create a coherent past out of the incoherent fragments of his memory. The fact that he might be getting it all wrong—out of the scattered stones on the ground, the detritus of a score of successive superimposed cultures, create a temple which had never existed—didn't matter.

49

Winter Rain

He would return home and call Stephen. He must reach Stephen (783-5962). He walked now through the rain toward home, toward the Piston, his neighborhood bar. A last drink. None of it was any good if he couldn't get his father to understand. There would be enough money for Amos. Michael would forgive. Gaetano would solve everything. He would call Horace in the morning and get his help.

And finally, after the Piston had closed, Alec found himself at just before two-thirty in the morning leaning up against a brick wall six blocks from his apartment, his hands in his pockets, waiting for the sudden, heavy downpour to stop. He tilted his head up, his mouth closed, his eyes closed, and felt the wet chill on his skin. The colors of the night were the pale yellow gold of the street lights, the intense red and green of the traffic signals (blood of plant and animal kingdoms), the blue-to-gray of everything else. So soaked was Alec that he didn't think, sensed only that he was cold and wet, felt he had to go home. He stepped out into the rain and lurched down the sidewalk, almost run over by a stretch limousine.

"Hey, Mister—"

Alec kept on.

"Hey, Mister—"

Although he was the only other person in the street, he was able to think this voice wasn't for him.

A figure stumbled out of a doorway behind Alec, toward him, hand outstretched. "Hey, Mister"

When the hand, the long claw-like fingers, touched Alec's shoulder, dragged down across the slick rubber-like material, Alec came to life for the first time, jerked away just as the hand clawed at him again, raking the fingernails this time down Alec's throat.

"Hey Mister—"

Alec, coming up out of his deep senses where he swam, suddenly found his voice. "What—!" At the same time, he swung around toward whatever it was behind him, his arm out.

His turn gathered momentum as it came around, and his arm, outstretched, led by the edge of his hand, gathered force, and connected, hard, against something even before Alec saw what it was. The pain, for a moment, was intense, on the edge of his hand. Then the other man was gone, his sharp edges melted into the shadows, leaving Alec alone in the street again. Later, closer to home, Alec forgot about the pain, which was dull and diffused across half his

50

hand and no longer sharp just at the edge. He couldn't think, couldn't do anything beyond the impossibly difficult job of staying upright and moving his feet one in front of the other without falling over them.

In the morning Alec found Michael in his bed. He stared at him, his head on the pillow, his line of sight across the white sheets a foreshortened depth of field, Michael monstrously distorted, trying to put together what he knew about yesterday from this fact of Michael asleep in his bed. Michael had called him. They had discussed this yesterday, and he was here because they had discussed it and decided that his coming here was the right thing to do. Or Michael (Michael had his own key) had, for reasons of his own, come in the middle of the night, after Alec had gone to bed. He slept peacefully, no tension around his eyes or in his jaw.

Eventually Michael woke up. When he opened his eyes and saw Alec staring at him, he closed his eyes again. "You don't remember last night." He drew his hand over his forehead. "Of course, you don't remember last night. You were drunk last night." He threw the covers off and swung his legs over the side of the bed. "You were too drunk last night to leave with Amos so Gaetano called me. I'm here to look after Amos, don't you remember. Stephen called last night all night long. I think he was drunk. Finally I turned the phone off." Then he turned back to look at Alec. He put out his hand toward Alec's face. "What happened to your head?"

Alec didn't have a clue.

3

When he called Stephen back, he got the answering machine. The bombing was on the tube again. While he sat at the end of the sofa, watching the pictures, punching in the numbers (783-5962), the phone in his hand rang.

"Alec—" His father's voice could suggest surprise and complacency and distaste in a syllable. Alec himself had cultivated a plainer speech. "—I have found you at last. I have news."

"What's that?"

"Bernice and I are in New York. On our way home, we have decided to swing by Boston and to pay you a visit this afternoon. We'll be arriving after lunch and will check into the Ritz after we get into town. Can we expect you for dinner at the hotel?"

Alec found himself agreeing to the arrangements. Then he hung up. He would be angry about this in five minutes. He wanted to hit something, hard, and cause pain. He wanted a drink. He heaved himself up off the sofa.

"If you are going to shout like that—" Michael stood in the door. "—you will disturb Amos. He's restless as it is, and uncomfortable."

Alec brought his arms up, his fists together, and then brought them down. He wanted to bellow. He turned away to the windows.

Alec was forty-eight, and his father put him on a leash and jerked him around, He felt wrong, inadequate. He hated him, hated himself, looked back at Michael—"Go fuck yourself"—and pushed past him to the kitchen, where there was alcohol.

"What the fuck is the matter with you?"

Alec felt Michael watch him as he jerked open the cabinet door, threw a glass onto the counter and reached for the bottle, unscrewing the top while he was bringing it down from the shelf—"Little early for that, isn't it?"—while he felt he would explode if he didn't get it into him. He poured it in, splashing some, drank two swallows, looking out the window over the sink, into an airwell, at a brick wall opposite, then said, "I have to reach Stephen." It was something he had to do.

"What happened to your hand?"

Alec ignored him. He had to reach Stephen. He felt unmoored, and he You never said."

He took another long, desperate, thirsty sip. Across the air well, he watched while a woman, a foreign student from a Near Eastern or North African culture, poured bird feed on the windowsill for the pigeons. There was bird shit on all the windowsills.

Things were cracking up, falling apart. His mind, made of porcelain, was crazing and cracking up and falling apart, piece by piece, starting at the edges. Why didn't he have work? There was something about him, something that even Alec didn't know, which potential employers could spot when he was interviewed, which told them not to hire him, some twitch, some jerk of his head, that told them he was crazy, dangerous, couldn't be trusted, would turn violent and self-destructive.

"Look, I've got to go."

Michael always left at the tough moment. He was tall and slender and the type of young American manhood (strong profile, strong chin, long columnar neck, strong mouth, steady gaze, open face), and he ran like a rabbit every time, tail in the air.

"Amos is sleeping."

He turned away, got a coat from the closet, gathered his things, filled a bag. Alec watched him abandon him.

"He's had all his medications until noon. Can you handle it?"

He was concerned. His face showed concern, and Alec hated it that he was able to make his face show anything he wanted it to. Alec himself was trapped inside a face that showed rage only. He knew, if he tried right now to twist his face into an illustration of—indifference, say—he would fail, end by having a face showing a demonic, twisted attempt to cover rage with indifference. He wanted Michael out of his life. He wanted his father out of his life. His "mother"!

Winter Rain

"Are you going to be OK?" Michael approached him, put out his arm slid his hand around behind Alec's neck, pulled him close and kissed him on the lips. "Will you be OK?"

Alec squinted, the muscles in his face grew taut, will I be OK? and allowed himself to be kissed.

"I worry about you—"

Later, after Michael was gone, while sitting next to the bed holding Amos's hand, Alec sipped a drink and, like a pearl diver, dove deeper and deeper and deeper into the sea, down where the sun shone little or not at all, into a permanent twilight, last light before night, down far from the choppy waves, down where the currents were slow and wide and deep. And with each drink during the long day, the interval between waves became longer and their amplitude greater, and the feelings with which he had be gun the afternoon—anger, rage, envy, self hatred—resolved themselves into one rhythmic pouring out of grief.

At one, Gaetano was with Amos, and Alec was in his car. In the paper, there had been two ads for managers for convenience stores and one for the manager of a bookstore. He answered the two classifieds for night manager positions in stores at the edge and at different ends of his district. He drove over, double-parked, ran in, filled out applications and was told he would be called. He bought a copy of the Classifieds. The manager at the counter, a darkskinned man with an accent, interrupted a conversation with another darkskinned man in a language Alec didn't recognize to take his money. Then he double-parked and, putting his shoulder against the rain, he walked down the street to a pharmacy and picked up medications. Each time he put his hand into his pocket to pull out change or for protection against the cold, the raw, sore edge of the heel of his hand was raked by the edge of his pocket, and he winced with the pain. It hurt when he drove.

Near two large ornamental pillars marking the entrance to the fens, he crossed the street from the pharmacy. A pair of hookers in black plastic raincoats and spike heels glanced at him and then away, allowing him to check them out. As he drove along the edge of the fens, an old man trundled by pushing a wire shopping basket with large green plastic garbage bags of bottles, mumbling to himself. Under the roof of an old building falling down in the middle of the fens, an old man waited, looking for sex. People had varying

57

opinions about these beggars. They needed to be institutionalized, but the government couldn't afford it. On the other hand, in a high tech society like ours, there were bound to be people who couldn't hack it, who didn't have the education or the brains. Some said it was a question of character. These were failed human beings.

Driving around the fens was difficult—there was a system of one-way streets circling the park—and traffic was alternately very fast on winding parkways and clogged on the short narrow straight streets. Alec drove fast wherever he was, used his brakes liberally, kept one hand on the wheel and the other to push back his hair from his forehead. Driving fast, causing the tires to scream, expressed the tension he felt, and it was satisfying to him to know his car, roaring through the quiet streets, caused people to scatter, and to stop and look.

Alec, leaving his paper and his bag of drugs in the car, stopped by the Piston. The tv was on: pictures of planes taking off and landing, GI work crews refueling planes, convoys across a desert, nighttime black and white shots of bombing: ordinary bridges, schools, factories in the universal modernist architecture exploding and collapsing in a cloud of dust and a pile of rubble. These were followed by still pictures of Saddam Hussein, a stern, handsome man with a shock of black hair and black mustache, characterized as a "Hitler," "a psychotic," "powermad." The President said the war was America's righteous response to this madman, the rising up of Good against Evil. People on tv said this Hussein killed babies. While the contest was defined in terms as ancient as the Old Testament, the style of the pictures on the screen was late twentieth century entertainment: movies for children about wars in space with high-tech special effects—Armageddon weapon systems, dazzling technology which defeated nature. "We can see in the dark!" No bomb missed its chimney, no rocket its missile. The Mother of All Battles was being brought to the living room of the American public, cartoons made real.

There were men sitting at the bar, nursing drinks, watching these pictures on a screen which ordinarily showed porno flicks. Alec threw his keys on the bar and ordered a drink. The men watched impassively. The screen was on the wall of the bar devoted to AIDS posters and Safe Sex posters, and a man watching the bombing could see, around the edges of the screen, portions of the AIDS posters which hung on the wall behind it.

"How is Amos?" The bartender, Donald, slid a drink down the bar.

"He sleeps."

"Who is with him?"

"Gaetano."

Donald grinned. "He's a hunk."

When he brought Alec another drink, he paused at the bar. "How's the work search?"

"I'm not really looking—"

Two of their friends had been laid off. "Not given any notice at all. Just told to clear out." Donald wiped the bar. "Neither one of them has anything." There was nothing separating Alec from the two men laid off. He was himself only a couple hundred dollars from being on the street. They watched the pictures of the bombing. No weapon in the last ten years had been too bizarre to be bought by the people. Sitting in the dark bar, the men watched the stuff perform.

On the way home, he passed the entrance to a straight bar, which two men were leaving. As he approached them, they looked him up and down and smiled.

"Faggot."

Anger was suddenly there at the surface, and the hatred which had been there all along was in his mouth. He calculated the size of the two men, who else was on the street, and considered whether he could take them, how much damage he could inflict on them and how much he would suffer himself.

"Asshole." It was a measured escalation. In the ne xt step up, he slowed and let the two men get the measure of him. They were fat and greasy and out of shape. "Assholes." He said it in a slow whisper. They would be able to understand the shape of his lips even if they couldn't hear his word. They hesitated, glanced at each other, didn't smile, continued to move away from the bar door across the sidewalk to the line of cars.

Alec came almost to a halt. He now had the advantage. His arms hung down to his sides, holding the paper and the bag of drugs . Barely perceptibly, he moved his body toward a crouch. He showed he was ready to drop what he had in his hands. His eyes squinted.

He said it again, miming the word this time with his lips: ass hole.

The moment passed. They moved on across the sidewalk, and away from him, and Alec passed them, feeling their stare in his back, listening for the sound of any movement on the concrete other than his own feet. Any city was a dangerous place for a gay man, and Alec had perfected the ability to be aware of other movement on the sidewalk before and after him and never walked down the street without knowing who was behind him and where.

It was only when he was free again that he realized he had left his car at the bar.

Amos was among the first of their friends to test positive. At that time, a positive result was said to be a death sentence, and, never having known anyone under sentence of death, Amos's friends treated him as if he were mysterious and awesome, who knew things they couldn't know, being still on this side of the line between the living and the dead. Amos's friends watched him and watched themselves, and learned how to be around someone under a sentence of death. While they were learning, others of their friends, who had tested later, tested positive and died from PCP or Lymphoma or KS or CMV or something mysterious that happened in the brain. That is, Amos's friends were discovering that each person with HIV was living at a separate speed. For some, the intervals between a positive test and the appearance of the first symptoms to the onslaught of illness to death were as short as twelve months. Others went for years without a symptom, years between illnesses. Amos, among the first of their crowd to be tested positive, attended the funerals of a dozen of their friends who had tested after him. It was only in the last year that the speed of his illness increased. It was as if the whole lot of them were running down the beach, each at his own speed, their crowd stretched out for hundreds of yards along the sand. Behind them came this black hole which caught up with one and snuffed him out while others ran on ahead. Then this black hole picked out another of their crowd, running at a different speed, followed him until it caught up with him, snuffed him out, too, leaving his body on the beach, while the rest of them ran on. And it was impossible to know who was going next. Some said this difference was attributable to the age of the infected person. Younger men had a slower curve than older men. Others said it was a difference in attitudes in the way they responded to the invasion of the virus. It was said that men at peace with themselves seemed to survive longer than men who were angry. Some said there was no real difference in the curve of infection, the difference was only apparent, caused by the uncertainty of determining the moment of infection.

Winter Rain

On his way in, Alec ran into Margaret in the hall. She had, as she usually did, a mop in one hand and a bucket in the other, come from cleaning up the waste of the building. She looked, as she usually did, exhausted.

"How's Amos?"

"OK—" He shrugged. "—sleeping. He's not well."

She worked her jaw muscles, shook her head. She looked directly into his eyes for a long moment, then she went on past him without saying anything.

Alec sat on a straight chair next to the bed, which had been his grandmother's, the weak winter sun, in one of the few breaks in the rain, lighting the square of the shaded and curtained window. Amos's attention was mightily concentrated. Each breath seemed to be the result of conscious choice: I will breathe in now. I will breathe out now. Alec held Amos's limp hand. He allowed Alec to hold him. He was oblivious to the bedcovers, to his position in the bed, to whether or not his mouth was open. Alec watched him concentrate on breathing. He asked Amos if he wanted water, and Amos responded with a slight move of his head and returned to his concentration. It showed the barest notice of the question, had the instinctive rejection of a hand smoothing a hair when one was watching a movie. The move was inconclusive.

"Do you want water?"

Amos jerked his head in a way which was just barely more noticeable than before: no. He showed impatience by the alteration of a line across his forehead. It occurred to Alec that Amos could as easily have answered yes, that he didn't care whether he got water or not: he didn't want to be disturbed while he was about this important labor. Alec, holding his hand, sat by the bed, absorbed by Amos's concentration in this single activity. Alec had had difficulty getting his father's attention. Watching Amos die made it critical to Alec to find Stephen. As the minutes passed, gradually Alec let go one by one of his tense and mechanical responses to the demands of his own life, his father's quarrelsome nature, Michael's distance, even the things that gave him pleasure—his flute, sex. He heard the phone in the living room, turned off in here, and the answering machine kick in: "For God's sake—" It was Arabella's voice. "—where are you? I have to talk. Oh, Alec. I need help!" He gradually replaced them with a spreading and engrossing interest in the thing Amos was most interested in: his breathing.

61

Winter Rain

During the long afternoon while Michael was out of the house. Alec sat with Amos, concentrating on Amos's breathing and aware with a degree of precision every time Amos hesitated to begin the next breath—or paused after exhalation before beginning the long uphill climb toward filling his lungs again. When these little aberrations in the carefully timed sequence suggested that something was wrong—he had stopped breathing—Alec would become alert until the familiar sound began again, the hoarse intake of air down Amos's wind pipe. He couldn't leave him even for long enough to get a drink.

Occasionally, after a long and exhausted exhalation, the pause seemed interminable, and Alec realized he didn't know what he should do if Amos didn't resume breathing. Just as Alec was becoming aware that the feeling he was experiencing was fear, Amos might not breathe again, he noticed a spreading stain in the bedcovers (pale, moist, yellow) and, at the same moment, heard Amos resume breathing. The crisis had passed. Alec got up and changed the bedclothes and got a drink.

During the years of comparative health, before this current year of trauma and sickness, Amos had attended to "things." He had made a list of people with whom he felt he had to come to terms. Alec had watched this process, been part of this process, as his friend looked at his life and gradually, in a step-by-step manner, detached from it. Amos told stories of coming to terms with his father, his sister, from whom he was estranged, various people he had worked with, old lovers, friends who had moved to Pasadena and Tucson and Madison. Gradually, the things that he had had to deal with were found closer to home, the issues more immediate: who would do his laundry and to what extent would he be visibly grateful for that favor. Those who saw Amos every day—Alec, Michael, a few others—found themselves being dealt with, as if he were announcing, Now I am dying, Now you owe me. He put his head back on the pillow and had closed his eyes, opened his mouth, and, finally having declared truces, victories, defeats everywhere, gone home, retreated inside his head, to deal with the great struggle there.

Alec wanted to talk to Amos. What was it like to die, to come up against the end of everything, to have no future, no possibility of altering the course of events, of saying, tomorrow I will do better, to have memories but no hope? He wanted to ask the other questions that had never been asked. How had he dealt with his sister's hatred? Had he forgiven Alec when Alec had fucked the man from the bar in

Winter Rain

Provincetown that summer? Had he known that Alec had loved him?
Was it easier to forgive when you were dying? But it was clear now
that Amos no longer thought about any of these things, didn't give a
shit. This process had now brought them to this point where Amos
had not spoken in three days. Amos on his journey was far beyond
coming to terms. He didn't give a shit about Cardinals. What terms
he was going to come to, he had come to—or not. Faced with other
struggles, he no longer cared that it was his friend, his former lover,
who changed him, cleaned the urine off him, changed the sheets. He
no longer offered thanks, no longer complained.

Amos, slipping away in front of him on the bed, represented a
major instance of failure to bring closure; his death represented an
asymmetry in Alec's life, a failure to have done it and a recognition
that now it would never be possible to bring closure. Alec's father
presented the question of whether age (Death's spy) had arrived and
made a closure impossible. Stephen had left home and now refused
to answer his phone (783-5962). It seemed to Alec that he was
surrounded by people with whom it had suddenly become impossible
to say the last word. He fixed a drink and contemplated the
discovery that the last word had already been said, that now the only
person who could give the last word had moved on, was no longer
interested in the game, had turned to other things.

The light in the window had softened t o a rectangle of pale gold.
He clenched his hand and released it, feeling the ache in it. While he
held Amos's hand with one of his, he gripped his other and opened it
to look into the palm, to look at the discolored portion along the
outer edge. He couldn't remember how it had happened. How it had
happened seemed irrelevant, under the circumstances. He could
have fallen against something. He had gotten very drunk. Once he
had come home with a dent in the car fender without knowing how it
had gotten there.

Michael had asked him about the scratches on his neck, his arm
crossed on his chest, his eyes narrowed: "They're the kind of thing
that happens when you're making love. One or the other of you turns
into a cat and starts clawing—"

Alec had laughed. He hadn't known he had scratches on his neck.
He couldn't have picked up someone last night.

"I wouldn't put it past you."

"Hey, man. I'm in love with you. I don't fuck around —" He thought, I don't fuck around. I don't think I fuck around. I fuck around.

"You were drunk—"

"—even when I'm drunk—" I don't fuck around.

"When you're drunk, you don't know what you're doing."

"I know what I'm doing at the moment I'm doing it —" I fuck around.

"I've seen you—" I don't fuck around. "It's only later—"

"I've seen you paw Gaetano."

"I don't remember later. I know about it at the time. Gaetano knows I don't mean anything. I don't fuck around. So do you."

"You think it's cool, not remembering, coming home with scratches on your neck and a hand swollen like you were in a fight and not knowing how you got them. But it's not cool. You say you're monogamous. You say we're monogamous. Are we? How can I trust you, when you don't know where your dick was last night? What are those scratches on your neck? What did you pick up last night? Did you pick up a virus last night?"

What do I do? Alec hated Michael when he dredged up muck. "I'm not like that." I don't fuck around. I fuck around. What if I fuck around.

"When you're drunk, you don't know what you're like."

No. When Alec was drunk, he knew what he was like. But when he was sober, he didn't know what he was like when he was drunk. The possibility that he had been careless or indifferent last night proved the potential that the life one had was not the life one thought one had. Michael had said to him once, "You've got a skewed vision of reality." Well, of course. Ordinarily, when he couldn't remember, it was the morning after he had been out with Michael or Gaetano or Arabella, and the potential that what he couldn't remember was something horrific was minimal. They would have remembered —and told him of his sins. But sometimes, what he couldn't remember was a block of time when he had not been with anyone he knew, and the next day, piecing together last night, he knew there was someone in the city who remembered what he had done or where he had been last night but whose paths with him would never cross again, and what he had done last night, that chunk of his life, two, three hours, a half a day, was therefore irretrievably lost. And, worse, it was also possible that, a week hence, or a month or a year, Alec could walk into a room and some man or woman across the room would stand up, walk over to him, throw a drink in his face, and say, You shit. This particular lost past would not be lost any more: It would be dripping all over his face. What vision of reality encompassed his hurt hand?

His hand encompassed Amos's, who concentrated on his breathing. That was a reality which was inescapable. Late in the afternoon, Amos awoke. His eyelids fluttered, opened slightly; he took a deep breath and sighed and shifted slightly in the bed. The afternoon sun, prevented from entering the room by the shade, caused the room to glow thick yellow.

"How do you feel?" Alec often spoke to Amos, not expecting a reply.

Amos did not open his eyes. "Fine." The word reverberated through the room like the sound of a cello in a hall.

"Did you sleep well?"

"Oh, no. I have not been asleep."

"What have you been doing?"

"I've been busy, all morning."

These were the most words Amos had said since he arrived from the hospital. With each question, Alec pushed further to get Amos to come out of his sickness.

"What have you been doing?"

He sighed, again. "Shopping. I went shopping. Then I went to church."

"Did you enjoy that?"

Amos smiled, his eyes closed. "Oh, yes."

"Then what did you do?"

He didn't answer for a time. "We went out to eat. Everybody was there. I've been busy all day." He lay there for a while in the pale expiration of the light, his breathing almost imperceptible under the bedspread, Alec holding his hand. "I've been busy all day."

"Who was at the restaurant?"

This time Amos didn't respond. It was a letting go around the eyelids; he had lapsed again into his torpor.

Alec settled into the chair, his hand holding Amos's fingers, the light settling around him. He composed a letter in his mind, applying for the job to run the bookstore, advertised that morning in the paper. Since he had managed a restaurant and an all-night convenience store and had taught school, he was the perfect man for this job.

The phone rang again, and the machine answered it.

"Why aren't you there?" Arabella, she of the crisis and the drama. "Look, I'm on my way into town. Stephen called me. I think if you

65

want to see him, you can do it this afternoon in an hour, at the Bookstore Cafe. He'll be there. But what I'm calling about is this. I want to see you. I'm going to be at Paradise tonight at nine. I expect you there. This is Arabella. It's three o'clock. If you don't come, you're a shit. I love you."

Alec turned the drink around in his hand and stared at the ice as it melted. It was said there was a God who ordered things so that all the fault lines ran together and created a moment of crisis, during which character was defined. From his window, he watched while a man walked down the alley toward the trash dumpster, carrying a bag of trash in one hand and a small brown paper bag concealing a bottle of whiskey, from which he took sips, in the other. The man walked with tiny little steps (eight inches, ten inches) as if were he to walk at a greater speed, he would be in danger of falling over. Eventually, he made the dumpster, carefully lowered his trash inside, turned and walked back toward Alec, his tiny little steps keeping him upright, as if the segments of his body—his head, torso, pelvic region, thighs and calves—were not connected, were merely stacked on top of one another and that a too-quick or violent movement would cause the whole delicately balanced assemblage to fall to the concrete and shatter. Life carried a risk—stray gunfire (the article tomorrow would be about him: A Boston man, sitting at his window reading, was killed by stray gunfire yesterday), an out-of-control car on the street, a collision of subway trains in the dark tunnels, an encounter with a psychotic, armed mugger. In an anxious, tense city, death could come from any unexpected quarter. There was no such thi ng as safe. One was more or less, approximately, relatively in danger. Alec was continuously in danger of being in the wrong spot at the wrong time and of having a question, a proposal, a statement made (a gun discharged, a drink thrown in his face) whicah had nothing to do with him but which had the effect of exposing all his weaknesses, all his deceptions and self-deceptions, his failures, about which he himself had known nothing until the moment of sudden explosion.

It was a question of being exposed to the thing Alec had not prepared for. The lucky man was the one who never met the unexpected danger, who, having prepared to do rescue work with drowning victims, met, continuously, half-a-dozen times a week, cases of persons dragged from bodies of water —in which what was needed was what was known. Alec assumed the joke was that one prepared to revive drowning victims, which guaranteed that he would meet only burn victims for the rest of his life.

Winter Rain

After Michael arrived, Alec told him that Amos had waked enough to speak.

"What did he say?"

"He felt fine."

"Oh, terrific. What else?"

"That he'd been shopping."

"Oh—"

Their eyes were on the tv screen playing silently in the corner, the woman in fatigues holding a microphone and lit in the harsh glare of floodlights which shone on her lipstick. They watched her lips and her shiny lipstick making words (number of sorties, total tonnage, missile kills) while Michael came to terms with this new and worse stage of Amos's deterioration.

"I'll be back at six-thirty. I'm going to find Stephen."

"Is your father going to call?"

"Who the fuck knows. I'll be back in time to deal with him —"

Then he pulled on his coat and went out through the door and down the hall out into the wet cold dark afternoon (it had begun t o rain again), out onto the street and turned left toward downtown and toward the Bookstore Cafe. The last image he had of the apartment, as he closed the door behind him, was of Stephen's jackets hanging in the closet, among his own, and of Michael, staring at him as he pulled the door shut, looking as if he were being abandoned by a person he had expected, from the beginning, to be untrustworthy.

It didn't matter. There were no fewer homeless on the slick streets, and when he passed the entrance to the subway, there seemed to be more of them, huddled in the doorway there out of the rain, clawing at him from under their blankets and newspapers.

"Got'ny spare change?"

He was suddenly in a rage and, drawing his hands out of his pockets, threw them out in a great circular movement, clearing the space around him and striking a man as he did so, hitting him on the shoulder. The danger was that he could be out on the street. If he missed one month's rent, he could not catch up the next month when he got a job. There was no slack to take up, no fat under the skin to be absorbed, and any slip of the knife was fatal. The money he was spending on Amos already meant he couldn't make next month's bills, and the crisis which had been avoided by his paying for Amo s's medications had been transferred to him, to a crisis which would unfold at the end of the month when the rent came due.

Winter Rain

And when he got to the bookstore, inside, in the warmth, out of the rain, and ordered a drink, what he was looking for —but couldn't explain—was to get down under the fear he felt, which alloyed his anger and made it brittle, down to the anger itself, to escape the confusion of his feelings (anger called up fear, and hope despair) into something cleaner, deeper, smoother. Arabella said, "I never know what is going to set you off. Suddenly you ignite, and there is no talking to you until you burn out. Go away and drink. That's what you need." Michael and Gaetano and Amos, when he had been less sick, had understood this, and had left Alec alone.

He wandered through the store, down the aisles of new, shiny, hardback books, looking over the tops of the bookcases at the crowns of the heads of the other customers, hair of different color, quality, length, style, looking for the long curly dark hair that belonged to Stephen. He came around the end of the aisle and bumped into a young man (at first it seemed like him), but he had a beard and was heavy. Arabella had said he would be here. Why was he coming here? He was to be here, she had said. Alec passed through Fiction and Current Fiction and Biography and Autobiography and Photography and Dance and Theatre. He passed through Psychology and Self-Help and Men's Books and Women's Books and Gay and Lesbian Books, Poetry, Philosophy. He squeezed around men in heavy overcoats carrying umbrellas and passed women dripping water on the floor and stepped over people kneeling in the aisles. Stephen had to be found.

Stephen must come home. Stephen had been in therapy since he was fifteen, and Alec had imagined his sitting in an armchair, his head resting on the heel of his hand, staring off into the corner of the room, searching his memory: I don't remember. I was twelve, thirteen. I don't know. I had a blue snowsuit. I was on a sled. My nose was cold. The sky was dark and the cold was biting. As he sat there in the armchair, his head resting on his hand, the memory would take form, each detail remembered, called forth, added to the picture, each stroke of the brush. My blue snowsuit. What had he worn? The pause. The concentration on the picture which had thus far been assembled: the sky, the dark, the snow, the cold, the blue snowsuit, the sled, the nose. What had he worn? Had he even been there? He would have been there at some point, wearing something. But was he there then, and what was he wearing? What had he said? The silence, the pause. Have I ever been in this room before?

Winter Rain

Alec could remember giving a fully realized picture of some event in his past and the other man asking, When did that happen? and being unable to supply a date and then on analysis discovering that the picture he had given had internal contradictions (his father had not let his hair grow long until after Watergate, they didn't live in that house until he was in middle school) and then losing faith that the memory (so clear, so vivid) was of anything at all, was anything more than a composite of many times, was anything more than a fantasy. Had it happened? What was the source of the vivid image in his mind? So vivid he could still taste the adrenalin in his mouth when the image played itself out?

He pulled books down from the shelves, flipped through them, and replaced them in their slots—*I, Claudius, The Wasteland and Other Poems, Speak, Memory, Remembrance of Things Past*— looking for something that would hold him. Stephen would be looking for the one image that explained it all, and it was essential to Alec that he be there to say, *But I didn't buy the corduroy pants until two years later, when we moved to the brick house.* Stephen had to be found before some severe and permanent damage was done. That happened, but only once. There had to be someone who could say, *No. That didn't happen,* or if it did, *it only happened once.*

Why had Arabella thought Stephen would be here in this book store at this hour? It was now four-thirty. He was to have been here between four and five. Stephen returned to the bar and ordered another drink. A double. Life becomes more complicated. At some point in his youth, it had been possible for Alec to dream his own dreams. But then he had grown up and now it was necessary for Alec and Stephen to have the same memories of the same events, to sort out similar moral inventories of their shared past. Alec, shoving a book back onto the shelf without looking at its cover (it was a copy of Walter Lippman's *A Preface to Morals)*, grimaced. Alec's father had to be taken into account. The message on the answering machine had been this: "You've never been a steady person. Do you expect people to depend on you if you don't answer telephone calls?" It would be difficult to enjoy getting drunk if his head was cluttered with all these people, and it was Alec's practice to concentrate on one of them, his father, say, and then to concentrate on one aspect of his relationship with his father—a letter he had written to Alec when he was at summer camp—and then to allow the single, unadulterated feeling to burgeon and flow until it flowed copiously enough to swim in.

Winter Rain

His fear, which he had had to admit to regularly in the last year, had been that what Stephen was remembering, for he was in the process of reassembling all the bits and pieces of his memory, from his childhood was something revolting, something truly repellent about Alec himself, something worse than that he had merely beat him or had battered him. It had come as a shock to Alec, when he had not yet come to terms with his own father, who was still in the process of reassembling the bits and pieces of his own memories, to discover that he was the emerging villain of his son's memories. He was attempting to secure Stephen as an ally in his war against his own father. Could he get to Stephen's memories before Stephen himself could get to them?

He was in among the poetry books. Stephen had said, "It didn't work out the way it was supposed to—." It was the first time he had made a judgment about his life, and (he had been fifteen thereafter the comments came with increasing frequency. "Why did you leave Mom?" he had asked when he was seventeen. Why didn't you take me with you?

Once, walking into the living room on Saturday morning, he had found a bar glass in the middle of the living room floor. It was a mystery how it had gotten there. Amos (they were lovers then) had leaned back in his chair at breakfast and said, "Well, did you enjoy Paradise last night?" By listening carefully and putting details together, his memories came back to him. Ah, yes. Amos had come by at midnight and invited him to go to the bar. Gradually most of the hour or two spent at the bar would be retrieved, some comment Amos made releasing in Alec's mind some new part of the memory, the glass in the middle of the living room floor no longer a mystery.

It was essential that Stephen remember what had been good so that Alec's own memories, in which his good life had been destroyed by his father, could be preserved. *But why do I feel the way I do?* Stephen had cried out, just before leaving a month ago.

He was in among the AIDS books: *Living with AIDS, Medical Help, Safer Sex*, Paul Monette's book on the death of his lover. He had had unprotected sex with Amos since he had been infected. Since that time, he had had unprotected sex with Michael. Even now, at the end of sex, he looked down on Michael's belly and saw the small pool of semen lying on his skin. He pondered the route the virus had taken through their crowd. Safer Sex.

Two days ago, Stephen had read a curious item in the paper. A man had been killed in a robbery. It was not clear whether the man was the robber or his victim. On his death, organs and tissue from his body had been "harvested"—removed from the cadaver—and preserved and sent to 170 separate places around the country for use in transplants and medical procedures involving blood, organs and tissue. Standard tests had been run to detect HIV, with negative readings, but these 170 separate organs and bits of tissue were the common factor in new cases of infection around the country. Tests showed that this man had been infected with HIV so recently that antibodies had not had time to appear before his death and did not appear until after these organs were transplanted (along with the HIV virus) into new bodies. It appeared that 170 people would develop AIDS from this cadaver, which they had been told was free of the virus. The man whose body became the cadaver died not knowing that he had the virus and not knowing that his body would be cut up and dismembered and dispersed to the 170 separate places around the country, becoming the vehicle by which the virus would cross the continent.

It was five o'clock. Alec put down his drink and pulled on his gear, stuck his hands in his pockets, turned his back to the door and pushed against it, going out into the rain. He had missed Stephen. He had come earlier—or would come later, or not at all. Maybe he had come in, seen Alec, and left before Alec had had a chance to see him. Alec was anxious and deflated. He would write Stephen a note: Stephen, *I wanted to see you. No. Stephen: I love you. I hope you —. Stephen. I love you. Will you call me? I need —. Stephen, I am very sorry—*

He could be at the gym. He could be with Arabella. She had said he would be here, so she must have been in touch with him. He could be at Horace's. With Alec's father at the Ritz. Right now he could be trying to reach Alec at Alec's apartment. Alec looked for a phone.

"How is—" Alec was managing his umbrella, the phone, his change, hunching his back against the rain. "Amos?"

"Sleeping. How are you?"

"Has Stephen called?"

"No—"

"I have to reach him. I'm—"

"You're a mess. But you're much sought after. Arabella is trying to reach you. She says be at Paradise at nine. She's left Horace. Stephen has not called. Your father is looking for him, though. Your father is looking for you. He's at the Ritz. Your whole family appears to be falling apart. Are you all right?"

"I'm all right—" Why shouldn't he be all right? Since he'd left a decent home, there was something wrong with Stephen. Since he was on his fourth marriage and managed to indicate an interest in Alec only after his divorces, there was something wrong with Alec's father. There was something wrong with a country that was using its strength like a tyrant. But there was nothing wrong with Alec.

"You sound like a mess. Are you sure?"

Michael picked and picked without knowing what he was picking at. Invariably he stumbled on the wrong target. "I'm OK. I want to find Stephen. I'll call later. I'm exhausted."

Alec needed to have a talk with Michael when he got home. There was something, something big, that he needed to say to him, that they needed to talk about. He knew that much. He was about to formulate what it could be that he needed to talk to Michael about (*I'm sick of you being*) but it wouldn't come. It was there on the tip of his memory, right there at the end of it where he could taste it, but it was so evanescent that he couldn't lodge it between his teeth.

"Michael."

He heard Michael hesitate. "Yes?"

"Things can't go on this way—"

"What do you mean?"

"Well—"

"What 'things'?"

"Ah—"

"What do you mean, 'this way'?"

"Look—"

"Alec?"

"Ah—"

"What is going on?"

Alec could feel it coming on, the anger, rising up from way back in his throat, sour and nauseating. "You get in my way. I can't find Stephen, and you're so goddamn—"

Michael laughed. From where Alec stood, he could see back down the block to the entrance of the Bookstore Cafe, and he watched the people coming out and going in. The rain obscured his vision, and he could not be sure he wasn't seeing Stephen.

"Alec?"

He was pulled back to the conversation.

"Yeah?" He craned to see.

"What is going on?"

But the conversation didn't go anywhere. Alec hung up and walked up Boylston through the Prudential Building into the South End, toward the gym. The conversation didn't go anywhere because Alec didn't know what it was he had wanted from Michael. The news that Stephen had not called. But he didn't know what else he wanted —the news that Amos was still sleeping—to reach the ache. He passed a bar and, noticing it, stopped and had a drink.

His father was at the hotel. He would understand. He would hear him. And Alec began to look for a phone, as he walked toward the gym. For an hour or two, now, while he had been looking for Stephen, his father's message had been waiting at home: *I'm here, call me.* Suddenly, it seemed it would be good to be with his father, even with Bernice, who wouldn't get in the way. His father's brother had died, and Alec's father had been there with him. He knew what that was like. His eyes raked the streets, looking for phone booths. There was one ahead, in front of the Hardware Store.

He dropped in the coin and punched in the numbers and heard the sound of the ringing.

"Hello?" An unfamiliar female voice.

"Bernice?"

"Yes?" The voice was guarded.

"This is Alec, I got your message—" What he wanted was, he suddenly realized, for this unfamiliar female voice to overwhelm him with warmth and affection.

"Ah—"

He wanted more than the hesitation. "I'm near the hotel —" He was changing his plans even as he spoke, speaking even before he had thought about what he was going to say. "—and I could come by now—"

"—ah, well—"

"—if that were OK. We could talk about dinner—"

"—well, you see, our plans have changed, and it is going to be impossible, as much as we'd like—"

Impossible to go to dinner, even though Alec wanted, but you see, Alec's father and "mother" were very tired, after their transatlantic flight, and it was, as surely Alec would understand if he thought about it, asking a great deal of them (after all, Alec's father was not as strong as he had once been) to go dinner on such a short notice when it had been such a long time since any of them had seen each other. She referred to the strain of social life. It was impossible, even, for Alec to speak with his father, who was resting.

"No, I don't think there is any point in calling back later."

Hurtling down the street, past the great pile of the Christian Science Mother Church, his hands thrust hard and deep into his jacket pockets, his shoulders hunched over and his head down against the cold rain, Alec chewed his rage. He had believed him. For a fucking second, Alec had believed that his father wanted to see him.

But the worst was that Alec saw inescapably that he had wanted to see his father. Alec was able to go sometimes for years at a time without ever having to admit to himself that he still wanted to be stroked by the old shit. There was a gay bar around the corner from the gym. It was called The Hawk, and Alec found it and found a stool, found a drink, found in the alcohol a way of escaping his anger, which was violent and murderous, into the only other haven available to him, self-pity.

Alec, who suspected that his friends thought he was an alcoholic, found Gaetano at the gym. Gaetano, unlike Michael, could be counted on never to bring up Alec's behavior when he was drinking. Gaetano watched Alec attack the weights. Alec threw the bar into the air as if its resistance were personal, as if he could hurt it. He grunted and exhaled and grimaced, the muscles of his face tight and swollen with exertion.

"Take it easy—"

Alec, who thought he was taking it easy, grunted.

"Have you found Stephen?"

Stephen didn't want to be found. He could search, but if Stephen didn't want to be found. He pushed against the bar, up off his chest, up, and up, and up. He couldn't do what Gaetano invited him to do. He couldn't talk about it. He pushed the bar off his chest. He pushed the bar off his chest. He couldn't talk about it.

"I called."

Alec didn't answer.

"Michael said that Amos was better today. He talked."

What was it that he couldn't talk about? He would find Stephen. He would search for him to the ends of the earth. He would never be able to hide from him.

"Michael said your old man's in town."

Alec sat up on the bench. "Is that all the fuck you have to talk about?"

Gaetano shrugged. "That's the new business, isn't it? Your dad arrived today with his new wife?"

"I don't have anything to do with him—"

Gaetano laughed.

"Leave me the fuck alone."

"What's the matter—" They fought like old friends: they knew where the old wounds were, and went for them. "—it pisses you off to know we all know he's in town and you don't give a shit about him —" He paused. "—or is it that he doesn't give a shit about you?" He laughed, took his foot off the bench, turned to the next bench. "It's driving you crazy that he's here—" He dropped the bar onto the rack and began carelessly to slide on plates.

Alec pushed the bar off his chest. Then up, again. Then up, again. Furiously, he drew in his breath and blew it out, in again, and out, in synch with the movement of the bar, not answering Michael , watching the black dull iron come down to his chest and go up the length of his arm and descend again.

"—don't you tell him off? tell him to go fuck himself this time? " Gaetano was laughing.

"Go fuck yourself."

"I would if I were you—"

Gaetano lowered the weight against the rack. He sat up. "On th'other hand, I prob'bly would'n either." He slapped his thighs. "My old man's a shit too. He don't even want to see me. When we're finished here, le's go get a drink—" He was afraid, sometimes, that he was going to push Alec too far, and then Alec wouldn't come back. He didn't like Alec's anger. Sometimes he was afraid of it, but Alec was important in a way he didn't understand and couldn't have spoken about. There were moments when he felt that Alec was deep.

An hour later, Alec was in the Paradise, looking for Arabella. He found her leaning against a bar on the upper level, watching the dance floor with the look that said, while she was dressed and ready for it, she had done this before and didn't expect any surprises.

She kissed him. "The trouble with your family is that none of you know when to give up." She put her hand behind his neck and kissed him again. "You've been drinking." She lit a cigarette. Her husky voice was pitched beneath the music and carried just far enough to reach his ear. "Come with me."

They got drinks.

She led him up the stairs. As she climbed, Alec watched her rear end move from side to side in the tight shiny material of her skirt. She was a beautiful woman. They were going to the bar upstairs, away from the dance floor. The sight of her legs and her buttocks moving under the shiny material was arresting. In the dark room, she found a banquette and sat down, placed her purse on her lap and crossed her legs.

"Can you believe it?" She held a cigarette in one hand up by her face, her elbow resting in her other hand. She looked away, blowing smoke in another direction. She looked back at Alec and raised her eyebrows.

He didn't know what she was talking about.

"Every time I think I can concentrate again, I forget and turn on the radio—or the tv—and I'm pulled away from whatever it was to our planes."

"I don't have time for planes, Arabella —"

"—you're right—"

"—or energy. Get to it."

"—that's not why I called you. I don't know why I expected it not to happen to me. I watched it happen to your mother, after I was married, but it never occurred to me that it would happen to me. You're all alike. All the men in your family. Your father, Horace, you. I feel so sorry for Stephen—"

"There's nothing wrong with Stephen—"

"Oh, I know. Nothing wrong with him. Just look at his family! Bad genes, every one of you."

"I don't have bad genes."

She laughed. "Your father! Still strutting his stuff at 82. That's an equivocal message. It's not genes anyway. It's the way you all raise your children—"

"It's Stephen avoiding me, not the other way around. He didn't show this afternoon—"

"You were late. Did you get there on time?"

"I was there an hour. Why did you think he would come?"

She shrugged. While she was smaller than Alec, when she looked at him she seemed to look down on him, her eyelids slightly darkened with eyeshadow, her long lashes veiling her eyes. Her eyes seemed less to look at him than to rest on him, to caress him but at the same time to mother him.

It was a peculiarity of Arabella's that she didn't often close her mouth. It was open now, in her odd asymmetrical way, showing a bit of the teeth on the right side and none on the left. Her open mouth suggested willingness, an eagerness even, a sensuous and sexy abandon.

"I didn't know he would be there. I thought that was where he would be going this afternoon—"

"Why?" This was a mystery to Alec. What did they have between them? "What—"

"Why, we were talking about a book, and I told him that bookstore was where he could get it. He said he'd go after four, when he got off work—"

"I don't understand. When did you talk to him? Where —"

"Oh, Alec—" She put her hand on his knee. "—he calls me almost every day." Her green eyes rested on him, watching him suffer, her mouth slightly open in her way, ready to say something to ease his hurt.

"What book—?" Every day. It had been a month since Stephen's call. He would call Arabella, but not his father. He didn't owe Arabella anything. He didn't mean anything to Arabella. They were nothing to each other. Not shit to each other. *He calls me almost every day.* The little shit. I'm his father.

"He calls me—"

"What do you talk about?"

She shrugged. "His life, his family, what else?"

"Me."

"You and Gloria."

"Holy hell. Why you?"

"Why not? I'm married to one of you."

"So during all this time when I was trying to reach him and he wouldn't call back or tell me where he was, you've been seeing him every day—"

"—talking to him on the phone most days—"

"Why wouldn't he answer me?"

She shrugged. "Oh do get me another drink. I'm dying with all this heavy talk." She looked out across the room at the people milling about.

"Why wouldn't he answer me?"

She looked at him, at his mouth, waiting perhaps for him to say something else. Her characteristic way was to look you in the eye, then to drop her eyes to your lips and to watch them.

"Why wouldn't he answer me?"

She looked him in the eye again, her head tilted back slightly, her eyelids darkened by eyeshadow. "All the men in your family are abusive." She reached for her purse and for cigarettes. "I think he has just come to that." Then, after she lit a cigarette, she blew smoke above their heads and watched him, settling down into a waiting silence.

So.

"Want that drink?"

She smiled, nodded.

"Same?"

OK. He moved through the crowd toward the bar. His father had arrived today, and the message which Alec had been expecting had come in the afternoon: *Bernice and I are in town. Call us. We can meet for drinks. Bernice and I would like it if you were to join us tonight for dinner.* The old shit.

When he brought the drinks back to the table, Arabella thanked him and put some bills on the table partially under her cigarettes.

"I know you don't have money. I want this to be on me." She sipped hers through her straw, her head down, pursing her lips, her eyes open and watching people around her. Then she leaned back against the banquette and looked at Alec. "You're all shits."

Alec threw his drink back and grinned. "If that's all you have to say."

She smiled. "Do you think I don't love you, just because I say you're a shit?"

"I don't know."

"Stephen needs someone to talk to."

Yeah.

"You've got the same thing your brother has. Both of you are —. It was just that Stephen needed to talk about the way you've been recently."

"How have I been?"

She laughed. "You've been driving him away."

"When?"

"You sound like Horace. When? As if you didn't know. Honey. This is me, Arabella. Lie to Stephen, but not to me. Horace says, 'I don't remember that!'"

"What?"

"Whatever I am telling him about, when he beats up on me. He pretends he doesn't know, doesn't remember. It's as if he thinks he doesn't have to know. You. You're so unconscious. You don't seem to know what's happening around you. You don't want to know."

"What's set all this off? I thought—"

"You thought I wanted to meet you because I was leaving Horace. I'm in crisis, and I needed to talk to you. You came here prepared to help me out of whatever mess I was in. I can get myself out of my own messes. I'm a successful, professional woman, remember? I have my own money. I wanted to meet you because something horrific is happening in your life, and you—you're such a coward you won't face it—"

"Face what? What are you talking about?"

"Oh, do get me a drink." She reached for her purse. "Here's some money. And Alec—" He was rising from his chair, but he stopped and waited. "—you do know I love you, don't you?" The look she had—her lowered eyelids, her partially opened mouth— suggested she wanted him to answer at the same time she doubted he agreed.

He glanced at the money. "Oh sure. Sure. I know you love me." He went away through the crowd, men and women whose attention was nervously divided between the person they were speaking to and everyone else, toward the bar. The sense of crisis was made more urgent by the music, hard and loud, and by the light show. The patrons of the bar were twelve feet under the epicenter of an electrical storm. Alec's mind saw dangers everywhere —in Stephen, in Amos, in Michael, Gaetano, Horace, his father (Bernice!), his joblessness, each of whom threatened Alec's assertion that he was OK—and nowhere. Since he depended on no one else, there was nothing that anyone could do to him.

He was unprepared, when he returned to the table, to hear what Arabella said to him.

"You molested Stephen when he was small."

He had been in the process of putting down the drinks and of lowering himself into his chair when she spoke. It was a moment before he heard that she had spoken. What she said was unclear.

"What?" He looked up at her, almost, but not quite, certain that he had heard something incredible.

"Stephen says you molested him when he was small."

The thing was so stupefying—even yet it didn't make sense—that he wondered if he could have misheard her.

"Molested him?"

She was hesitant. "You know." She paused. "Sexually molested—"

"Stephen?"

"Yes! That is who we are talking about."

"Molested him! He says that?—"

She nodded, watching him warily.

"—that shit!—"

She laughed a small laugh. "That's the ticket. Attack him. Don't let him hold the advantage."

Alec was confused for a moment.

She laughed a larger laugh. "Listen to what he says, Alec."

"He's accusing me of being a monster —"

She put out her hand and touched him. "You're about to be angry with me. You're feeling I don't love you."

"Do you believe him?" He searched her face.

"I believe he believes it."

He slid down on the seat, lay his head back, and groaned. "Oh great. Oh great." He sat up straight on the banquette again and looked at her. "I didn't do it. I never molested him —"

The thing was there, and there was nothing he could do. The charge had been made, and even a denial left him with tar on his soul.

He laughed. "I thought this was about Horace —"

"Horace? That's all over. I've moved out." She grinned, and rolled her eyes. "Gaetano!"

Later, she told him that Stephen had gone to the Ritz this afternoon and had spoken to Alec's father. She said that Alec's father had asked Bernice to leave the room so that he could talk to Stephen, that he had expressed shock and fury. "I doubt that he will ever speak to you again—"

Alec bought them another round of drinks. There was a hopelessness and a fury about him that showed itself in the steadiness of his drinking. He put them away, one after the other, staring off through red eyes into the crowd under the lightning. Arabella grew silent, accepting the drinks he brought her, getting up once to go to the bathroom and once to buy cigarettes, but otherwise sitting still, her lidded eyes filling with tears.

At one point, she asked, "When did you start drinking —"

It was an odd question. "I don't know." Then, "Why?"

"I just wanted to know." Their sentences came out one after another and lay there in little pools of silence until they had absorbed all the silence—they were like sponges that soaked it all up—until one or the other of them threw out another sentence: "You seemed so drunk already when you got here."

"You mean tonight—"

"Yeah. When did you start drinking today? this morning?"

"I thought you meant, *how old was I.*"

She was staring toward the bar. She didn't say anything, and he didn't, and then she asked the question again: "When did you start drinking this morning?"

He looked at her to try to figure out her meaning.

He took a stab. "My father called this morning. After that."

She was quiet.

"Is that what you mean?"

"Do you suppose we drink too much?"

It lay there soaking up silence.

It was like tar, the question, and it didn't need an answer. The continuous, rolling crashes of the music taking place all around this silence moved in closer until all the silence was soaked up. The lightning flashed above their heads.

"—never hung up on morals, really. I always knew my mother wasn't telling the truth about sex. She didn't know the truth about sex. None of them did. The priest. They didn't tell the truth about sex anymore than the President told the truth about race. I found my own way—"

Sometimes the music obscured her words. Alec wasn't listening anyway. Her words were part of the noise of the room.

"—these things happen, and you wonder how they could have been prevented, and maybe they couldn't have been prevented, but nobody tells you that, you know? It's the risk you take being alive, that everything you were ever told turns up inadequate, and you find yourself in territory where nothing you ever learn ed is any use—"

She placed her purse on her lap and held the clasp with both hands, staring off into the crowd of dancers.

"—I was so pretty. Just straight out of bed. In jeans and a tee shirt. I was so smart. There wasn't anything I couldn't do. I believed in myself. Do you remember how we were when we were first married? Jesus, he was a handsome man. I clung to him. Just being with him made me feel—endowed, gifted, terribly lucky. Now I don't know what that means. Now I'm a ball-breaker. That's what I

81

am. I can see myself. I used to think all my success was because I had talent. And skill. Charm. Now I think anything I do is almost an accident. By chance. I used to be one kind of person, and now I am another kind of person. I changed. I have become the kind of person who hurts people. I couldn't measure how much I enjoy hurting Horace.

"I like to see him suffer. The way to his heart is through his dick, and I attack him whenever I can. I belittle him, point out where he fails, increase his anxiety. I've told him I was disappointed when we first made love. I told him I only stayed with him because of the money—"

The first time Alec saw Arabella was in a restaurant after a wedding. Horace had brought her. The crowd of them sat around at table—six or eight around a table too small for two —the men in white tie, the women in long gowns. Arabella's was a long dress of some stiff ivory-colored material. The exhausted gaiety of an after-the-wedding party. She was at the other end of the table, and Alec had watched her (Gloria was opposite him) as if she had been a young ballerina alone on a stage, performing for herself. She listened to what was being said, to one after another of the speakers, her head tilted like a bright bird's. She sat sideways in her chair, almost perched on it, and oddly he remembered her saying, "—the color was pure—" He couldn't remember now what she was talking about, to what the words had referred. Then she had begun to expand on some point, her elbow on the table, her palm up, her fingers slightly spread and bent, like a statute's, and it would have been perfect if cool clear water had run out of her palm down between her fingers, to drip into a bank of ivy. Her words were lost to him.

She had closed her mouth firmly. Alec even knew what he himself had looked like at that nightclub table. There had been a picture taken and the members of the wedding party had decided to commemorate the occasion: His thick hair, wetted with a gel, was parted and brushed back. Alec saw himself smiling into the camera, his tailcoat pushed back from his waist, his head thrown slightly back, ease and elegance suggested by the casual way his fingers toyed with a silver cigarette case (his mother's gift to his father, his father's initials) to the white tablecloth. His face showed amusement, self-confidence, a light disdain for the scene. It was as if, despite the dress and the place, Alec felt himself slumming. In his mind's eye,

Alec's eye lingered on the breadth of his shoulders and the taper to his waist. He had been 26.

"—your friend the stockbroker—"

He pulled his mind back haltingly. The stockbroker.

"—who used to be transvestite prostitute—"

Him.

"There are so many questions. How did it feel to be a stockbroker after you've been a prostitute? Did he want to go back?"

"What?"

"Go back. Be a prostitute again. Did he miss the color? Can you go back? How did it feel to be so different?"

There was a series of photographs of Alec sitting next to Stephen in wooden lawn chairs under an apple tree. It had been parents' weekend at a summer camp Stephen was attending. Stephen was ten —or twelve—and sat next to Alec, listening to him under the blue sky. Everything in the photograph seemed new and fresh, the leaves on the apple tree, the luxuriant green grass which was so thick it hid their shoes, their skin (he was aware of the wreckage of his face), and the grief he felt was for unavoidable loss.

"There is no way a transvestite can imagine what it would be like to be a stockbroker. Do you suppose?" Then, "Can you remember?"

He had hated his life then. The picture had captured him at a moment when he had been most successful at playing a difficult role. Was there, in the fact of disguise, of hiding something primal a bout oneself, of selling some version of what one was, something which united the two? Two different prostitutions? Something that could give meaning to the man's life? Or was there nothing to it? He did this and then did that, pushed the moment to an overwhelming question.

"Stephen hates you."

When had it happened? What had he missed? "I—" He didn't know how to begin. "I—" What was there more to say? "I—" There must be a way to present his case. "But you see —"

"Your father is contemptuous—"

It was last call, and the bartender wouldn't sell any more drinks. The lurid lights, the electrical storm, the pounding music. Then the bar closed. Alec and Arabella collected their coats and umbrellas from the coatcheck and went out into the rain. She said, "Get me a cab," but she didn't tell him where she was going. Then he was on the street alone. Almost alone. A young man in the middle of the block came toward him, leaning on a cane with one hand, the other holding up an umbrella. Alec watched his shuffling step approach.

"Got'ny money?"

"No."

"God bless—"

The young man was on his way, a lame bird, hopping down the street, his dark form reflected in the pools of water on the pavement. Alec could not have easily described what he had done since noon today. It was impossible to recover the remote past. How many years? Stephen was 21 now. Ten. Twelve. When Alec was 40. What had life been like when he was 40?

The photographs which still existed of him at 40 showed someone still young. A search of an unlined face in a photograph didn't show what he had been capable of when the photograph had been taken. The more pointed question—what had he done?—couldn't be answered. Coming up upon an intersection, he had turned right —or left. And at this distance of twelve years, during which he had come up upon thousands of intersections and had turned right (or left), there seemed no way to rediscover, to resurrect the moment when he had arrived at this particular intersection—the wind from the southwest blowing his hair in his eyes and the sun from the south in his eyes, the trailer truck stalled, and the beggar woman, caught in the silver light of late winter afternoon, transfigured by the light into an angel of hunger—and had turned right into the wind and the sun toward the moment which was now completely lost to him. Had that happened? Had he dreamed it? How, in the years since the time when Stephen thought he had been molested, could all the moments when he had approached an intersection an d turned left be retrieved and sorted out? Arabella: "Stephen remembers." Alec: "Oh shit, what does Stephen remember? He doesn't remember the most important moments of his childhood. I know. I've asked him." He had not paid attention. The thing had been done, his character permanently altered, he hadn't noticed and had forgotten entirely.

What had been the fact which had made him what he was? When had it happened? Alec had remembered the powerful odor of his father's aftershave, the delicate, stiff clutch of his mother's embrace. He had forgotten what was important. He pulled his jacket close around his neck and held his head up. The light rain wet his hair and ran down his face into his eyes. Gusts of the rain came at him up the street, causing waves of dull gray in the shining water. It couldn't be escaped. His chest was wet with it.

In the middle of the cold, wet, bitter street, Alec threw his head back and called out—loud enough to be a scream, meant to be heard and answered, in sounds that did not make a word. He listened for an answer. The bars were closed. He wanted a drink. Arabella had gone somewhere. He should have asked her where she was going. Alec could go home. Michael would be there with Amos. How was Amos? How was Michael? The pavement lurched suddenly, and Alec sought his footing. How was Stephen? This part of the street was built over railroad tracks. The whole railroad yard, which stretched from here for a mile into the center of the city, had been covered over in pieces since the thirties, and what seemed to be the ground—the surface of the road—was in fact a bridge thirty or forty feet above the tracks, which now ran underground.

He would go to the Ritz. He would tell him. He turned around and started walking back toward where he had come from. This time, the rain was against the back of his neck.

He would explain to his father everything that had happened —his own childhood, Stephen's childhood, why he had gotten married, divorced, what it mean to be queer. He would tell him he was as much a man as he was. He would explain why it was necessary for Arabella to leave Horace. The concrete beneath his feet seemed to swell and grow. He found it difficult to stand. He made it to the side of the road, falling once, and put his hand on a brick wall there, which steadied him, but the ground came up and he fell. When he was able to stand again, he wedged himself for safety between the wall and the road (it was a doorway) while both swelled and billowed and shrank and receded from him—and swelled again and billowed again.

The rain was driven in clouds between the street lights, and what fell on his face stung and burned. "—I asked if anyone was there, and you didn't answer. Why didn't you answer! I have called and called, and you didn't answer. You sit there in the dark. I see you there! your eyes shining shining. Why didn't you answer! I've been calling out for all my life—"

His voice rose to a screech. He held his arm up before his face, and he peered over it as if over a cross. "—they've called me and I've answered. I've answered! But you never answered. You sat there in the dark—"

Winter Rain

In the doorway, there was a form, wrapped in a blanket, standing up, leaning against the brick. The blanket came down far enough over the face to cover the features (it was Amos!) except the tip of the nose and the chin. Alec conjured it. "—you won't answer. I've hated you. Filthy pig. Fucking filthy pig—" The concrete lurched again—a long slow oceanic swell—and Alec clutched the brick. "—you won't answer. You come on and make your ultimatums and announcements, and before I have a chance to speak, you send your bombs—" He grasped the brick firmly behind him and rose up to his full height. "You say I am guilty. I am not guilty. I have never done anything but love my fellow man—" The rain came down stinging and burning. "I loved you. Once. I haven't loved you for years. You're a pig—"

"Hey, mister—"

"—don't speak. It's too late. I thought I'd explain it all, but it's too late to explain—"

"—hey, mister—"

"—you committed incest on me—"

"—hey, mister—"

"You're a shit."

"Got'ny money?"

"It's gone to rent and taxes so he can drive around in a car with sirens and bomb'em back into the stone age, back into the rocks—"

"I haven't got'ny thing to eat—"

The sky lit up from horizon to horizon (black buildings like a mountain range under a flourescent sky) with the first flash of lightning. Alec saw the man in the light.

"You hungry?"

"I ain't got nothing to eat—"

"Poor baby—" Alec reached out to touch the man. "—aint got nothing to eat."

"Hey mister, sick—"

"Sick? You sick?"

"I'm cold. I'm wet—"

"You sick? Can't you see a doctor either?"

Alec touched his forehead.

"—don't."

"Poor baby—"

"—don't touch me—" The man pulled back.

"Poor baby, he's sick and hungry, and they won't feed 'm—"

"Don't touch me—"

"Poor baby, got AIDS too?"

"No! I don't got AIDS. Stop—",

"And nobody'll love ya? Poor baby?"

"Look, ya fucking faggot—"

Alec looked hard, tried to focus his eyes, tried to hear and couldn't make sense. The ground swelled and heaved, the sky flashed and thundered, the rain came down and stung and burned.

"—get ya fucking fingers outta m'hair—"

He held the man's head against his chest, looking up into the heavens, listening hard.

"—ya fucking faggot, let go 'a me—"

He heard. Faggot! You called me a faggot. I told you I was getting a divorce, and you called me a fucking faggot. You called me a fucking faggot. *You called me a fucking faggot.* He had his hands on the sides of the man's head, stroking him and then clamped vice - like against his skull.

"Oh, you shouldn'a done that. You shouldn'a said that, ole man. I always said you shouldn'a said that. It was goin't'a come back t'haunt ya—"

"Ah— ya hurt'n me! Let go—"

"Ya shouldn'a said that, ole man. Ya shouldn'a said that —"

"Ya hurt'n me!"

"Ya shouldn'a said that—"

"Ah, let go—"

"Faggot—"

"Don't—"

Then, rhythmically, Alec began to beat the other man's head up against the brick wall behind him, holding it by the sides as in a vice, and beating it against the brick.

"Ya shouldn'a said faggot—"

The man began to scream.

"Ya shouldn'a said faggot."

But no one heard. Alec did not even hear. He was deep inside his head, hearing the word faggot and saying over and over *ya shouldn'a said that*, his eyes closed, oblivious to the storm above them and to the blood on his hands.

4

The tv seemed to be on all the time during these days of the war. Pictures on the screen now showed piles of rubble where buildings had been, and the nation's breath was collectively held in anticipation of the ground war. Alec and his friends rarely watched these violent images any more. For weeks, they had hardened themselves against what they had seen and turned their attention to the things closer to home.

A state of suspended—if violent—animation described Alec's apartment, where Amos's health waited before it showed what direction it intended to take. Amos's defenses were destroyed by the disease, his body fought over by rapacious and fatal infections. Some days he seemed almost lucid, almost aware of what was happening to him. He was able to raise himself up onto his pillow and to look about the room. Other days he was out of it completely, immobile and unaware.

The gang came by, rang the bell briefly, knocked softly, tiptoed in. "How is he today?" They brought things—covered dishes and clean laundry—and stayed to ask, "What does he need?" or "What can I do for you?"

Alec greeted them with a drink in his hand and a deep red face. He oversaw the operation, bought food, cooked, cleaned the house, kept Amos clean, received the visiting nurse, kept charts of the medications, maintained contact with the doctors and the AIDS service organizations, seemed in charge. He moved about his chores with an air of purposeful efficiency. Michael borrowed his car, and

Alec gave him a list of things to pick up at the store. Gaetano called to say he was coming by, and Alec told him what to pick up on his way over.

Often at three or four in the morning, Alec waked in the quiet dark apartment and found Michael next to him in bed. As he rose to consciousness, he heard Amos's breathing in the bedroom and listened to these two men, both of whom were—or had been—his lover, breathing while they slept, one with a harsh searing sound in the other room and the other more quietly, through his nose, next to him in bed. The more regularly he went to bed drunk, the more often he woke at three, hungover and anxious. Waking at three or four, Alec felt weak and cowardly, terrorized by what was there in the dark that he couldn't see. At that dead time of the night, when the fears of every unknown thing were magnified, when his own failures seemed unforgivable, Alec rehearsed his life—the breakup and divorce from Gloria, Amos, the loss of Stephen's confidence, the wreckage of his relationship with his parents, the deaths of friends. He listened to the sounds of their breathing, and the sounds of the city, which never quite died out even at three in the morning, as if life never quite lets go, and wondered if he could hang on, if it wouldn't be better, easier, simply to die now rather than to wait and die later of the virus. He had it, he had gotten it from/given it to Michael. Or die in a rain of thousands of tons of screaming iron and explosives falling on his head from a dark sky, of humiliation at having failed again after so many tries. In the dark apartment, to the sound of the staggered breathing of his two lovers, he would turn on his side in the bed, his head thrown back, his hands clasped between his knees, and vibrate with fear.

"I never thought it was necessary for Amos to come here. There were other men in town whose obligation to him is as great as yours. Why are you doing this? Are you still in love with him?"

Michael had fumbled when he tried to say no.

"I think you are."

"No, I'm not." It caused him pain to say it.

"Why you, then!"

"I was in love with him."

Michael raised his eyebrows.

"Don't jerk me around about this."

"It sucks helping my lover look after a man he's still in love with." Michael's feelings showed in every rigid angle of his body as he went about the apartment doing chores, helping Alec look after

Amos. Even when he dropped on the coffee table the money he contributed to Amos's upkeep, he dropped it with a kind of fury.

Alec scooped it up without looking up at him, tapped the bills mechanically and slid them into his wallet. It was necessary always to act as if you had not committed murder. "Why are you doing this?"

"Because I love you." Michael stood across the coffee table from him, looking at him defiantly. Michael's obligation to Amos was as great as Alec's, and Alec's was no greater than that of a dozen other men.

"What do you want?" *From me* was what Alec didn't say.

"A drink."

Alec heard the refrigerator door, the ice tray, the glass and the water running. He called, "Get me one too."

Michael was back, fury in his face. "My t-cell count is down to 370. I'm afraid—"

On the coffee table were the coffee cups half filled with after-breakfast coffee and the newspaper. Headlines: *The President: All economic indicators show that the corner has been turned; girl shot and killed on school ground.* In the midst of these Michael placed the drinks. It was the confusing time when morning was shading over into day.

"You don't have time for me."

"You said you wanted to be left alone."

"I do."

"I thought I did. I'll give you what you need, when I know what it is."

"I want to be paid attention to."

"I do."

"Will you!" He gestured to where the money had been on the table. "I'll need all my money for myself before it's over —"

All my money for us all, before it's all over. Somebody had to look after Amos while he was dying. It was a minimum requirement for civilization. Someone had to sit beside his bed, hand on his thigh, ready to say, Amos, it's me, I'm here. You're not alone. The President: It is America's duty to stand with the forces of right in this great struggle. Alec could not think who it might be, if not him. You will not die alone. "I have to do this —"

"Do you love me—" Michael's anguish showed in the hard inflexible angle of his neck as he stood in front of the coffee table.

"You take away from me to give to him—. I come to your place because I am afraid, and what I find when I get here is Amos —" His voice was unsteady. "—what I am afraid of—"

Without either of them taking the lead, they turned and together moved the coffee table out of the way and opened up the bed, so recently folded up, and pulled back the covers. They sat on either side and pulled off their boots and tee shirts, lay on the bed and turned toward each other, their arms around each other. Alec could feel Michael's breath against the skin of his chest.

"You're driven—"

Fighting the wars. It was said that people all around the globe were hot with admiration for the President of the United States, who so promptly and effectively marshalled the forces of a grand alliance of nations against naked aggress ion. The President said there was no anti-war movement. The sex between Alec and Michael was like hand-to-hand combat. Alec wanted to be gentle with Michael, but everything was a struggle, and he couldn't escape the need to defeat him first. His body took over, and he fucked him hard, and ignored Michael's whispers to go easy, please.

He had met Michael in the gym, three years ago. He was a friend of Gaetano's, and the three of them had had a beer after their workout. Michael had the polished exterior that suggested careful thought and a belief that life could be controlled. His short hair was brushed back away from his forehead, and he was clean shaven. He wore simple clothes—jeans, a shirt of dark purple, blue and magenta —and had a simple clean silhouette. When Gaetano left them alone in the bar, Michael was direct: "Do you have a lover?"

"No, not now."

"Recently?"

Alec shrugged. "Four months ago."

"I'd like to date you."

Alec had smiled. "What do you want?"

"I like older men."

So. They had gone to a movie together and then to another bar, where they sat on a banquette in a back room and Michael talked about himself until the bar closed at two. He was a decorator, did expensive city condos in new buildings for rich lawyers' and stockbrokers' wives. They went back to Alec's and made love. Michael made it his business to please Alec. Alec's duty in this was to be pleased, and, when they were not making love, to listen to the story of Michael's life, who had been abused but who learned to look after himself by a kind of quid pro quo: *Love me, and I will please you.*

Love me meant listen to me. They became lovers. Their time, aside from the drugs and sex, was spent talking. Michael talked and Alec listened to the ways that Michael's childhood had been raped from him and to his search for a man who would let him have his childhood again. Alec had asked him what he wanted. I want new memories. They lay on the sofa, Alec on his back, his head against the arm, Michael lying on top of him, his head resting on Alec's chest, Alec's hands clasped in the small of Michael's back. As he listened, he stroked Michael's back, down the long blonde slope from shoulder to waist, and kissed him in his hair, saying, *Remember this: I love you.*

The city was frozen in the middle of winter, rigid with the cold. The rain had finally stopped, leaving ice on every street and step, every tree branch. People fell, tree limbs snapped and broke. Cars, their brakes locking, skidded into each other i n a loud crunch of steel. People cracked under the violence. The anguish Alec felt now arose from this inability to be gentle with Michael, from this accumulating failure of his civilizing, moderating impulses, leaving exposed the raw greed for power, which was abusive and violent in his love-making.

On Sunday, the morning after Alec went to the bookstore looking for Stephen, the ground war started, and he woke and found blood on his hands. The thing came through to him, through the confusion of first looking at himself in the mirror, as something so natural that the first thing he did after seeing the blood was to look for a cut. He turned his arm over—first the right and then the left —and looked at the far side of his hand and forearm, his elbow, and what he could see of the back of his upper arm. There were no cuts or bruises. He did find a scrape on the knuckles of his left hand, but nothing else, and the scrape had hardly bled. The blood on his hands was embedded in the crevices around his fingernails. As he woke up and was more able to think, he found that the blood had been washed off, washed off badly, leaving evidence around his fingernails. He spread out his fingers and inspected his nails, ringed with dark dried blood. The sight made him sick. The nausea came up in him—it was the alcohol from last night still in his stomach and the sight of the blood —and he put his hands on the sink and stiffened his arms and leaned, his head down. He waited for the vomit.

But it didn't come. Worse, it stayed where it was, and after a moment, swallowing to keep it down, he ran the water over his fingers, found a brush and cleaned his hands, scrubbing hard until there wasn't any sign of the dark line around his nails. Last night. He had gone to the bookstore, the gym, Paradise. He looked for Stephen. He talked to Gaetano at the gym, but he couldn't remember, now, why he had gone to Paradise.

He had made columns on his yellow pads so that he could check off each of Amos's medications as he administered it and could determine quickly that each had been given at its correct time and interval. Now he checked his lists against his watch. It was 9:40, and the boxes for four, six, and eight had not been checked off. There was no way to tell if the medications had been administered. He had been asleep. The nausea came back. Having no medical training, Alec didn't know the effect on Amos of skipping medication.

He sat by Amos's bed, holding his stiff dry hot hand, watching him breathing. His breath seemed to come regularly. Alec took to counting between inhalations, and Amos's pulse, though weak, seemed to be no weaker than it had been yesterday. He checked the pulse again, holding his fingertips against the artery in Amos's wrist, and wondered if it was not perceptibly weaker. He checked it a third time, feeling for the pulse through the skin of fingers that seemed now to be made of cowhide, too tough to sense the weak pulse of the blood. Fear came up in him. He had forgotten to give Amos the medication, and he would die.

On the chest of drawers was the array of Amos's medicines. The three bottles that contained the drugs which should have been administered to Amos would have the date the prescriptions were filled. He would be able, by counting the capsules in the bottle, to tell whether any dosage had been missed. His fingers were shaking as he poured out the pills on the bedspread and counted, but the number wasn't what it should have been. Alec counted again, this time getting a different number. He began to sweat. He glanced at Amos. Was he breathing? Was it faster this time, or slower? He began to count Amos's pulse and then thought he should finish counting the capsules instead. He stopped and counted the little pills again and reached a third figure. Alec panicked. Would it be better to give him his medications now, even if he didn't need them, or would that be worse for him? He didn't know.

The phone rang. The phone had been removed from the bedroom and now, not knowing what effect the capsules were supposed to

have, Alec felt if he left Amos for a moment he might die. The phone
rang. If he left him for even a moment, since he had been incorrectly
medicated, he might go into convulsions and die. It would be a result
of his own failure. I am causing him to die. The phone rang again.

He ran to the living room. "What!"

"I beg your pardon—"

"Who—"

"This is Mrs. Carl Frederich Argento—" Mrs. Carl Frederich
Argento. His mother. Alec's mother had been dead for seven years,
had died in convulsions in Alec's own arms, still at war with him (age
hadn't softened her), unwilling down to her last breath to give a kind
word, preferring judgment and condemnation. Mother! "—Bernice
Argento. May I speak to Alec Argento, please?"

Bernice. "I can't talk to you now, Bernice—"

"Oh, I know, this is intrusive, and I do apologize but can you just
answer one quick question?"

The hopelessness of things (his mother would find out that he had
failed to administer the drugs properly), the impossibility of
retrieving the past (he would have explained to her) defeated him.
But I can explain— She would respond with a torrent of words. "It
is a mystery to me why you don't have more respect for your father
and me. Elemental human decency would require that a boy so
nurtured and cared for—" There would be nothing for him to say,
nothing to feel but shame.

"Could I ask that of you? One small request, if I may? And then
I'll let you get back to your important occupations —"

The voice was soft and sugary, threatening. Alec's tormented
mind raced from the suffocating voice on the phone to the bed in the
next room. He tried to hear Amos breathing and couldn't: "What do
you want?"

She paused to register offense at Alec's tone. Her own became
more polite. "I would like to know if you know where Arabella is,
Horace's wife? She has not been home since yesterday, and Horace
is beside himself— I thought I might be able to help."

"I don't know—." He ran his hand through his hair. "I don't
know—." I don't know where Stephen is, either. I don't know if
Amos is dying. And, after Bernice Argento, Mrs. Carl Frederich
Argento, had thanked him and gone back to her own important
occupations, telling him first that she needed to speak to him also
about Stephen, but that that could wait, Alec went back into the
bedroom where Amos lay, dreading to see him and then relieved to

97

see that he was still breathing, acknowledging to himself that he
didn't know what it would feel like to have caused someone's death,
what shame felt like on such a scale.

Amos was alive. Alec fixed himself a drink. His hands shook as
if he were old, and he sat for the rest of the morning beside the bed,
holding Amos's hand, without moving except to give Amos his
medications at ten and t hen at twelve, and to fix himself a drink at
10:30 and almost twelve. In any endeavor the result might not be
what one had sought, might instead be a disaster, caused by
carelessness or ineptitude or the odds, a disaster of such dimensions
that it would overwhelm all attempts to explain or to sort out
responsibility. The visiting nurse arrived and checked Amos's vital
signs and the medications charts, administered the IV and cheerily
announced that all was as it should be. Alec didn't tell her about the
blank boxes on the yellow legal pad. There was no way of making
certain that one was safe. Holding Amos's hand, he felt danger all
around him, in what suddenly seemed like the impossibly complex
schedule of medications which had to be administered, too complex
for any one person to master, in the temperature of the room, in the
foods that he had to prepare for Amos, and the stakes, represented by
Amos's harsh, unsteady breathing, tremendously high. Amos had
come home to die, but he had to die in his own time and not because
someone around him had failed to give him what he had needed at the
moment he needed it. Alec wondered if he had in fact failed. There
was no way of discovering whether the medications had been given.
Sitting there in the darkened room holding Amos's hand, the weak
winter sun lighting the rectangle of the window and causing the
mullions to seem like bars across the opening to the outside, Alec
twisted, suffered a war with himself.

When Gaetano came, he let himself in (the gang all had their own
keys now) and tiptoed softly to the bedroom door and peered in.
"Everything OK?"

In the living room, Gaetano lowered himself into a chair and
looked up at Alec. "You're amazing."

Alec couldn't think what Gaetano meant, He thought, *I am not
OK.*

"I mean, looking after Amos this way. I come in and find you
holding his hand in a dark room, hour after hour. I couldn't do that,
give myself up to it that way. How do you do it?"

Alec shrugged. Where would you start if you were to explain to
Gaetano? He fixed them drinks.

"I feel like a slug beside you."

This was painful.

"Everyone talks about how devoted you are—"

"Everyone is helping—"

They talked about the visit of the nurse and of what she had said about Amos, about food in the house and the state of the laundry. They seemed to use up all the towels every day, and the sheets had to be changed once a day, overwhelming Alec's small supply. They talked about the details of life, the temperature in the room, whether the window should be opened slightly, and briefly, about the ground war.

"They had to begin fighting, there was nothing left to bomb."

It was difficult for Alec to focus on their conversation. He was surrounded by dangers; his own strengths seemed inadequate to what had to be done; he felt ashamed, and he had to rehearse in his mind Gaetano's questions, think carefully what they meant before he could speak. Gaetano asked if Alec had heard from Arabella.

Arabella. Bernice. "Bernice called. I don't know." He had forgotten.

Gaetano smiled. "She spent the night with me last night."

The idea was so foreign that Alec couldn't assimilate it.

"We talked—"

We talked!

"—ah, that's all we did. We talked and then she stayed over. I slept on the sofa. She's at my place—"

"Gaetano—" Stephen called her every day.

"It's OK. She's going through a hard time, and she needed someone to talk to—"

"Gaetano, you—" He didn't know what he wanted to say.

"She was pretty drunk last night after being with you."

She was with me last night. Paradise. The blood on his fingers. He would have to deal with that when he had a minute. Stephen (783-5962). Where was Stephen? Whose number was that?

"When you didn't want her to come back here, she didn't know where else to go. It was late, after two—"

"I never said—" The vomit was back up. The fear was on him again, of everything he didn't know, of being betrayed by his ignorance, by his trust that what he didn't know wouldn't rise up out of the dark and breathe fire, devouring him.

"Why did she go to you?" But why did Alec tell her she couldn't come to him?

Gaetano shrugged. "She—"

"You're nothing to her."

"She was drunk—"

"She's married to my brother—"

"—and she didn't have anywhere to—"

"She had a key here—"

"She says, you told her she couldn't come here —"

"What did she say?"

"—about—"

"Did she talk about me?" Then, in a rage, Alec almost screamed. "What did you do to her?"

"Nothing, man, nothing! Cool down! We talked about what a fucked up family you have." Gaetano laughed. "I never heard anything like your old man. How did you survive?"

"What'd she say?"

He shrugged, held his hands out in front of him, palms up. "His sense of humor—"

That.

"—leaving you on the street—"

(he'd be holding his hand, trotting along, the hand up by his ear, seeing everything, the cars stopped and moving in the street, the grownups coming toward them and passing them, in heavy coats, carrying packages, his own heavy coat hanging heavy on his shoulders, the cold wind on his face, his nose runny, and then the hand would slip away and he'd be trotting along beside his dad, looking at everything, and thinking it was scary to be out, the loud horns blowing, then suddenly aware that he wasn't there, he'd look and he wasn't there, he wasn't there on either side of him or in back or in front, he wasn't anywhere, and Alec was just a little kid alone on a street in the middle of all the grownups going places, into the doors of the buildings, not knowing where his dad was, where he had gone, or who would take care of him, he wanted his mommy, then it came up from deep inside him, and he started to cry, just a little kid alone in the big street with no one to take care of him, his whole body aching trying to get enough air in his lungs while he cried out as loud as he could)

"—while he hid from you. Arabella says that was his favorite pastime, taking you downtown and hiding from you, you and Horace—"

Winter Rain

(then he would be there, come from somewhere, standing the re
laughing, slapping his knees and laughing, howling with laughter, his
face all wrinkled up with laughter at little Alec)
   "—and then mocking you—"
(crybaby crybaby little girl)
   "—while you were crying—"
(wants his mommie!)
(little girl)

He hated his father. Alec went into the bedroom and sat beside
Amos—*Amos, It's me, Alec*—and listened to the sound of his
breathing, counting between inhalations. Alec knew the number of
breaths in a length of the swimming pool at the gym (fourteen down,
fifteen back) and he now knew the interval between Alec's breaths.
Once his father had played the trick on Horace and Alec together, and
Alec had tried not to cry. Having Horace there with him made him
strong, but Horace had cried anyway, and when their father had
reappeared, he laughed at them and swept Horace up into his arms.
Alec had trotted along behind them on the way back to the car,
feeling brave and alone. He held Amos's hand. He had become as
intimately familiar with Amos's hand as he had with Amos's
breathing. He had learned to tell, from the slightest pressure,
whether Amos knew his hand was being held. Sometimes there was
no response, the hand seemed lifeless. Other times there was
something, a movement of the fingers. Now he felt the slight
pressure as Amos's fingers curled around his. It was comforting, that
slight pressure of the dry, hard fingers. He wondered what he was in
contact with, how much of Amos was responding to him, how much
of his mind was at work.
   "It's me, Alec." What memories did he still have? Alec wondered
if he were able still to remember their times together, the three years
they had lived together, the choice of pictures for their walls, choice
of food, their sex, Alec's betrayal of him. Was all that gone, now. He
rubbed the fingers softly. There was a movement at the door.
Gaetano was behind him, leaning at the jamb, watching. It was
possible that Amos found his fingers, the gentle rubbing, to be a
distraction from more important business. There was no way to tell
what was brought to connection, there in their fingers, of all the
times their fingers had touched one another, their words, their eyes,
breath intermingled, making, reminding, renewing memories, hurting,
comforting, falling into or out of each other. For Alec everything, all

101

the rich past, was now distilled into the touch (he was wrong in thinking Amos responded) of their fingers, all their time together, the sense of slight warm moisture, even in the cold hard hands, which was all of their touching over years. The ache which Alec felt (Arabella had gone to Gaetano, Stephen had gone to Arabella, crybaby, crybaby) would eventually come to this, where everything was distilled down to warm moist touch, this ache of jealousy losing itself among all the other aches of jealousy felt in a lifetime, among all the other pains (betrayal, guilt, shame), everything he had felt during thirty, forty, years of life, distilled down until location, time, quality were all lost in a faint evanescent sensation in the palm and fingers of a hand. Holding Amos's hand, watched by Gaetano, Alec felt the difference between them. He and his feelings were still tied to time, and Amos, beginning to float free, was above him, beyond him, showing him his future.

"It's beautiful, man."

Alec turned, looked over his shoulder at Gaetano.

"It's fucking beautiful."

He rubbed the hand once more, gently. The answer to the question, how would it end, was here. He leaned over and kissed Amos on his open lips, making it slow and lingering, hoping to f eel on his lips a response. It was not clear whether Amos was aware. He kissed him again.

Then he stood up and went into the living room, and Gaetano followed.

"It's beautiful seeing you with him. You're like a fucking mother—"

Gaetano said he shouldn't have talked about Alec's father. "I guess all that stuff is pretty raw, huh." He was awkward and embarrassed. "I didn't mean to stir things up for ya."

Alec wished he would go. Then he remembered that Gaetano was here so Alec would have some free time away from Amos. It was Alec who was expected to go. So he did. He left Gaetano with Amos and the yellow pads and the drugs, took his address book and went in search of Stephen.

"Hey, can I borrow your car tonight?" Gaetano called to him just as he was shutting the door behind him.

Alec stepped back inside. "Sure. And if you talk to Arabella, tell her to call me."

Winter Rain

Margaret, carrying a mop and pail, was coming up the stairs as he went toward the front door. She walked heavily, as if she had gained 100 pounds and her frame had difficulty handling it, as if it hurt.

"What's up?" Alec fumbled with his keys, preparing to lock his apartment door.

She stopped, heaved a sigh, glanced at him. "It's the front door again."

"What's the front door?"

She was turning away, headed down the hall. "It has to be cleaned up."

He followed her out.

"Somebody does it regular now. Comes right in the front door and pisses right there under the mail boxes —"

His car was cold, and in this weather would not warm up before he was home again. He drove the perimeter road around the fens, staying close to the inside, pulling out around cars when he was able to, swerving in and then out when a space opened up ahead, making it through a light before it changed, his eyes passing over the buildings which dressed the fens, the broad icy walks, the trees sheathed in ice, the gray patches of ice on the road reflecting the sky turning momentarily black when cars passed over. A siren screamed in the area behind the buildings.

He parked behind Symphony Hall. The cold was sharp and burned his cheeks. He ran half a block to a door with four names, none of which he recognized. McKinnon was the third. Stephen used to have a girlfriend who lived in the building named McKinnon (or McKinley, McCannon, Cannon, Kinnon, McKinnon). He pushed the buzzer. There was no answer, and he ran next door. It might have been this building. There was no answer. He ran back to the first building and left a note (it was difficult to write with gloves) taped to the glass: "I am looking for Stephen Argento. If he is staying here, would you call Alec Argento (859 -0815). Thank you."

Alec ran across the road to the pharmacy to pick up Amos's drugs (three weeks food, a round trip flight to Province town), cotton swabs, diapers, then out to Massachusetts Avenue to the South End and another door with names. "I am looking for Stephen Argento. If he is staying here, would you call Alec Argento (859 -0815). Thank you." At a third place, double-parking and running in and pushing a likely button, he heard a voice in the speaker say, 'Yes?" It was polite, open, female.

"I'm sorry to intrude." He leaned over, speaking into the small microphone. "But I am looking for my son, Stephen Argento, and I remember he once knew someone who lived in this apartment —"

"No. I don't know any Stephen at all. Sorry."

He wanted to ring the next buzzer down, and the one above. The next building over, on either side. The address book he was following was his own, but interspersed among the hundreds of names in his own handwriting—friends, people he had worked with, sexual partners—were several, half a dozen in all, in Stephen's. Coming upon them in among these personal pages had the shock value of finding someone else's memories among one's own. Alec had called them all. Not one of the people who answered admitted to having ever heard of a Stephen Argento.

While a name, an address and a phone number seemed to be immutably connected, sometimes, particularly among kids who prided themselves on having so few possessions that they could be carried on a bike, a phone stayed with an apartment while a member moved on. Or a number would leave with a tenant, following him to a new place. It was possible for a name, a phone number and an address suddenly all to be separated, and what had before come to seem so intimately connected with a person that the mere thought of him would call up his number and address could, overnight, become attached to strangers.

Alec stood on a stoop, holding onto the railing, facing a young man who had pulled open the door. The ice fell in waterfalls behind him down the steps.

"Stephen? Yeah. I think that's his name—"

"Stephen Argento."

"Yeah. That's him—"

"He's my son."

"I just knew him by Stephen, though."

The boy looked Alec up and down. "What's up?"

"Is Stephen here?"

The boy hesitated, thought. "Nah. He ain't here. Nobody's here but me."

"But he lives here?"

"I dunno."

"But he's been here?"

"Yeah. He's been here, all right."

"Recently? Was he here last night?"

"Uh-uh. Not last night—"

"When—"

"I don't remember. Sometime." The boy looked Alec up and down again, satisfied.

"But he's staying here—"

"Nah. He's not staying here."

"You don't know whether he's living here—"

"Uh-uh—"

"But he's been here—"

"To sleep?"

The boy laughed. "Man, I guess so—"

"Do you know if he's coming back?"

"I dunno." He shrugged. "I dunno, maybe I don't know this Stephen." He looked perplexed for a moment. He tried to look helpful. "Maybe if you came back, some of the other guys —"

"Could you tell them—"

"Well, you see, I don't know all the guys very well —"

The boy looked at Alec, his eyebrows raised a little, waiting for Alec to say something. He'd said it as you'd say, *I don't know what's in God's mind,* expecting agreement and sympathy. The boy looked cold there in the open door in a thin baggy tee shirt. Alec was cold, his feet were cold, and Alec shrugged and thanked him and walked back down the steps, holding onto the railing.

Sirens drowned out the noise of the street. Alec stuck his hands in his jacket pockets and walked back toward the car. The quality of winter in the city—the colors were black and shades of gray, the texture was harsh and brittle, and things shattered instead of bending —flattened out the emotions, stretched them until they became thin and tight. Cars in the street were like tanks, their occupants totally enclosed, and people's faces, coming toward Alec down the sidewalk, were armored by cold flesh and inaccessible. Arabella could help find Stephen. Bernice said she wanted to talk about him. To get to him, he had to find Arabella or Bernice, who would have left with Alec's father this morning to return to Pennsylvania. The city in winter —like the frozen surface of the stream in the fens, like Amos's mind, like God's mind—was impenetrable. All the color had gone, and it was necessary to press on even if he had forgotten what he was going toward.

Why was he trying to reach Stephen, who didn't want to be reached? Why was he caring for Amos, who didn't give a shit anymore? In his car, he turned on the ignition (it was slow starting, to demonstrate the difficulty of life) and floored the accelerator, pulling out into a break in the traffic, almost running over an old woman, wrapped in grey scarves, carrying bags walking along the edge of the road, and drove to the Piston, had a double and watched the porno flics, the AIDS posters showing on the wall behind the screen, then drove to the gym, down Huntington, and found a parking place in front of a shop that sold Near Eastern food, moved through the crowds of students crossing the avenue and waited for a trolley to pass before crossing and entering the gym. He had two hours before he had to relieve Gaetano.

He could make the weights move. He could put eight 25 -pound plates on a bar and using the force of his pectoral muscles make them move up the length of his arm. He could swing the dumbbells with six ten-pound plates from in front of his groin out to the side and up above his head using his deltoid muscles. He could lift a dumbbell straight above his head and then bend his elbow and lower it behind his head, stretching his triceps muscle to its maximum. But everything else seemed out of his control, and when he arrived home, two hours later, and found Michael with Amos (he had relieved Gaetano), in the cluttered apartment, the souvenirs of the twelve years since he had left his wife overburdened with the paraphernalia needed for Amos, he found he didn't have anything to say, couldn't formulate a sentence which would suggest that he had a goal or a plan or a design.

"Your father is in Pennsylvania. Horace called to say that. He's looking for Arabella. Gaetano had to go early—some emergency. I'm here. I want to go out to dinner, let somebody wait on me, and then I want you to fuck me." Michael spoke from the sofa, an arm along the back, a leg along the cushions, looking at Alec through the door in the hall.

The ice wouldn't come out of the trays whole. The cubes stuck and then shattered when he tried to force him, and he filled his glass with the shards, which looked like broken glass. He poured the whiskey and stood at the counter and raised the glass to his lips and drank, two, three deep swallows.

"What?" He stood facing Michael, the coffee table between them, the drink wetting his hand.

"Horace called. He's having some sort of business emergency. He needs to find Arabella and can't. You should call. Stephen called. I think he was drunk. He sounded like it. He didn't say where he was." He had a drink on the table, and he reached for it and drank. He looked at Alec. "Do you know where Arabella is?"

"No, I don't." It was all Alec could manage. He felt he should ask about Amos, but he couldn't make himself formulate the words.

"What's the matter with you?"

"I don't know what's in God's mind."

Michael studied him. He was waiting for something more, and Alec couldn't think what more to say.

"I—."

Alec went to the bathroom to take a shower. Then he came back into the living room and sat down next to Michael and dialed Horace's number.

"Have you seen my fucking wife?"

His brother was a jerk, and he surprised himself by saying, "No, Horace, I haven't—"

"I thought you two were together last night —"

"No—" But then they might have been, he had no memory of last night, why he had been at Paradise.

"I need to find her. The auditors were here all day today, and I'm being eaten alive. She's the only one who knows about some things I did last winter—" Arabella was an officer of Horace's company. "I'll need her signature—"

The conversation wandered on, Horace explaining in a disjointed way the connection between the need to find Arabella and the auditors. "Dad is pissed. I took them to dinner last night, and all they could talk about was you. There's some problem with Stephen."

Alec's eyes moved across the pictures on his wall —the photograph torn from a magazine of a nude man at a rugby match in England, his graceful body surrounded by policemen, one of whom held a hat over the man's genitals, a reproduction of a painting of a mythological subject by Titian. Alec's hand groped for Michael's on the sofa cushion.

They ended the conversation. Michael pulled him toward him and kissed him.

"You were with Arabella last night. You met her at Paradise, don't you remember?"

When Gus came, who was to stay with Amos, they got their coats and went out to dinner. Michael left his keys for Gaetano so he could use Alec's car. They hailed a cab and drove through the streets of the city, across the river to Harvard Square and went to the Harvest, the cabdriver sullen and silent, Michael and Alec quiet in the back seat.

The waiter took their order, and they sat silently, looking in different places in the restaurant, the waiters moving about, the maitr'd, the large expressionist landscapes, the other diners, avoiding each other's eyes, moving their drinks around on the linen. Alec felt accused and didn't know how to begin without apologizing. Anything he said would open him up to admissions he didn't want to make, didn't know how to make.

"They say the ground war began this morning."

The other side had a million infantry soldiers. Alec's image was of a desert black with troops fighting in close combat. The carnage would be appalling, thousands dying at once.

"How do you feel?"

Michael toyed with his drink, moving it back and forth, wiping the moisture from the stem.

"Tell me."

"I am angry. I've got this thing now in my blood—. I feel fine. I get up, I've got energy, I can think, and I want to get on with it, and then I remember I've got this thing in my blood, which means that despite how I feel, I'm weak as a baby and there's nothing I can do to protect myself from—. I think of Amos, shit, I see Amos every time I see you, and I see that is how I am going to end up —blind, immobile, out of my head, covered with lesions, hideous, incontinent, 70 pounds, disgusting. I want to hit somebody. You, I'm so angry with you, all I want to do is hurt you, humiliate yo u in some public way—" He looked around the restaurant. "—here, stand up and call you a shit and make a scene, throw a drink in your face. Why is it you who's negative and me positive? I have things I want to do with my life, and this virus in my blood won't let me, tells me I'm going to die—"

He was not looking at Alec. His eyes moved from one end of the restaurant to the other, not lingering or stopping on anything, focussed on some middle distance. "—I am helpless. What was it I did that was so horribly wrong that this would be a fair punishment? Had sex with a man? What did Amos do? I never liked him. You'd been in love with him and I was jealous. But he was a good man. He didn't murder anybody. He didn't cut up their bodies and stick thei r heads in the freezer. What did he do that makes this OK? How could anybody say Amos deserved this? Does anybody say I deserve this? I have this compulsion to ask people. Do I deserve this? *This*? I am afraid of suffering, of it hurting. I hear people say, I'm not afraid to die. Maybe not. I don't know what dying is, being dead. But I can see in front of me, every time I go to your house, what is happening to Amos, what has happened to Amos, and I am afraid of that —of

At length, Michael started again. "—I knew that I wouldn't get any help. I learned that when I was a kid when my father beat me and took my money, and I learned how to take care of myself. I hid my money and learned to take the beatings rather than tell him where I had hidden it. I figured I was as smart as anybody else, and I could make my own way. And I have. I used to think you could do things over again, make them right this time. I thought, even though I missed out on it as a kid, I could find what I missed in you, that you'd give me love.

"Now I know that's not going to happen. You can't do it. I don't know whether somebody else could have done it, but you can't. I'm angry about that, too. You fucking betrayed me. You were going to love me and help me, be strong for me. You promised more than you delivered. You're a big hunky strong man, but you turned out to be weak and inadequate, good only to look at, good only for fucking —"

At length, the waiter, disapproving, came and took away their untouched plates and brought them another round of drinks and then a check and they paid and left, walking out through the emptying dining room, past men and women toying with brandy and cigarettes and coffee, voices hushed and deadened by the carpet and the concrete walls and the oil paintings, candles making bright cheekbones and foreheads and lips.

In the cab on the way home, across the iced-over river and through the city, Michael sat on his side of the seat and Alec on his. They stared out through their separate windows as if passing through different landscapes, Michael seeing Beacon Hill and Alec seeing the CITGO sign. Neither man tried to talk, and neither of them reached out to the other. Their hands lay on the seat beside them, separated by fifteen inches of brown vinyl. At home, Alec paid while Michael left the cab and went into the building.

"You were the most beautiful man in the bar. I think I fell in love with you the first time I saw you. It was your eyes —"

Alec had dropped his coat in the hall and had gone directly to the kitchen, fought with the ice tray, and poured them drinks. Now he sat in a chair at the end of the coffee table. Michael sat in the middle of the sofa, his feet up on the coffee table, talking. His hands were in his lap. As he talked, he looked down at them and then up, at the wall opposite, at the pictures pinned there—the streaker, the Titian, the theatre posters—then down again at his hands.

110

"—they weren't bright, like kids eyes. You weren't a chicken —"
He glanced for a second at Alec. "—that was for sure. You'd been
around some, and it showed in your eyes, in the wrinkles around
them, and in the way you had of looking at men and letting them
know you didn't care about the game everybody was playing. Your
eyes showed you'd lived, and it had worn you down, but you were
still strong, and I thought you were wise. I thought that was what I
saw in your eyes.

"I thought, this guy can teach me something. I could learn
something from you, how not to get too worn down. I bet this guy
has dealt with tough stuff before in his life. You remember how I
was that year I met you. This guy looks strong enough for both of us.
He's been through it and survived and knows how and he can show
me.

"I kept up with you when you came to the bar. Then I saw you
there once with Gaetano and I knew Gaetano, so it was easy after
that. I fell in love with you, and I thought this is what I've wanted all
my life, someone who'd be strong for me, protect me, make things
easy. It would be wonderful, going through life with a man this
strong. *Nothing bad can happen to me if Alex Argento love me.*

Alec stood up and without saying goodbye or goodnight went into
the bathroom and brushed his teeth. When he came back, he was
naked. He asked Michael to stand up so he could make up the bed.
Together they pulled it out, and Alec got in under the covers and
turned on his side, away from the center, and closed his eyes, leaving
Michael standing, fully clothed, beside the bed.

5

—to reach him under his arms, but my fingers slip on the sweat. My neck is in the crook of his elbow and he squeezes. I begin to choke. The lights—huge and white—are in my eyes. My fingers slip on his skin, try to find a place along his arms, his shoul ders. I reach for his neck, under his chin, and push. His head goes back and up. I can't breathe. My eyes begin to hurt, and I fight for breath. He is choking me. I fight for breath, I can't fight him off, it is dark, my chest heaves, I am going to die it is still night, I am in bed, Michael beside me, sleeping. The sheets are wet under me. My lungs fight for breath, and my heart beats hard (THUMPthump, THUMPthump, THUMPthump) and loud, the only thing I can hear. I am dying *I think I am going to die.* He was bigger than I was, and I couldn't fight him off. I am safe in my bed in my own apartment. I am safe. My relief, sudden release from unbearable stress, leaves me lightheaded: I am alive. I breathe deeply, try to get my heart to calm down. My whole body is wet. The crack of light around the shades marks the windows, shows faintly on the mound made by Michael's body in the bed, picks up the glint of brass candlesticks, the edge of the bookcase. I feel the hard clutch of muscle in my stoma ch. I try to regulate my breathing, gain control of the spasm of fear that jerks my heart. I turn on my side, facing Michael's back, slide my hands between my knees, lower my head, clench my eyes shut. There is nothing to be afraid of in the apartment. The door is locked. I listen hard. It is difficult to hear over my ragged breathing, over Michael's long shallow inhalations. I can hear nothing. There is someone there. He's bigger than I am and powerfully built, and he's trying to kill me. I am afraid. I lie in bed, and my body trembles. I try to sort out what is real from my dream. There is no one in the apartment but Michael and Amos and me. The room is dark and filled with movement. I hear Amos breathing. I count intervals. I hear a phone. Arabella said something. Stephen. I open the door quickly and find the room empty. Stephen is trying to reach me, calling from payphones all over the city. I was gone all afternoon and most of the night. The phone rings. *I hate you, Dad.* It is like a blow to my neck. *Did you call just to tell me that?* Just that. I want to shake him hard, hurt him, make him see. Make him suffer. Rebellious, insolent shit. He has abandoned me. I turn in bed, the phone rings. Stephen! *I hate you, Dad.* Stephen, where are you? The phone grows slick with sweat in my hand. I'm not going to tell you. I'm never coming home. Stephen, I love you. I don't care. I want to make him love me. If he doesn't. I love him. I hear the sounds of Amos breathing. I hated my father. Stephen doesn't hate me. I caught him under the arms and swung him up, high above my head and around. The white sand and the blue-green sea and the blue sky swirled around behind us, the sand giving under my feet. He laughed his high bell-like laugh, against the sound of the surf. His laugh, the sun, the surf, the sea, his brown skin—the moment was out of time, our senses suspended in the air, our skin touching, the sand between my toes, the salt water drying on our skins, encapsulated by the high dome of the blue sky. He hit me on my back and head. My head ached. *I hate you, Dad.* I grip my hands between my knees. A siren makes a high tense cry along the street, the sound deeper and more penetrating, more saturated, in the night air. The phone rings. Stephen! *I hate you, Dad.* Stephen, I love you. He is silent. He doesn't hate me. I put my arms around his shoulders and feel his thin body against my chest. He's young, it's his time to suffer. I never wanted you to suffer. I never hated you. I caused Stephen to suffer. I can't remember the last night we were together. Arabella said something. I don't know why he has gone. He hates me. I want to ask, *Why did you leave?* The day the war started. The day before. We struggled, always. His whole life with me has been a struggle for survival. What have you got in your hands? Nothing. Show me. No. Show me, now. No. Stephen, do what I say now! No, I won't do what you say now! You're a bully! suddenly enraged, and I hate you! I whipped him. I had to make him obey. I didn't know what else to do. What would I be if he didn't obey? He showed me (his hands were empty), because I was bigger and could beat him into submission. I turn in my bed. I turn again. My joints ache, and the bed feels like stone. I hurt him. I would do it differently, if I were somebody new, different, who could do it differently. Petty fights over nothing pitting me against him, fighting to win, afraid of losing, afraid of what it would say about me if I lost. I wanted to kill him. I wanted to kill him. I was afraid. The red numbers say 2:17. When did I get in bed. How long was I asleep? He's been willful, rebellious, sullen, devious. Arabella said something, there on the tip of my mind. What are you hiding? Nothing! I'll teach you—*Be on my side!* I feel fear in my stomach. The payphone in the street rings, unattended. I turn again. My body aches. The phone rings. Stephen! No one is there. I listen to the payphone ringing. Someone, for whom it is meant, doesn't hear, and it rings and rings. Stephen! The man was in front of me on the street, crouched, his legs apart, his arms spread, his head up from beneath massive shoulders. The night was full of noises, and the branches, blo wn over the sidewalk, whipped back and forth like arms reaching out for me. When I tried to pass, he shifted to the left and then to the right to prevent me. My arms were filled with bags. I was afraid. He ran at me, and I tried to run, but he caught my legs. I fell on the ground, my bags splitting and falling everywhere. I fought. I socked him, grabbed his arm, I tried a scissor lock on his torso. I kicked him, I hit him. He was stronger than ten men. I am sucking air, I can't fill my lungs—

—his arms are around my chest, squeezing, my arms are helpless, I kick back at him, I try to get his groin, I throw my head back, he pulls out of the way, squeezing me so I can't breathe, I cry out I lurch up out of the bed and am standing in the door, my hea rt is going like crazy, hurting the inside of my chest, the room unfamiliar with the bed out (I've never been in this room before), Michael's body outlined by the faint light. I don't know why I am awake, standing in the door. I hear the phone ringing. I take a deep breath. I hear the phone ringing. It is still night, I am in my home. It is the payphone in the street, calling for somebody, anybody. Please answer. I stand in the doorway, listening, my heart pounding against my ribs. It was nothing. What seemed for an instant like everything was nothing. I go into the bathroom and lift the lid and piss. This is something. I lean on the wall behind the john, my thoughts disordered. I go back to bed. The thing in my head was nothing. The payphone rings. Stephen. I am not there. Stephen. It's been years since we had a decent talk. She joins me at the kitchen table, her elbow supporting her head, her fingers running through her thick black hair. What's there to talk about? Stephen. She looks up at me, weary having to tell me. Your son. What's there to say? Don't attack me. I think he hates you. She made a frown, daring me to contradict her. He hated her in those years. Gloria is dark, and her coloring is dramatic, black hair, red lips, her gestures large, belonging on the stage. You're teaching him to hate you. Everything was drama and crisis with her, accusation and condemnation. I walk into the kitchen, and she stops me, coming around the end of the counter, wiping her hands. She stares at me through eyes hard with indignation. It's been years since we had a decent talk. Fine, let's talk. But she is suspicious (not when you're in that mood), narrows her eyes, backs away. Look, you want to talk, I'll talk. I'll tell you what I' m thinking. You're always asking what I'm thinking. I think you're a goddamn bitch, Gloria. I don't remember the words I used. I shouted louder than she could, screamed at her, drowned her out until she fell silent. It was satisfying when I made her cry. She cried from frustration, which showed I'd won, and all I had to do was keep on beating on her. She sits at the kitchen table crying. I see her very clearly. The phone rings and nobody answers. She cries and cries. I was angry, but I can't put words to my anger, and I don't know what the fight was about. We'd drink, and we'd fight—then violent sex all over our bedroom, under the anger the hurt and under the hurt the need. You're such a weakling. I was very tired. I was afraid of her. She could accuse me of such things. I am very tired. I can't get comfortable in my bed. Stephen. Arabella said something. My shoulders are sore, and my back. I lie on my stomach. Michael is undisturbed, nothing bad can happen to me if Alec Argento loves m e. The life of the city, sirens going by, the phone ringing, goes on, and he is oblivious.

—I am breathing heavy, my chest is pumping like crazy, I try to get loose, duck my head out of his arm, he holds his wrist and pulls and my neck is in the vice, but I can't, I kick at his groin, butt my head, his arm closes tighter, my chest heaves, sucking in air, I try to find a place on his arms, his shoulders, my fingers slip on his sweat, I suck in air, I'm choking, I'm going to die, my body arches My chest is pulling in air. I can breathe. I'm going to die I'm in my bed. I can't get enough air. I touch Michael beside me. He was going to kill me. It was a dream. It is dark. The red numbers say 3:07. I am in my own apartment, in my own bed, Michael beside me sleeping, I am not going to die yet, and the fear in my heart, the knot of hard muscle in my stomach, was terror in a dream—attacked in a dark street by a man crouching, his legs apart, his arms spread, preventing me from passing, grappling, losing, feeling weak against him. I try to breathe more regularly, breathe in, breathe out, get the fear under control. I listen to the sounds of the apartment. I can hear nothing over the thumping of my heart and the roar of my breathing. The fear is stil l on me. Gradually, I am able to hear the sounds of Michael breathing, shallow, steady, above the buzz inside my ears. A siren in the street going toward the hospitals, someone being taken to the Emergency Rooms, the large white van, red lights flashing front and rear weaving in and out of traffic, slowing for lights, easing through, speeding up, the siren screaming out over the neighborhood emergency, emergency. My breath subsides. I lie in the dark beside Michael, sensing danger. There is someone in the apartment. My body, instead of relaxing down into sleep again, lies rigid in the bed, covered with sweat, the sheets damp under me. I listen, strain to hear the creak of floorboard, the sound of door opening. I hear it, I don't hear it. My anxiety obliterates my ability to think. I hear Amos breathing in the other room, his jagged breaths a different rhythm from Michael's next to me. I am surrounded by dangers in the dark, figures that slide from shadow to shadow. I went to bed hearing Mom and Dad fighting downstairs and woke to the certainty that there was someone in the closet, slowly pushing open the door. I know the man in the dream. He comes every night to kill me. He has a shaved head and massive shoulders, is strong and hates me. For years he has come to kill me, and I escape from him, wake gasping for breath, my heart pounding, struggling up into consciousness, terrorized in a dark room. I have never seen his face. My breath, calmer, steadier now, subsides into long exhalations followed by a long pause. In a spasm, I inhale. I make my long slow exhalation and pause, and, in a spasm, inhale again. I am surrounded by dangers, and in the dark I am defenseless. I turn on my side on the damp sheet, toward Michael's back (nothing bad can happen to me if Alec Argento loves me). I can't protect myself. The virus is in my blood and makes me weak. I don't know if I have the virus. It will grab me in a sudden sickness so devastating there won't be time for fear. I have given Michael the virus. I live, get up in the morning, tend to Amos, look for a job, breathe, have sex, play my flute, talk with friends, go about the city. The burden of my shame bends my

119

spine and contorts my face, too heavy for me. My friends say one thing and mean another. Michael tells the truth: *You have betrayed me.* I promised him love and gave him the virus. I shouldn't be allowed to live. Someone should murder me. I should commit suicide. I would admit to anything, incest, rape, child battering, indifference, if Stephen would come home. I grip my hands between my knees, arch my back and throw back my head, strain to get the knot out of my back. Michael wants love. He looks at me, arms out, eyes pleading, waiting for something from me, and I can't speak. What I need to say I can't say. I couldn't stand his eyes. The man comes toward me on the street, arms out, crouched, legs apart. I have lived out my life afraid of the dangers in the dark, figures that slide from shadow to shadow, planning to tear me apart. He couldn't forgive me. I have never been forgiven. People don't forgive. My father, his face tight with anger, *I will never forget what you have done to me,* and me standing in front of him (the sun never entered his study), waiting for something more, some sign that what I had done, rebellion, sullenness, disrespect, was forgettable, forgotten. Everything is remembered always. Alec Argento murdered his lover. Alec never admitted he murdered his lover. Alec abused his child. Oh, God. Paradise. The dancers, the lasers, the shimmer of Arabella's dress on her thigh. Stephen. This was what she said last night: *You molested him.* Hello, Stephen? Stephen! Where are you? Will you come home? I hear him, and it would feel like a reprieve from the axe. I love you. I'll wait for you. The bed is wet with sweat and stinks. My joints are sore, and I turn, looking for a place for me. I have to get a job. My rent is due, unemployment is not enough. I have not tried hard enough. I have been la zy, believing that a check would come, that some reprieve would be delivered, that he would turn and say, but I forgive you. The real sound of hell is not the screams but the silence: there's nobody to hear. The payphone rings in the street. A pusher uses it to take orders. He hears the ring and runs down from his apartment and answers. It rings, the sound of someone needing drugs at three a.m., seeking oblivion, the sound of someone from whom need has removed the skin, flayed alive (in the summer, I play my flute in the meadow beside the stream under the great uncracked dome of the blue sky, a long unbroken line of dark sound floating over the bushes and shrubs around the trees and monuments), the sound of someone calling across the city to a telephone on the street, seeking oblivion in ecstasy, special K, coke, the brain waves smoothed out to an oceanic swell, the phone ringing and ringing in the empty street, anything to obliterate the electrical impulses across the synapses of the brain that are the here-and-now, life-as-it-is, defined as the cuts and scrapes— the flood of blood—as the skin is removed. I am told my mother loved me. I remember nothing. I am placed on a cold steel table surrounded by a cluster of masked people in white, staring down on me. They move to my head, their hands reaching toward my eyes. I cannot move. The circle of their heads, eyes only showing above their masks just above my face, their hands, sheathed in latex, pulling back my eyelids and fixing them immobile. Hands work on each eye. I see the scalpel and feel—as a kind of itch—the blade slip between the cornea and the iris of my eye. The blade detaches my cornea and lifts it from my eyeball and carries it away. I am sad, but I am not in pain. Then, like a change of scene in a play, these masked figures leave and another group appears, staring down on me. These ones are interested in a different part of me. I feel the point of a knife at the top of my abdomen, at my sternum, feel it enter, an itch, then a kind of tear. An incision is made down my stomach to my pubes, blood runs cold down the sides of my torso onto the table. Cool fingers pull my skin apart and expose my abdominal muscles to the air. Blood runs down my sides from the incision, and deft hands mop it up, tie off arteries, cauterize. My abdominal muscles are separated. I feel an itch, and the cool fingers, the eyes above the masks gaze down into the hole in my body, probe my insides. I lie immobile, unable, even if I had wished, to move. I feel an immense sadness. The fingers slide under part of me and lift it up (I feel lighter) and pull the part of me (I feel and hear the scissors) out of the cavity of my thorax. For a second, the cool fingers hold it up above my chest. Blood drips down on me. It is my liver. Other hands take it, and I see it disappear toward a small cart near my table where there are clear plastic containers. I feel cool air in the space where my liver had been. The masked figures around the table disappear, replaced by a new set. More cool fingers probe me. My pancreas is lifted out. I am aware of the space where the pancreas had been and of the feel of the cool hands handling my bodypart and carrying it toward the small cart. The containers have labels (liver: Biloxi, pancreas: St. Louis). The masked figures around me move quickly from my table to the cart and back again, carrying away pieces of me. I feel progressively lighter, more aware of the cool air of the room on my insides, more hollow, as I am dispersed to the small clear plastic containers on the cart. My body is being harvested, what is still useful being removed and preserved and stored for shipment around the country. I am cold, and although I am watching all this from a great distance and without pain, I am afraid. My blood spatters the fronts of their smocks, and their hands, sheathed in latex gloves, are covered with my blood to their elbows. They have had to reach deep inside me to remove my organs. A new team arrives and remove both my kidneys, one at a time (Iowa City, Schenectedy). Cool fingers reach under and lift up my intestines, pulling them up out of me like long, slick, steamy hoses. I am crying. It takes several pairs of the cool hands to bring them all up. They loop down, festoon the raised pairs of hands. They place them in the steel bowl on the cart, where they lie, hot and steaming. I feel the cool bowl. Without my organs I feel light and windswept on the inside of my abdomen, like the breeze which gets in under a coat to the bare skin. Tears run down my cheeks onto the cold table. I feel wind where my skin has been removed. I hold my breath to stop my body from being wracked with sobs, but they don't stop. I grip my hands between my legs and hold my knees close together and close my eyes tightly to shut out—my head thrown back, my mouth open—whatever it is there in the room with me, but whatever it is is inside my head, inside my eyelids. The weightlifter has the bar across his chest, straining to push it up, his face red and swollen, contorted with the effort, his eyes squinched closed but open and looking up, the ends of his mouth pulled down, the effort pulling down the ends of his mouth until his teeth show, his face a mask of pain as he strains to make the lift. Stephen in agony, standing at the end of the kitchen table, looking from me to his mother, at the moment of hearing that we were to be divorced, his face about to break up into a cry, his eyes fighting between closing and opening, the ends of his mouth pulled down and opening up to reveal his teeth and tongue. The agonized face of Christ on a crucifix. Amos's head—all bone and teeth, the skin barely there, the eyes deep sockets with their large protuberant balls—like Pharoah's eyes, vacant with terror at his nightmares, dug up after three thousand years. Michael holds his breath against what is to happen to him, his eyes squinted, his teeth clenched, his face hard. *You betrayed me. I hate you.* Regret, sorrow, guilt, shame. The plastic mask of a monster. The phone rings in the street. I can't control the pictures in my brain, projected on the inside of my eyelids in the black room. *You betrayed me.* When he climbed up into my lap and hung his arms around my neck, he snuggled into my arms, feeling my strength and my protection. I hold him, fondle him,

Winter Rain

stroke the back of his head against my shoulder, carry him to bed. He is so small. I couldn't protect him from me. A siren. My father is a drinker. The odor of alcohol and cigarettes and his irrational anger. Mother said he was like his father. Behind him his father's image and behind him his father's image, receding into infinity, drunk and angry, identical in the distance, toward the distant past, all drunk and angry (identical DNA). And me, and Stephen. We inherit our anger with our genes and chromosomes. Arabella: You've all got bad genes. Stephen is unlucky in his parentage. Arabella: You're all alike. I know, I married one of you. She has run away. I would run away—from myself. We are unlucky in our parents. We ride in ambulances careering through city streets, sirens wailing emergency, emergency, people and dogs scattering. Who were Arabella's parents? I should be neutered. The cool fingers probe, lift, separate, and I feel the knife open the scrotum, sever the vas, cut the vessels and the arteries. They look like peeled figs in their small, separate, plastic containers. Why did you have me? To honor me. I need him too much to love him merely for himself. *Honor me.* A little girl, naked, ran toward the camera, her arms out, her hands limp at the ends, face contorted with terror and pain, running from napalm. Honor me. Are you single? Yes. I circled the dance floor, alone, looking into the dark where the flashes of light ill uminated shirtless men, their torsos glistening with sweat, dancing, hunting for a man, Amos at home, too sick to leave his bed, my eyes squinting through the smoke and the dark. I breathed deeply, regularly, my eyes moving from man to man, checking out t he way his body fit together, my need for something that was there in front of me overwhelming and irresistible. I felt the men's hot stares. A man, dark, semitic, strong features, curly dark hair, large brown eyes, returned my stare, smiled, invited my attention. I pursued him around the room, to the bar—"Double, and whatever he's drinking," nodding in his direction, four feet away—and finally to an exchange of words: "Thanks." He raised the drink in a salute to me, looked at me over the rim of the glass. I nodded. "Dance?" but thinking sex. What happened next was unforeseen. "Are you single?" "Yes." I can hear me saying it now yes. It would not have changed what happened later, if I had said, no. The sex with this dark stranger was not the betrayal, it was that yes. I told him my name, and the next day, he told a friend who knew Amos about Alec Argento. He said he was single. Amos confronted me: You denied me. No matter what I did, he remembered I had betrayed him. I was transformed. Yo u denied me.

Winter Rain

There are photographs of me at seventeen in cutoffs and teeshirt, hiking boots, a baseball cap turning backwards, carrying on my back in a knapsack the paraphernalia for a hike. I look into the camera with an open grin, steady eyes, ease and assurance. There are no photographs of me dark with rage. I have become this when I used to be that. Stephen, on a playing field, ran down the course toward me. The sky was deep blue and the occasional clouds, white and puffy, slid off to the left in the face of a wind which caused the trees to rattle and bow. He ran toward me, his arms bent at the elbows, his knees lifted high and pumping, his head held up and his hair, blown by the wind streaming out behind him, like a horse's mane. I waved to him. He waved back, his left hand cutting an arc high above his head. As he drew nearer, he grew larger in my vision, and —the sun caught him, and he went all gold—he seemed like a young prince. In the street a car alarm screams—loud, demanding, complaining—a wail of distress through the silence. Someone has attempted to break in. The device itself has broken down. The alarm goes on and on. Things break down, people, machines, the social order. The odds are against a car being broken into on the street. The odds are against contracting HIV, being shot by random gunfire, being run over by a truck at an intersection, losing all your savings in a failed bank. The odds are against winning the lottery. The alarm continues its rolling howl in the street. The odds are low enough. I turn to Michael and slide my body close to his back, fitting my curves to his. He is warm. I hear the alarm, highpitched, mechanical, piercing. He doesn't respond to me. I betrayed him.

—I push hard against his chest, trying to get him off me, turn quickly and try to get my elbow under his arm, grabbing for his wrist, pull, hard, breathing heavy, but he is too strong, he has his arm around my neck and I begin to choke, I can't breathe—I wake up gasping for breath. I almost died. The alarm. I didn't almost die. It is my apartment, my bed, Michael is in bed beside me. The red numbers say 6:00. The alarm is ringing. My chest heaves. It is still dark. When I go back to sleep, I have the dream. It is four. The alarm for Amos's medications. Two at four. It is cold. I get up and slide into my jeans and pull on a sweat shirt, get a glass of water from the bathroom, turn on the nightlight in the bedroom and stand by the bed, observing Amos, counting his breathing. "Amos?" He doesn't respond. I sit by his bed and slide my hand up his thigh. "Amos?" I slip onto the bed and lie next to him so I can slide my arm under his head to raise it. "Amos?" He groans. "Can you wake up enough to take your pills?" No response. I a sk again, and he makes a noise which may be an assent. His mouth falls open. I take each capsule and place it inside his mouth, feeling his teeth and his moist tongue, now showing signs of thrush. My tongue has played with that tongue. I raise his head and put the cup to his lips and tilt it. Some of the water runs out the side of his mouth. I lower his head slightly. I think I see him swallow. I give him more water, and he swallows. He is asleep, again. I lie next to him, my arm under his head. He doesn't care that it is me. He doesn't care what is being done for him, to him. I doubt that he cares that there is a human being here. He may sense the warmth of my body, but what more is he capable of sensing? that I regret the way things ended? that I want to say that I am a failed human being? that I would like him to forgive me? I lie next to him, feel the heat from his body on my arm and against my side, everything we shared now reduced to this exchange of heat. The cool hands move toward me with a scalpel, insert the point at my sternum and expertly make an incision to my throat. They peel back the skin. Quickly my sternum is severed deftly, and the hard bright metal apparatus inserted in my chest, which is suddenly hugely expanded, like doors opening on a never-before-pillaged tomb. My heart (THUMPthump, THUMPthump, THUMPthump) now beats in the cool open air, my lungs behind it expanding and contracting in sudden bewildering freedom from the constraint of my ribs. My table is crowded by people masked in white, their long latex gloves spattered with my blood. Half a dozen pairs of hands reach toward me, lift my heart (cold hands around my heart) and suddenly I feel my arteries being severed, sudden reduction of pressure in my body, and my heart lifted out of my chest cavity and carried across the room, dizzy from the height, to a container on the cart, with my other parts. I see it steaming, beating alone, fully visible in its plastic jar on the roll-around cart, throbbing—THUMPthump, THUMPthump, THUMPthump—in time with Amos's. A whole new team has moved in, more cool hands reach in and lift my lungs, move them up and out, one to each side of the table, the arteries, the windpipe severed so quickly it was done before I knew it. I see them inhaling and exhaling in their containers. My energy dissipates around the room, diffused into many centers—and weak. Sadness weakens me. I am conscious throughout the room. I want your body! Arabella's laughing, mocking face. She harvests me, reserves to herself the right to use me (Oh, Alec, he calls me every day), patronizes me,

murders me. I hear, from the other room, the sound of my heart —
THUMPthump, THUMPthump, THUMPthump. I slide closer to
Michael and, lying on my side facing his back, fit my curves to his,
my arm encircling him. He is afraid. I will hold him, and whenever
he trembles, I will comfort him, soothe his fears, face the dragons
breathing fire with him. I hear my heartTHUMPthump,
THUMPthump, THUMPthump. I want his body. I sl ide my body
against his and feel my erection between us. Desire, need, proof
against fear, I am still alive. He is alone, and he needs me. He is
warm—

—with my arms around his torso, the heel of his hand under my chin,
pushing up, forcing my head back and back, I try to move my head,
but he prevents me, and I lose my breath, I can't breathe, I choke —I
gasp for air. My lungs suck in air. I'm in my bed. Michael's arms are
around me. I'm going to die of fear. My heart pounds —
THUMPthump, THUMPthump, TH UMPthump, THUMPthump. I lie
on my side, Michael's arms around me, my hands between my knees,
my head back. I will die if I go to sleep again. I feel myself fall
back toward sleep and catch myself just before I fall. He will be
there and will try to kil l me. I will die, my heart (THUMPthump,
THUMPthump, THUMPthump) will spasm (jerk, jerk, jerk) and quit,
and I will die in a convulsion of pain. I can't go to sleep again.
Michael's arms around me. The door opened so slowly I couldn't be
sure it was moving until I heard the creak and knew somebody was
opening the door and entering my bedroom. I might have run
somewhere but I was too afraid too move, and I lay in bed, my hands
between my knees, watching the door open wider and wider, the light
the pale silver reflection from the new moon illuminating the white
wood of the door as it moved. I am little, and I am going to be hurt.
I can't breathe. I watch for what is behind the door. I wait, watch,
rigid with fear, hold my breath for an interminable moment. Then,
shrieking through the dark: *Boo!* It is a scream, and I jump a mile. I
can't breathe. I am crying. *I hate you!* I am afraid of you. My heart
is going like crazy. A reasonable man knows that there is nothing to
be afraid of in the dark. He stood by the bed, watching me while I
sobbed, pronouncing his sentences from his great height. A
reasonable man knows there are no such things as monsters. Outside
an unearthly howl rises to a screech and falls, rises again, a siren —an
ambulance, a violated car, the police—crying out emergency, crime,
breakdown. I cry and cry. He beats me. Men don't cry. I feel the

hot stinging slaps on my bare bottom, and I sob and gasp for breath, feel my dick stir. Men don't cry. Well, she said, they don't, loo king at me annoyed, resentful, exhausted from the stove where she stirred something. You shouldn't have been scared. My sobs wrack my body. The dark room is not illuminated by the light from around the window so much as merely outlined by it. My breath subsides gradually, and I hold my hands between my legs and cry softly. I am absolutely alone. I walk through the dark night, the city turned inward on itself, the faces that turn to me dirty, stubble of beard, spittle, contorted with pain and grief, eyes red and rheumy, fingers reaching out toward me like claws can you spare a quarter. Can I spare? I have nothing spare (can you spare a heart?). I have no strength left. He overpowers me. Stephen: *You sexually molested me.* That was what she said, Paradise, the lasers, the cool shimmer of her dress. I committed incest on him. I turn in the bed, away from Michael, in agony. The memory, which has been on the edge of my thought, stealthy behind the door, comes back to me irresistibly now, I don't know from where, now moves to the spot between my eyes. Inescapable. Perhaps Amos needs water. Do I hear a siren? I have committed incest. There is no one to know what I am thinking. I try to think of something else, Gloria's lurid lips, but Stephen is insistently there in front of me, between my eyes. Stephen, thirty -six inches long, in the bathtub, on his stomach, splashing, his rear end, wet and pink, rising out of the water like two porpoises. I soap him. I feel his skin under my fingers, wet, warm, slick, firm. The pleasure I had in washing him—I try to remember what its components were—the water, his slick skin, his pink body, the articulation of his small joints, his utterly beautifully formed limbs. He kicked and splashed. I try to remember what I felt—did I breathe more quickly, more shallowly, what did I see. What was happening to my blood? I turn again, my hands between my knees, clenched. I know what I feel now: a shame so vast, so choking I can't breathe. The cool hands remove my heart. It lies steaming, throbbing (THUMPthump, THUMPthump, THUMPthump) in his palm, his fingers extended and slightly curled, dripping blood. If it were true. It is true that he thinks it is true. It is true. What do I know? I know what I feel. I know only what I remember. Stephen comes running toward me across the sand, his wet hair stuck to his forehead, his trunks drooping around his hips, Dad! Dad!, and jumps up into my arms, careless, trusting. I hold him tight against my chest and swing him around, the sand and the surf swirling behind his head. Dad! *Did*

you see that? I rode the waves! The image, like the image of
sweating dancing bodies illuminated by the strobe light, lasts only a
second, and there is nothing before or after to explain. What did I do
after, in the dark. When was that? Where were we? What beach?
But I didn't cut my hair until 1977. When did I cut my throat? Can't
you remember? I try to remember —the continous current of feeling
which is my life now lost, and what's left, puddles in the mud like a
river gone dry. What was the exact nature of my pleasure in washing
Stephen? I have stood behind Michael in the shower, soaping his
back and rear, running my hand over his slick skin and around to his
front, feeling his nipples, running my hand down the crack of his ass,
and encircling him with my arm, soaping his cock and balls, feeling
both of us aroused by the intimate touch of skin, soap, water. And
after, in bed, his rear raised up to me, I have slapped his buttocks
hard, until my hand stung and his skin grew red, showing the print of
my hand before we tumbled about on the bed, when lust took over.
But with Stephen. Lying in bed next to Michael, his back turned to
me, the mound he makes outlined by the pale light fr om the crack at
the window, feeling nothing but fear. What is he going to tell me
about me when he tells me about this? Nothing bad can happen to
me if Alec Argento loves me. Stephen, Michael, Amos, Arabella,
Gaetano, my father, Gloria, my mother. The odds are. Michael lies
in bed next to me, the edges of the room touched with the pale light,
suffering his resentment. I ignored him, was afraid he'd accuse me.
Michael expected me to be strong for him. Strong. I hit Stephen
hard. I hit Michael hard. I can never satisfy. My father's cold face.
The applause seemed thunderous from the auditorium, when they
brought me to the front to take my bow, a solo part in the school
orchestra performance of a Bach orchestral suite. I looked out into
the dark auditorium, the light from the stage showing the smiling
laughing faces, clapping hands of the audience, searching for my
parents, somewhere in the audience. The applause seemed louder and
to go on longer than I had ever heard (I had done well), and I
searched for them among the bright faces. Afterward, the other kids
crowded around, congratulating me, patting me on the shoulder, and I
looked over their heads for my parents. I found them waiting for me
on the concrete at the front of the building, and we w alked quickly to
the car. On the way home, my parents in the front seat talked
between themselves—his drinking, his cruelty, her nagging, Horace.
We parked in the driveway and entered the house, Mother to the
kitchen, calling out to me as I went upstairs , "Take a bath!" and my

father, sullen, angry, indifferent, to the living room, a drink, and a
book. Nothing bad can happen to me. I went to bed. I played like a
fucking angel. I had played to an empty auditorium, put the flute to
my lips and blew my fucking brains out and there wasn't anybody to
hear. My hands are between my knees, and I press them together. I
am tired. When I had my flute to my lips, I could tame monsters.
She looked at him before speaking (*Don't bother your father with
that*) and told me I made her life hard. He thinks Stephen's glories
came out of nowhere and are a reproach to me. I am fourteen years
old, my hair cut short and slicked back with hair tonic, my flute
under my arm, taking a bow, searching the audience for his face,
looking for delight. I am hard. I don't believe it when Michael says
he loves me. In the end it will turn out that he merely needed me,
needed my muscles, my strength, my experience, my dick, didn't love
me. He'll betray me and blame me. My mother, lying in her hospital
bed, the tubes up her nose and down her throat, an IV in her arm:
You were supposed to be a comfort to us. The phone rings in the
street, the insistent sound coming up from the street into my living
room, demanding an answer. The person on the other end, strung out
on heroin, in the strait of withdrawal, joints aching, confused, body
hurting everywhere, seeking help. Answer me. The bell on the
phone rings and pauses, rings and pauses, rings, the mechanical
sound suggesting it could ring forever, without fatigue, without
despair of an answer. There is nobody to answer. I feel my mother's
stiff cold mechanical hug. I am tired of this electrical storm in my
brain, the torrent of images. They assault me, leave me sucking air.
I want to die. You're only good for fucking. I am not drunk any
longer. I want to be drunk, put my brain to sleep. I should get up
and fix a drink. A drink would calm me, shut out all the voices. I
can't go to sleep. I mustn't go to sleep. If I could sl eep without
dreaming. I am surrounded by danger. The man, his arms out. I am
a fool to fear dying. It is happening to Amos —the extinguishing of
consciousness—and there's nothing there to fear. He doesn't care that
the phone rings in the street. It ri ngs for someone else. The Tobin
Bridge. I stand on the railing, my hand on the steel strut, the wind
buffeting me, my hair blowing in my face, all of Boston before me,
and incredibly far beneath me the water, steel gray and from this
distance solid as concrete. What would it be: to lean slightly
outward, to push off, gently, from the strut, and then as I fall to feel
the weight on my feet lighten until, as I gain speed downward, my
feet too leave the railing beneath and behind me until I am free of

anything solid, sailing out and down, my arms now over my head, diving down toward the water two hundred feet below, steel gray and solid as concrete, the wind so loud in my ears I can hear nothing else, no ringing, no crying, no soft click of scalpel. Murmur ed accusations, the look of betrayal—I would have left all behind on the solid steel railing, on the steel strut, falling free through the cold air, falling toward an obliterating instant. Over. A train. A crowded platform, a train coming up out of the tunnel at high speed only just beginning to slow down. It would take only a step toward the edge, then a leap—and oblivion in an explosion of blood and flesh. Obliterating pain. Then nothingness. I stretch out in the bed, my arms over my head, my legs flexed and pointed, relax. I feel the damp sheet under me and am aware of the warmth of Michael's body. There are on the chest in the bedroom, twenty or thirty bottles of pills for Amos, among them powerful painkillers. A sufficient number of drinks, a handful of pills, an enervating sleep, a slow fall of my body temperature, a slowing down of my breathing, of the images in my brain, to end it all. To go on, watch Amos's slow dying, be witness to Michael's decay, and to hear in my mind, if not from their throats, their accusations: Alec betrayed me. I know over and over (people never tire) how I have failed. Some of their accusations are true. I am guilty at least of some of what they charge me with. Stephen says I molested him. What is the point? The urgent need to discharge semen, to make my mark, and when it is done to know that the need will come again, that it isn't over, that release is only temporary, and that what seemed like final achievement, escape from the here-and-now, life-as-it-is, was only a momentary illusion. I have thought that Michael and I join in some profound way in sex, and afterwards the seven inches of sheet between us seems still to be measured in mocking miles. We are betrayed continuously by our need for something tha t transcends the here-and-now. In the fens, I play my flute and hear the line of the melody, which seems to reach something unchangeable, and know that it is gone when I take the flute away from my lips. Transcendence is temporary, my thirst bottomless a nd continuous. I can't drink enough to quiet the voices in my brain. I can drink again, but I can't get enough, and tomorrow, today, I'll have to start again, the voices having come back. I am looking for Stephen Argento. If he is staying here, would you call Alec Argento (859-0815). Thank you. Call me. Call me before I go crazy. The call will come, he will answer, the connection made, and everything that before had been

Winter Rain

incomplete will be completed, all the pieces fitted in, the end of the measure. But he doesn't call, and when he does, it's to say, *I hate you, Dad.* I am tired. The phone doesn't ring for me, it rings in the street, looking for drugs, oblivion. My heart beats (THUMPthump, THUMPthump, THUMPthump) in its clear plastic container. It should stop. It will go on, in somebody else's chest, carrying memories, the primary colors of a transcendent morning on the beach, it will lurch in someone else's chest at the sound of a phone in the street. It has no loyalty. My fucking heart will betray me. My balls, peeled figs, will churn in somebody else's sack at the sight of a man. I wish this long process of dying were over. We die by parts until there's nothing left but the small weak light of sensation, the warmth in a hand, which burns a while and then goes out. What poor weak bastard would want this? Be kind to one another. We are unable to be kind without self-interest, and we are cruel in our dreams. What did I do to Stephen? I don't care anymore what they say. They'll say what they want, what they have to say, and tell me what I have forgotten. I am told my life. I feel the itch at my chest, and the masked figures lean over closer, a circle of them above my head. The scalpel cuts around my left pectoral muscle, beginning at my throat, down the center, underneath, and then up next to my arm. Cool fingers slide underneath and lift, detaching it from the ribs underneath until it is like a wing, attached only to my shoulder. It is peeled away from the bone and detached completely, lying resting in cool, latex-sheathed fingers and carried to the table, placed on wax paper, a fillet of red meat. My right pectoral is detached, the scalpel moving quickly and expertly around and underneath the meat. I feel my abdominal muscles pulled and separated and lifted out. I choke. The tubes in my nose and throat sucking and blowing. Then, all over me I feel the itch of the incision of knives —at my shoulders, my neck, down my sides, and on my legs. Pieces of me are carried away to the table and placed on the wax paper beside my pectoral muscles. I grow lighter still and feel the air for the first time on my bones, cool and fresh and disturbing. I hear the phone ring in the street, someone calling for somebody, anybody. I wish someone would answer. Tears run down my cheeks from my eye sockets. The masked figures murmer among themselves, talking of last night's party, the war, money, lay-offs at the hospital. I can see their eyes only, above their face masks, as they go about their work. M y biceps—long and full—is held up by one end by a sheathed hand and placed in two hands waiting to receive it. Blood runs down my sides from

131

incisions all over me—gaping holes—and other hands move to
staunch the flow with clips and cauterizing. My skelet on is by stages
revealed. All over me the tendons still attached to the bone hang
useless, decorate me like string. My intestines steam, coiled in the
steel bowl, and my muscles lie on wax paper—trapezius, deltoids,
latissimus dorsi, spinal erectors, triceps, biceps, forearm flexors and
extensors, pectorals, abdominals, serratus anterior, quadriceps,
serratus major and minor, soleus, tibialis anterior, gastrocnemius. I
am a mound of cut meat. How could I fight the man now? There is
nothing left of me, of my life. Asleep, without dreams, is
nothingness. What weak bastard would put up with it. You wake up
one day and remember what you had meant to be. It is inescapable
that you see what you are. What happened to the boy—dark-haired
angel—that used to be? If I were dead, there would be no phone in
the street, no calls from Stephen, no regret, no grief, no pain.
Silence. Stillness. Absence. I can't stop crying. Amos dreamed he'd
been to Paris, but when he's dead he won't go traveling in his mind—

—my neck, his fingers tighten around my throat, and I can't breathe,
I open my mouth, gagging, and feel the blood in my face, behind my
eyes, my body arches, my fingers slip on his slick skin, looking for a
grip, I am dying, I am afraid, I push hard against his arms, bending
them up, desperately strong, shoving his arms up until his grip on my
neck loosens and, then, suddenly, I am free of him, I twist and strike
him hard with my fist, then he has me again, he has the reach on me,
closes his arm around my neck again—I am gagging, I can't breathe, my
eyes go red, my heart is pounding I lurch up in the bed I am dying, my
back arches Michael, awake, is looking at me, *I am in my own bed, safe.*
"What's the matter with you?" I am not dying. "I had a dream." "Are
you OK?" "Are you sure?" I lie down again, Michael turns away,
exhausted, my chest heaving. I am still alive. I hear Michael's breathing
settle down, Michael, whose defenses are weak, whose body is vulnerable
to the slow, stealthy invasion of every virus. I slide next to him, on my
side, fit my curves to his, put my arms around him, feel the slow
expansion and release of his chest. He is not afraid. My nerves, a pale
translucent skein, hangs draped over a chrome frame, my tendons, like
shoestrings, hang in a row over another. My skin, empty now and torn,
is thrown over the back of a chair. Even my bones have been emptied of
their marrow, which is now in a row of small containers on the cart. I
am translated. It had been a cold, rainy August day and then had dried

up. The sun had come out, and I carried my jacket on my arm, feeling the warm sun on my shoulders and the wind in my hair. What clouds there were, were all white now—the darker ones with rain had moved East to the horizon—and the blue showed through, cleanly and intensely. The sun gilded the landscape. On the left across the field was a flock of boys playing soccer. At first, because of the angle of the sun, they were lit from behind, dark silouettes, running and shouting, the gang of them chasing one who came up the field toward me, the ball bounding between his feet. As they moved toward the left, the sun shown on them more from the side and illuminated their clothes, and I saw that some of them had on the jerseys of the grammar school. It was where Stephen went to school. There was a boy, one of the boys chasing the one carrying the ball, who might have been Stephen. He appeared to be twelve or so, slender, running awkwardly but with immense energy and abandon, his arms pumping furiously, his head crowned with a dark curls. It was Stephen. The boys started the ball back down the field, and the flock of them chased after the one who kept it rolling between his running, kicking, feet. Stephen was in the middle of the pack. I could see him trying to break loose from them, trying to get closer to the one with the ball—Were they on opposing sides? Was Stephen trying to get the ball from him? Or defend him against the savage onslaught of twelve-year-old players?—he moved in a nimbus of his own dark curls, his golden jersey, his pale, golden arms, flailing legs. And then he stopped, dead on the field, and the boys moved on, leaving him there alone, his face turned full toward me, his eyes — great clear blue eyes—equal parts delight and astonishment. He raised his arm and waved, wildly: "Dad! Dad! Dad, it's me, Stephen!" I was grinning like crazy. I raised my arm to wave. "Terrific! You're terrific!" And then I shouted at him—for we were alone now in the field, the boys having run off down to the goal at the other end—"I love you, Stephen!" But Stephen was already turned back to the game, had already begun to run down to the goal at the far end and so couldn't possibly have heard me say, "I love you Stephen." I watched for a while—there was a scrimmage down at the other end—but after a few minutes, I felt a splash on my shoulder. It had begun to rain again. I am sleepy. The red numbers say 5:59. My memory betrays me. I didn't know then what he was already feeling as he ran back down to the other end. He hated me. And the memory, like the clouds, grows dark with blood. I am harvested. I turn, and then I turn again, back to Michael. The bed is like stone.

Winter Rain

When I am dead, I will no longer remember Stephen. When wil l they reach the core of me? If you know a Stephen Argento, would you call —

—the pieces of me, tested, measured, treated, boxed on ice, scattered transplanted into new bodies, begin to breathe, beat, pulse, pump, contract, secrete, carrying with them secretly, stealthily, old memories—

The sheet is dank, Michael's body is cool, the light from the window outlines the furniture like a drawing. The bed is like stone. I drift off, unable to focus.

—hundreds of people across the country (Schenectady, St Louis, Albuquerque, Concord) infected, weaken, suffer, go blind, mad, and die, not knowing they knew me —

6

A number of things changed during the night. First, the phone rang, waking Alec. His initial thought was of his rent. He had to find a way to pay, and, thinking the ring was the phone in the street again, turned away to shut it out. Where can I go to get money to pay my rent? Then realizing it was the phone next to the bed, he put it to his ear without opening his eyes.

"Hello?" It would be his landlord.

"Alec! I've got tremendous fucking news —"

Gaetano. Alec opened his eyes and t urned so he could see the clock. The red numbers said 6:47.

"You're married." Enthusiastic Gaetano.

"No, asshole—"

"This better fucking be good. Do you know what time it is? "

"I won the fucking lottery! I won nine million dollars! I'm fucking rich! I just looked in the newspaper and checked my numbers, and there they were. There they were! It said, There was one winning ticket sold. I got it all! Every fucking penny of it. Nine million dollars!"

In the next few minutes, Alec got out of bed, waking Michael as he did so.

"Christ, I didn't sleep at all last night—" Michael was not happy.

Alec was thinking whether he really believed Gaetano, when he discovered on the tube that the ground war, which had supposed to be a carnage, was turning into a rout. The other side wasn't fighting.

137

And, in the bedroom, still thinking of whether it was possible for someone really to win the lottery, someone you knew, Alec found Amos awake, his eyes open, his breathing steady.

"What day is it?" Then, "Have I been asleep long?"

He was still thinking of whether lightning could strike so close, and he wasn't prepared for Amos being awake, for him having come back from wherever he had gone. Gaetano was coming (he wanted to borrow the car), and Michael was groaning in the living room that he had not been able to sleep last night, his groans heard over the newscaster's voice describing the battle, and here was Amos, apparently lucid. He would think of the rent in a minute.

"No. You went to sleep last night, and now you're awake this morning. How do you feel?" He sat down on the bed. The tv was on in the living room.

"I feel rotten. Tired. Did I sleep last night?" Amos looked around him. "Why am I here?"

"You were sick—" Alec stroked his thigh.

He rested his head back against the pillow, closing his eyes. "God, this is an ugly room."

Alec laughed. "You always hated it."

"Why am I here?" Amos had risen to the surface of his mind and was breathing air.

Alec didn't try again. "Gaetano says he's won the lottery —"

Amos turned his head away. "Won what?" His voice was a whisper.

Michael came into the room and was now beside the bed, but the phone and he went back in the living room to answer it. "Nine fucking million dol

"The lottery, the state lottery—"

"Gaetano's won the fucking lottery!" Michael was screaming from the living room, then he was back beside the bed. "Gaetano—"

"I know—"

"—know what?" Amos, eyes closed, was nevertheless tuned into what was happening.

"Gaetano's won the lottery."

There was a long silence. Then, it was unmistakably there. Both Alec and Michael saw it: a smile formed on Amos's face. His eyes remained closed, and the smile suggested some interior mirth. "So did I—"

Michael and Alec glanced at each other and shrugged, then Michael went to the kitchen to get juice for Amos.

"Tell me the truth." Amos's voice was strong.

The truth was there was no money. "You were in the hospital after the last bout. They said there was nothing else they could do so we brought you here. We're looking after you—"

He lay still. "I went to Paris."

"Right."

Michael was back, and they gave Amos his pills. Then they changed the bed linen and sponged Amos off. For the first time, Amos looked at Michael and said, hi.

"How did I do that?"

"What?"

The doorbell rang. Almost immediately, there was a knock at the apartment door, and Gaetano entered in a heavy coat, shaking his heavy shoulders from the cold.

"Nine fucking million dollars!" Grinning, he threw his arms in the air.

"Go to Paris."

Alec smiled. "I don't know—" He stood up. "Gaetano, cool it." He kissed him ("Congratulations"), then turned again to the bed and stroked Amos's fingers. "But you did. You told me."

Sensing that someone should stay with Amos while he was lucid, but without having to say so, Gaetano (whispering, "Alec, Arabella wants to see you today") and Michael left Alec standing by the bed and went into the living room. Alec could hear them, Nine fucking million dollars! and their voices pulled him away from a total absorption in Amos.

"I was there, but now I don't know how I got there. I don't remember coming home." He was silent for a moment. "It was fabulous—"

Voices from the tv were describing yesterday's battle. "The 2nd Marine Division crossed the berms at 5:30 a.m., local time, and breached Iraqi defenses. The 101st Airborne was dropped into the Euphrates Valley. The 1st and 3rd Armored Divisions and the 2nd Armored Cavalry Regiment—"

"—I met this guy—"

"—the plan has been to create a pincer movement whereby —"

Alec sat down on the bed again, slipping his hand into Amos's. He felt a noticeable pressure from Amos's fingers, whose skin was dry and papery and hot.

"—he was Arabic, North Africa, all in white—" Amos was smiling. "It was fabulous—"

The phone rang. Michael came into the room, stayed with Amos while Alec went to answer. It was an odd sensation, hearing Gaetano speak of nine million dollars while he felt such anxiety about his rent.

"Look." It was Arabella. "I've got to see you today. What time do you have?"

"It's—" Why would she want to know? Alec looked for his watch. "—7:40."

"No, stupid. I mean, what time do you have available today? When can we meet?"

Alec didn't know. "Sometime. Amos is awake. I want to be here—"

"I'll come there—"

He remembered. "Did you hear about Gaetano?"

"I heard." She was pissed about something. "Your father called. Stephen told him where I am. I need to see you—"

"What's this about?"

"I'll tell you." And then, before she hung up, "And this fucking war!"

Amos remained in his bed, but the other three men rotated among the other rooms—each of them spent time in the kitchen getting something to eat, Michael and Alec took showers and dressed. The two centers of the apartment were Amos's bed, where he lay holding the hand of whoever was in the room at the moment, and the tv in the living room, which continued to broadcast in its mechanical voice news of the war in Iraq to whoever was watching. For a time, Michael was in the kitchen making coffee, and Alec was in the bathroom taking a shower. Then while Michael was in the shower, Alec was in the living room getting dressed and was able to talk to Gaetano for the first time. He hugged him, "Congratulations, that's terrific," but he was still perplexed about how he felt. Gaetano sat with Amos while Michael got dressed, observed by Alec, who occasionally diverted his eyes to the tv. As they passed each other, they made comments, asked questions, answered each other. Michael was sitting with Amos while Alec and Gaetano were in the living room.

"So, you're rich." The fact seemed to remove Gaetano from their crowd.

Gaetano was stretched out on the sofa, his head on one arm, his feet up on the other, his hands behind his head. He smiled. "Man. More money than I ever dreamed of." His grin was revolting.

Winter Rain

"When can you get it?" Alec wondered if he was feeling jealousy. He found himself thinking of what he could do with the money. There was Stephen.

He checked his watch. "In an hour and a half. They open at ten, and you can cash in your tickets then." Suddenly he let out a whoop and threw himself up in the air, his arms above his head. He whooped again. "I'm gonna buy every fucking thing I ever wanted. Alec!" He was standing in front of Alec, his hands on Alec's shoulders. "I'm gonna get that bike! The one —" And then he began to list things he was going to buy—a car, a bike, a membership in a decent fucking gym, clothes, chaps, a new biker's jacket, a watch, "not one of these fucking black plastic jobs." He said he was going to Maui as soon as he could get it together—and, "My God, next week I'm going to the islands. Not another fucking week of winter—"

Alec, listening to this, pulled on his jeans and then a black tee shirt down over his body still damp from the shower. There was Amos.

"Warm weatha!" Gaetano threw his arms above his head. With his bodybuilder's body, he looked like he'd just gotten heavyweight class in a contest.

Alec rested his hands on his hips and gazed at his friend. The odds. Gaetano, Amos, Michael. What were the odds in favor of finding Stephen? Arabella was coming later. It was hard to be excited for Gaetano. "How does it feel —" His need for rent money seemed tiny and insignificant.

Gaetano looked at him as if he hadn't seen him for a long time —a year or two. "What do you mean, feel?"

"Feel. Be rich. When yesterday you were poor."

"Oh, man—" Gaetano moved his head from side to side. Words failed him.

"Do you rememember how it used to be?"

Gaetano looked hard at him. "Christ. Poor. I guess!" But it was clear he had forgotten already.

"Do you remember how it felt to be needy?"

Gaetano waited a moment to answer, analysing Alec's face. "You're weird."

Michael came in and stood behind Gaetano. He ran his hands across Gaetano's shoulders and down his arms. "Want me to go with you?"

141

Gaetano hesitated. Then, "Yeah, go with me. Hey Alec —" He was jovial and happy and shy. "—can I use your car?" He grinned. "I'll get ya some gas."

But before they left, Alec needed things from the drug store. He grabbed his coat and ran out into the raw weather. His car was cold and slow starting (everything seemed made of iron this morning), and the roads slick with ice. Twice he skidded, and once at a stop sign he almost hit a pedestrian, an old woman, wrapped up in old wool shawls, who, in the middle of the intersection, turned and gave him an energetic and angry finger. The papers carried headlines announcing the start of the ground war and a feature describing the preparations that had been made for evacuation of the wounded. Alec picked up the articles he needed and two prescriptions from the pharmacist and ran back to his car. Already it felt as if they had lost Gaetano, and, for a moment, Alec put him with the others he had lost or was losing: Amos, Michael, Stephen, Gaetano. He was pissed. On the way in he passed Margaret and her mop.

So Gaetano and Michael went to get Gaetano's money from the lottery, driving Alec's car. Alec stayed with Amos, who had drifted away into sleep again. This time, however, Alec noticed that his face had lost the agonized look which it had had for weeks. By the pale light coming through the shades, he appeared to be merely asleep. In the middle of the morning, the visiting nurse arrived and pronounced the patient "fine." Alec told her he had waked and been lucid, and she shrugged. "That happens." Then she was gone. Alec owed for February. That payment was 28 days overdue. He also owed for January and for December.

Arabella burst into the apartment late in the morning, finding Alec cleaning up. She had on a tight short leather skirt and very high heels and ran down the hall toward him with short steps, sliding her feet into the step and kicking up her heels behind her. "Oh, lover! —" She threw her arms around him, causing him to drop the vacuum hose, "—you can't imagine!" and kissed him.

"What, Arabella."

She pulled away from him. "Are you in a mood?"

"No. Yes." Then, "No. I'm tired. I didn't sleep well last night. I owe money. I don't know what I am going to do."

She held his arms, looking at him, eyebrows raised, lids lowered, as if expecting to find a visible sign. "You need a drink." And she pulled him toward the kitchen. "Fix me a bloody mary."

Winter Rain

In the living room, she sat in the middle of the sofa, her legs crossed at the knee and splayed out to each side, and lit a cigarette. "OK. You've heard about Gaetano. I know." She nodded, as if they shared an attitude. "We'll talk about that in a minute. And about your money." Her eyes took in the room, the stacks of books everywhere, the boxes of books, the posters and pictures on the walls, the silent tv playing out its pictures of the war, and came back to Alec. She drew a breath. Suddenly she remembered. "How is Amos?"

Alec shrugged. "He woke up, was lucid, now he's asleep. The visiting nurse came by. She says there's no change —" He seated himself in a chair with its back to the tv, where a picture showed an expanse of desert.

The phone rang.

Arabella, on the sofa, tensed, her eyes on the phone. "Horace!"

It was a wrong number.

She was satisfied. "Horace is in town right now looking for me. I expected to find him here when I arrived. He'll call here —or come by. He wants me to sign some papers backdated, and I know that if I do it will make me half liable for the things he's done—"

"What has he done?"

"—I don't know."

"He's dishonest—"

"I know. I haven't talked to him. I've been away from the house since the other night when I was with you—"

"Paradise—"

"Yeah—"

"—when you told me about Stephen—"

"Stephen?"

"—about molesting him."

That stopped her. "Oh. Yes. That. I had forgotten."

"I hadn't." He laughed. "You forgot! Holy shit." He drained his glass. "I want to know more about that." Alec was angry. It had been coming on him since he woke up, this anger, and now it was right behind his eyes.

She saw it. "Now Alec, why don't you have a drink and calm down." She pulled herself up out of the sofa. "Why don't I fix us another little one?"

"I don't want another one!"

But she was already gone to the kitchen, and in fact Alec wanted another one. He was desperate, didn't know why he felt the way he did, that if he was crossed again by one other person, he would kill him. He could feel someone's neck between his palms, and his muscles itched to squeeze.

"Here." She was coming through the door, a drink in each hand. "Here, this will fix you! Take this—" She handed it to him, expectantly, waiting, urging, even pleading, eyebrows raised, lipsticked lips parted. "Won't this make you feel better?"

"Sit down, Arabella, I want to talk." He said it evenly, with force. "What exactly did Stephen tell you."

She opened her mouth in that characteristic way she had — showing the teeth on one side. "He said—"

"—exactly, Arabella. Exactly. Every word."

She glanced around the room. "—he said, when he was a child you had molested him."

"When."

"Oh, I don't know. About two weeks ago, I would guess."

"When did he say I had molested him."

She clearly did not understand.

"How old was he. Where did we live. What house did it happen in. What room. What was he wearing. Answer me, Arabella."

She attempted to laugh. It came out as if she were being strangled. "Oh, I don't—"

"What did he say?"

Everything in the room seemed now to glow with a kind of energy, as if everything were being subjected to an electrical charge and were being viewed through an oscilloscope.

"He didn't—" She had tears in her eyes.

"Exactly what did I do when I molested him."

She opened her mouth as if she were a fish, breathing, tears in her eyes.

"What did he say I did with my hands?"

She ran her fingers around the sides of her glass, smearing the sweat. "I don't know. I don't know."

"Did you ask? Why didn't you ask? Why the fuck didn't you ask? Why in the name of hell didn't you say you can't make charges like that unless you know what you're doing?"

"Oh—" She was clearly frightened. "Oh, Alec, we love each other so—"

"Do you have any idea what it is you've done, woman? Why didn't you tell him to talk to me? Where are you hiding him?"

"Alec, he's so frightened of you."

Alec didn't care. He wanted to commit murder. His fingers opened and closed and opened and closed, the muscles of his arms and shoulders aching for a weight to lift, something extremely heavy to throw around. He wanted to hurt someone. He tossed off his drink and went into the kitchen to fix another.

When he came back, he stood in the door, leaning against the jamb, surveying his living room. Everything in the room seemed to pulsate with an awful, angry power, matching the pulses of his own angry heart, the sofa, the walls, the pictures and the books in their boxes. "Gaetano's gone to get his money!" He raised his glass. "To Gaetano's money!" He laughed. "To Gaetano's fucking money! And my rent!"

She looked about her for her purse. When she found it, she pulled her feet together, as if about to stand up.

"What are you doing?"

"I don't know. I can't deal with you—"

"You throw a bombshell into my life, and when it explodes, blowing me all over the landscape, you say you can't cope—"

She looked up at him. "You're all like this. Horace is doing something terribly dishonest, but he won't talk—"

"I'll talk. Talk to me. Tell me what Stephen said."

"I have. Now you need to talk to him. Ask him what he means. I'm done with it—"

She had risen and was now headed toward the door, picking up her coat as she passed a chair.

"Wait—"

"No." Her eyes rested on the tv screen. In the middle of the expanse of desert was a line of men in what looked like white pajamas. Some of them held their hands above their heads. Alec watched it also.

"What's happening?"

She arranged her coat on her shoulders. "It's been going on since this morning. They're giving up."

"Giving up?"

"Surrendering. They're not fighting."

"Not fighting!"

"Apparently whatever was behind them was not worth fighting for."

They watched the screen together for a few moments. "I feel let down."

She laughed.

"I want to reach Stephen. Do you know how I can do that?"

"I'll tell him. That's all I can do."

"You don't know where he is—"

"Yes, I know. But I'm not going to tell you. I'll pass on to him that you want to reach him."

Alec thought for a moment. "Thanks."

"Sure." She moved again toward the door.

"Arabella?"

She stopped and turned. "Yes?"

"What is this between you and Gaetano?"

She turned fully to him, as if she now couldn't escape this and believed it would hurt less if she took it dead on. "I've been staying at his place. I needed a place to stay—"

He looked at her for a long moment, trying to see what was there. "There's more to it than that."

"Maybe."

She had her chin up.

He looked at the chin. Then at her eyes. "Why didn't you stay here?"

She shrugged. "Amos—" She lifted her eyebrows. "—and this is the first place Horace would look. He doesn't know Gaetano."

He crossed his arms over his chest, settling in. "That's not it. What is it?"

The phone rang. Horace.

"Alec—" It was Horace. "—is Arabella there?"

"No, Horace—" He was checking out Arabella's response. "— she's not here."

She was not smiling.

"Are you sure? I'm gonna beat the shit out of you if I find you're lying."

"Oh, fuck you."

He hung up the phone.

She was defiant. "I've got to go before he finds me —"

"It's something between you and Gaetano—"

She wouldn't answer.

"Hey, we used to be friends."

"Used to be. There've been a lot of changes. Nothing's the way it used to be." Unexpectedly, she leaned over and, resting her hand on his arms crossed over his chest, she kissed him. "None of us, either."

146

Then she stood in the doorway settling her things, searching in her pocket for her keys and making sure she had her purse. "Now, I've got to go—"

"Why did you come?"

Pulled away from her self-examination, she didn't know what he was driving at. She looked at him, wondering.

"What was the crisis that made you drive over to see me? "

"Oh, Alec!" Then, as she went down the hall, she called back to him. "I'm going away. Out of town. I came to say good-bye. Don't try to reach me at Gaetano's. I won't be there. And I'll tell Stephen!" Then, just before she turned the corner, "I'm going out of my mind!" and she was gone. Alec assumed she was lying.

"I'm dying, aren't I?"

Alec sat on the edge of the bed, his hand on Amos's thigh, facing toward the head of the bed. After Arabella had left, Alec thought, now I have to deal with the rent. His idea was to get out of the apartment, at least go talk to his landlord, before Horace came. But before he could make a plan, he had found Amos awake. The window, a glowing square of yellow above the bed cut by the shadows of the mullions, lit the still figure with harsh highlights across the forehead and cheekbones.

"It's happening now, isn't it?"

"I think so."

"Right now."

"I guess."

"Yeah. It is. I feel it."

"It's been happening for weeks, Amos. The doctors say there is nothing they can do. But that doesn't mean it is happening right at this moment." He stroked his thigh. "You seem strong. You seem better today than you have since you came here."

"How long have I been here?"

"Five weeks. Six weeks—"

"That long. I didn't know I was here—"

"No. You didn't know much, apparently."

"You've been looking after me?"

"Yeah. And the others."

"Who?"

"Michael. Gaetano. Arabella some. A couple of others."

While Amos talked, his kept his eyes closed, and his mouth hung open in the fashion he had recently adopted. Alec thought, listening

147

to him, his voice being so suddenly so strong, that he wouldn't have known he was so sick. It was only in looking at him that he could see how desperate his situation was.

"And you."

"Yeah, me."

"You were always good that way."

Alec couldn't think of anything to say.

"Thanks."

"I love you."

"I know." After Amos said that, he seemed to fall back into his torpor again, and even though Alec waited a long time by the bed, he didn't speak again. While he waited in the partially darkened room, Alec rehearsed the conversation in his mind. He had blown an opportunity that wouldn't come again. He wished that he had spoken more directly. I love you. He wished he had said, I'm sorry. Forgive me. It seemed important now, if Amos would forgive him, that he say he would. I forgive you. It would be something to hang on to.

During the whole morning, since Gaetano's phone call had awakened him, Alec had felt that he was one millimeter from snapping. As each thing came up, Gaetano's winning the lottery, the sudden change in Amos, the war starting, Michael's leaving with Gaetano, Arabella's arrival, with, in the back of his mind, his fear that he was going to be evicted at any moment, a fear sitting on his mind on brood, it was only by closing down his mind that he was able to survive without going crazy. Now, the drinks he had had with Arabella had fully permeated his system, and the feeling of panic which he felt was large and deep. He was fully drunk now, and he knew it. If he spoke, he would not be able to control his tongue, and he tripped over his feet as he rose from the bed and left Amos's sleeping bony body and went into the living room. The feelings he had waked with from his dream had remained with him, had settled in to keep company with him as the sun rose, and, going back into the living room, they accompanied him and sat down with him.

When Gaetano and Michael returned, they came in bringing in snow on their jackets, laughter and money.

"Here." Gaetano had a broad grin on his handsome face. He held out his wallet and pulled out bills. "I've brought money. There's enough—" He counted out thousand dollar bills. "—to pay your rent and to get the medicines." He stacked the bills as if they were cards, and then he put them on the table. He stood facing Alec with his hands on his hips, grinning. Michael watched all this with a bright look on his face, his eyes going from Alec to Gaetano and back.

"There was a reporter there—"

Alec couldn't understand what was being said.

"A reporter. At the lottery headquarters. They took Gaetano's picture. He's going to be in the paper."

"You're rich." Alec didn't know anybody rich except his father and brother.

"Fucking A."

He picked up the bills. They were new and sharp and hurt his fingers. "Is this for me?" He had difficulty focussing. He was afraid to count them.

"For you, good buddy, and to use for Amos."

Michael looked disapproving. "You're drunk."

The thing was so disorienting that Alec felt sick. It came up in him from his stomach, had been sitting just beneath his heart since he waked up this morning, and now had risen into his mouth. He was aware of how he must look. He felt like a beggar and knew he must look like a beggar—cringing, obsequious—felt shame, and wished Michael and Gaetano, whose sleek fat beauty now seemed an unanswerable reproach, would go away. Everything felt backwards, upside down.

He struggled to his feet. The floor heaved. He steadied himself by holding onto the arm of the sofa.

Gaetano caught him. "Hey, hey. Sit back down. What's the matter. Everything's OK now. I'm rich. We can do what we want."

Michael, his arms crossed on his chest, watched this scene develop, his eyes narrowed, his teeth clenched.

Gaetano lowered him (his strong arms) to the sofa, and for a moment Alec relaxed into Gaetano's arms (his steady strength). Then Alec began to laugh.

"Come on Gaetano." Michael put his hand on Gaetano's arm. "Let's go out. Let's celebrate. He's no good."

Alec stopped laughing. He put his hand to his forehead. "Arabella was here. She's going out of town. Horace is looking for her. She wouldn't tell me where she's going. She wouldn't tell me where Stephen is. Bitch."

Gaetano fussed around him for a moment.

Michael kept his distance. "He'll be OK. He'll sleep it off."

"Are you and she going away together?"

Gaetano hesitated. "I think she's going to the Berkshires for the weekend."

They took Alec's car again, Gaetano calling out as they left, "I'm going to buy a car tomorrow." They didn't know what Stephen had charged Alec with. Alec sat on the sofa for a long time, unable to move, his eyes on the tv screen, which showed the long lines of men in white curving across the desert, surrendering to American troops. The thousands of men, their arms extended above their heads, waited in line to surrender. The picture lacked all detail, the bright sun leaching subtlety from colors, leaving primary shades: flat blue sky and bleached white sand and uniforms, black skin. Any shadow cast was black, and the expressions on the faces of the thousands of men giving up—it was in the whites of the eyes in the dark skin, the hollow cheeks—suggested, instead of a particular sorrow, a timeless patient suffering. It had to do with their waiting quietly in line in the desert for whatever was to be done with them. These soldiers, who yesterday had been called "crack troops" by the media, were now being called "hapless conscripts."

Alec fixed another drink. There was his rent. But first, he dialed the number and was answered by a loud blast of rock music and a tone. "I'm looking for Stephen Argento. Would you ask him to call his father, Alec Argento, at 859-0815. Thank you." Alec thought of writing Stephen a letter but had no address. Arabella was in touch with Stephen and could get a letter to him, but he had let her leave without a letter, and he didn't know now how to reach her. She had said she was leaving town. She was as lost to him as Stephen. Who else was Stephen in touch with? Bernice had said that Stephen and Mr. Argento had talked. Alec considered calling his father —and couldn't.

The question of money pulled him back. He picked up the bills which Gaetano had left and, for the first time, counted them. There was enough here to bring him up to date on the rent, to buy Amos's medications for the month, and to have some left over. A gift f rom Gaetano. The anxiety he had felt about his rent had not evaporated. He didn't know how close he was to being evicted, and his relief at having money in his hand (he had never held several thousand dollars in cash in his hand at one time) was alloyed with the odd way he had come by it. There had been no cause to this effect. He had done nothing to procure the money he held between his fingers. He had not had it, and now he had it.

Winter Rain

The phone rang. "Is she there now?" It was Horace.

"No Horace. I told you. She's not here."

"I don't believe you. Something is going on between you. I'm coming over. If I find her there—"

"Come ahead, asshole—"

They had left him. He was trapped. He could pay his rent, but he couldn't get out of the apartment. Alec decided to leave Amos and to go downtown to the landlord's. Pay his rent now. Amos would be OK. He would not have to face Horace. He grabbed his coat, turned on the answering machine, turned off the lights in the apartment — and ran. He would pay his rent, and then he would find Stephen.

Running down the stairs, afraid Horace would be there already, Alec almost fell over Margaret. "Would you—?"

"Show me to him—" Her face showed, in its grim set, that she had known all along it would devolve, finally, on her.

On the street, it was trying to snow. He ran toward the subway, cutting between traffic at the intersection and getting across just before a police cruiser screamed by, all its harsh red lights flashing. He stumbled over an old man in an olive drab overcoat and unlaced hightop boots pushing a shopping cart piled high with plastic bags with empties. He got to the subway just as a train was about to leave and jumped on board.

People whose coats were dusted with snow carried newspapers with the headline, GROUND WAR STARTS, and the article on the preparation for the evacuation of the wounded. Now the enemy was giving up. Events had overtaken the paper.

Coming up out of the ground into the snow in the financial district, he found himself staring into the window of an appliance store. A couple of dozen TVs were banked in the window, all to the same cable channel, showing the same picture of a fiercely sunlit desert and long lines of white-clad soldiers, hands in the air. He hesitated, stood for a moment watching the display, the snow wetting his hair, the many-times-repeated image becoming almost abstract, a cubist rendering so broken up it lost coherence. Three minutes later, he was in his landlord's office.

"There!" He counted out bills in front of an astonished receptionist. "Could I have a receipt, please?" Money meant power. Behind the receptionist stretched an office to the glass wall of the building. Alec could see past rows of desks to the windows and beyond them to the forested hills of the horizon. For a moment, this high up, the things he faced on the ground seemed small and inconsequential. From this high up and this far away, the events occurring in his apartment would seem to be repeated in all the apartments of his building, and in all the buildings on his block. He was for a moment dazed by the notion of the reiteration of his trauma throughout all the apartments in the city. His vantage made him feel dizzy with power. Everyone, everywhere, in every little block, was in danger. A man never knew when overwhelming force of an unexpected kind was about to be applied to him, and, instead of fighting, cause him to surrender without firing an arrow. What must it do to your philosophy, Alec wondered, to have a large office on t he fiftieth floor overlooking a big city and beyond to the forested hills? Would such a view, he wondered, such a God-like perspective, cause you to spend every moment in tears? Or laughter? He could see the dance through all the windows: a thousand figures propped up in a thousand beds through a thousand windows, and to them from the left, a thousand visiting nurses, a thousand landlords in black suits and slick hair carrying a thousand eviction notices, a thousand supers in broken-down heels carrying mops, a thousand friends, hands clasped over their bosoms, weeping in unison at bedside. What would it be to be able to see into all the rooms in the city? A great musical comedy number of grief and suffering, every hand wiping every tear in synchronous movement with every other hand, and the moment of death, the fall of the head back against the pillow repeated in a wave by a thousand other heads, to the accompaniment of celestial applause reverberating through the heavens. When he had been a child, he had tried to imagine God, somewhere out there in space, looking back at the earth, and having vision so finely calibrated that on the great smooth surface of the earth, he could see every particular person moving about. He imagined how difficult it must be to have to respond individually to each particular human who must be so very very small—almost infinitesimally small and therefore undifferentiated—to God. How close attention he must have to pay! The elevator, in a fast descent, brought him back down to earth, to the particularity of his life.

Being able to pay his rent, no matter where the money came from, made him feel lightheaded, and he walked back up from the financial district to City Hall and over the shoulder of Beacon Hill down Cambridge to Sporters for a drink. The drinks he had earlier with Arabella and afterwards were still with him, but the achievement of this one thing, the lifting of the fear in this one area —he wouldn't be homeless tonight—brought him back from a state of drunkenness to euphoria. Everything wasn't impossible. He had paid his rent, and now he would find Stephen.

The bartender brought him a drink, and Alec was seized with the conviction that if he walked home through the city streets, he would find Stephen. Stephen—crisscrossing the Back Bay on his bike— would appear without antecedent out of the traffic, dusted with snow, and say, Dad! He was grinning broadly, drinking his drink in great gulps. He would say, Dad!, his arms out, ready to embrace him. The conviction was incredibly strong, that now, at last, all this was about to come to an end. All he had to do was go out on the street to find him, it was no longer necessary to call that number (783 -5962) and leave messages *I have reason to believe that Stephen Argento is there. Would you please ask him to call his father, Alec Argento? 859-0815?* So certain was Alec that he was about to find Stephen, he would have another drink before he left. It was like being certain that your lottery ticket was the winning number. There was no hurry to check the number: It would always be the winning number, today, tomorrow, tomorrow, and tomorrow. He ordered another, savoring already the immense exaltation he would feel, putting his arms around Stephen, kissing him on his cheek, and feeling his thin arms tight around him. They would walk back to the apartment through the snow talking in full-throated voices of what their lives would be like now that they had found each other again. The snow would have given up dusting and have decided to come down, as in a dream, in thick flakes, turning everything in the city new and white and clean. He would take his hand, and they would walk through the snow, through the fens, hand in hand. I love you! I love you too, Dad! He put his head back and closed his eyes and experienced the dream. He had several more, before he left, enjoying the dream.

He was back outside in the snow, turned left down Cambridge and then left again onto Charles and moved down toward the bend in Charles, his hands in his pockets, a grin on his face, his eyes alert, checking out the figures coming toward him. One of them would be Stephen pushing his bike. Ahead of him, the dark red brick walls of the buildings on each side of Charles created a narrow canyon under the luminous pearl gray dome of the sky. The snow was coming thicker now, obscuring the edges of the buildings in the distance and dusting the pavement under his feet. People's shoes left prints, which rapidly filled up and disappeared. Two men approached, in dark business suits and overcoats, walking close together and turned

153

slightly toward one another, talking animatedly. Neither one was
Stephen, though they were handsome, and, in the energy they
expressed, had a presence on the street. Alec steppe d aside and let
them pass. Coming out of a laundromat was a young man, long dark
curly hair, who stopped in the sidewalk and looked up Charles, away
from Alec. That would be Stephen. He had the right height, size,
shape, posture. Then he turned (it wasn't he) and looked down
Charles, toward Alec. He had a different face. Stephen would be the
next one. Alec reached the bend in Charles and crossed the street.
He passed more businessmen in dark suits and long dark overcoats
looking properous and at home in the street, in groups of twos and
threes, and women dressed for business like the men, and other
women dressed for shopping in furs and hats, carrying discreet bags.
At each corner, Alec passed beggars ("Can you spare a quarter, sir?")
and derelicts in rags holding brown paper bags concealing pint
bottles of whiskey, lying on the pavement under the pearl -gray sky
and under a covering of snow. Alec found himself searching the
faces of each person he passed for Stephen's features and aware,
constantly, of movement in the corner of his eye. The figure leaving
the doorway as he passed might be Stephen going back to his bike,
Alec turning back to look, so that he would not miss this opportunity
which was being handed him. At the end of Charles, Alec crossed
into the Public Garden. He calculated he had been one-third of the
way home. He had ahead of him the twenty-minute walk out
Newbury to Mass Ave then the walk around the Back Bay fens, then
five minutes to home. There was still plenty of time to find him. He
imagined a view from fifty floors up of the whole Back Bay district,
seeing himself as a pulsating point of light moving into Newbury
Street—and Stephen as another point of light somewhere else in the
Back Bay. He imagined the satisfaction at being able to see these two
points of light moving on lines, straight, curving, zig-zagging, which
would intersect at—where? In front of the Bookstore Cafe, at the
Trident Bookstore, in front of the Boston Public Library, the Burger
King on Boylston, at the Morrison monument on Commonwealth.
Which route out the Back Bay should he take? What of the tragedy of
watching the two points of light assume a parallel distance from one
another, one on Commonwealth, the other a block over on Newbury,
and then to see them come within twenty yards of one another on
Mass Ave as they both turned left, but never to come closer than that,
as he veered off to the right on Boylston, while Stephen continued
straight, their distance from one another

growing with every step until they disappeared from the view of the one on the fiftieth floor? Alec crossed from the Public Garden into Commonwealth Avenue, choosing to walk down the promenade in the middle of the divided avenue, past the statues proceeding there. From here, he cast his eyes first to the right and then to the left, and ahead, searching for Stephen. He tried to imagine how he would feel, when he first saw him—relief, exhilaration, joy. Alec could think of those feelings, but he couldn't feel them in advance, couldn't replace the anxiety in his heart. Would he, feeling joy, remember what anxiety felt like in the muscles around the stomach? Does reconciliation remember loss? There were tall dark haired men aplenty on Commonwealth, and several times Alec almost cried out, then the figure would turn and it wouldn't be him, or something, some doubt from a great distance, would prevent him from calling. Alec was convinced that he would recognize Stephen, even from a great distance, even if he were wearing clothes, a ski mask, say, that covered his entire head but his eyes, which disguised him. I will know him when I see him. It won't matter how far away he is. He would feel that it was Stephen, in the muscles of his stomach and the rate of his beating heart. And he would be right. If their paths came within eyesight of one another, they would find one another. But his senses played tricks on him. He saw, coming directly toward him, down the middle of the Avenue, moving around the large Collins sculpture, a dark haired man with curls in a long dark overcoat, jeans, sneakers, dusted like the statues themselves with snow. The snow coming down obscured the man and Alec couldn't tell. It was Stephen. His heart began to race, the knot in his stomach to tighten. His mouth went dry. He opened it to speak. The other man had just come around the Garrison statue, and Alec was already forming his name ("Stephen!"), already beginning to feel the joy you feel when some joy undeserved suddenly descends, when the man looked fully at Alec and it was clear that he was a stranger. He was years older than Stephen, ugly, and, in some un-defined way, cruel. He stared at Alec, but he didn't slow down, and they passed with the syllables ("Stephen!") still unspoken turning to grief in Alec's mouth. But he would be the next one. He had to be the next one. Alec passed the cross streets—Berkeley, Clarendon, Dartmouth, Exeter, Fairfield, Gloucester, Hereford—becoming increasingly agitated that he might miss Stephen. With each intersection, the possibility lessened that their paths would cross, and by the time he turned left onto Mass Ave and then right on Boylston, toward the fens, he had become frantic that he had missed him, would miss him. His eyes now moved ceaselessly from one side of the road to the other, checking out every moving figure. He knew what was happening: At the last possible moment, when stress was at its greatest and despair most imminent, then there would be Stephen.

The fens were on his left, he had just passed the O'Reilly monument. There were two beautiful boys there! He made the slow curve around past the entrance to Charlesgate, heading into the Fenway, into Park Drive, when he heard a horn. It blew loud and insistently behind him, and he whirled around. Stephen in a car! Of course! He hadn't thought! He could have come home and gotten Alec's car. He had keys! He searched the road. Which car was he in? There was a car coming toward him, unfamiliar, expensive, new, slowing down. Its horn was blowing. The man was —not Stephen. It was Horace.

"You son-of-a-bitch, STOP!" So this was what Alec had sensed would happen. He had rolled down the window and had stuck his arm out and was making frantic gestures at Alec. "STOP!" He came to a halt in the street by Alec, slammed on the brakes, and got out. He had known he would meet somebody. Wanting it to be Stephen had made him believe it would be Stephen. "You're trying to hide from me, you son-of-a-bitch! I've been driving all over looking for you. I knew I'd find you—"

"Horace—" Alec managed to control his voice. He was so disappointed (it was grief that the lightning had not struck) that he didn't care about Horace, didn't care about his anger.

"No! Don't talk to me!" Horace stood in the street shaking with anger. "You've fucked me up so much already, that —" He sputtered and couldn't finish. "Where is Arabella? I'm not gonna leave till you tell me where you're hiding her —"

"I don't know, Horace. I hear she's left town. I don't know where she's gone." Alec felt beaten, defeated. He didn't care about Horace and Arabella and whatever it was they were up against. He was not afraid of Horace. Poor Stephen.

"Fucking faggot. What a dump you liv e in—"

Alec felt an alarm go off. "How do you know—?"

"I got the super to let me in. I told her I was your brother, that you had a man with AIDS in there—"

"In my place!" Alec was almost screaming.

Horace shrugged, grinned. "Sure. I found that man in your bed. He's asleep, or dead—. I beat it outta there."

156

Winter Rain

Alec jumped for Horace. Screaming, he leapt for Horace's throat (the two men were the same size) and connected with one hand, Horace caught the other. The force of his body hitting Horace's carried them both beyond the sidewalk down into the snow. They rolled down the embankment toward the bushes, Alec struggling to free his hand and Horace fighting to keep him off, Alec letting out a shriek. In a surge of strength, Alec jerked his hand free and struck Horace in the face—he felt the crunch of Horace's nose—and there was blood everywhere.

"My place? Amos?—" He was down on top of Horace again. He had raised his arms high above his head and now he brought them down and grabbed Horace's throat. Horace should have been as strong as Alec, but right now he couldn't fight him off, and Alec, choking him, began methodically to lift his neck up and to smash it back down, causing his head to strike the frozen ground over and over. Horace's face grew red, his eyes bloodshot, and he emitted strangled, gurgling noises. Alec was going to kill him.

Alec felt powerful hands on his shoulders. They were pulling him up off Horace, but Alec wouldn't let go and Horace came up off the ground too, before whoever it was behind Alec dropped him, letting him and Horace fall to the ground in a heap. Alec's chest was heaving, he wiped his face. He stared at a man in rags standing above him, his face and hands dark with grime. There was a cart on the sidewalk with green plastic bags of empties. Alec could still feel in his shoulder the man's powerful grip. Horace lay on the ground in the snow, his eyes closed, his chest heaving.

"You was tryin' to kill'im, I know that."

Alec was just getting his breath under control, but he still couldn't speak. He shook his head.

"Tha's whut it look like."

Horace struggled to get to his knees. By a painful process, he climbed up on first one foot and then the other. Then, he was standing up. He rubbed his neck where Alec's hands had been, looking at Alec as one might look at a very dangerous animal.

The beggar turned to Horace. "Whut ya gonna do?"

Horace could not speak. Finally, "DO! Holy shit!" He stopped to breathe. "I'm gonna get in my car and get the hell outta here. This fucker's crazy!" And he did. He walked backwards a little, as if he were afraid of Alec, then he turned and walked toward his car, looking back over his shoulder. But before he drove away, he rolled down the window and called to Alec. It was clear he fe lt he was safe inside his car with the engine running. "You're crazy!" He hesitated, rolled up the window, almost drove away. Then he reconsidered. He rolled down the window again. "You know what they say about ya? They say ya fucked ya son!" Then he rolled up the window and drove away.

So that's what they say about him. He flushed hot. The old man had heard what Horace had said. Alec averted his eyes. The old man, muttering, "Ya shouldn'a done that!" wandered off. After a time, Alec wandered off, too, his head hurting, not wanting anyone to see him. He wanted a drink. And when he got home, the first thing he did, even before he went into the bedroom to speak to Margaret and to check on Amos, was to go into the kitchen and fix a drink, which he drank, standing at the sink. Then he fixed another, took a swallow, and he went into the bedroom, where he found Amos awake.

He stared at himself in the mirror. How many people now were saying, *Ya fucked ya son*. He'd been a fool, thinking he'd run into Stephen in the Back Bay. There were, what, half-a-million people in the Back Bay in the daytime? Had he expected to find the one he was looking for by chance? And there had been no certainty that Stephen had even been in the Back Bay, or even in the city. There was only a chance that the odds were as low as one in half -a-million. He sat down on the bed with Amos, putting his hand on Amos's hand, and stroking it. He wanted to die.

Amos looked at him. "I didn't die."

It took Alec a moment to connect. Then, "No. You didn't." He stroked the hand.

"I thought I was dying."

"You are. Sometime. We all are—"

"No. I mean today, this afternoon."

Alec stroked his hand.

"I kept waking up, choking, thinking I was dying—"

Alec was able to smile. "Not right now—"

It was now late in the afternoon, and the light through the shade was very weak. The shade was dark, luminous orange, and the room was in deep shadows. Alec could see only the outlines, the sculptured contures of Amos's face, the beak of his nose, the ridge of his eyebrows, his cheekbones just under his eyes, but what he saw suggested a relaxation of tension, a greater serenity than he had seen since Amos became very sick. Amos was ready.

Winter Rain

The phone rang at some point, after Alec had been sitting in the darkening room for half-an-hour or an hour. He went into the other room. It was Mrs. Carl Friedrich Argento ("Bernice"). Alec listened to her in the dark room. What did she know? She said that she had been asked to call Alec and to tell him that Stephen Argento wished his things mailed to him. Her instructions were explicit. "When you have everything packed up, would you call this number?" She gave him a number. "The people at this number are movers, and they will come and pick the things up from you. They will be given instructions on where they are to be delivered. Stephen has asked me to ask you particularly not to try to find out where the things are to be delivered. The movers will be given instructions not to tell you." After she was sure he had all the instructions, she asked, in a very careful, polite, voice, "Will you do this for me?"

"Yes, Bernice." He read back the number to her to make sure he had it right.

"Thank you very much—"

They hung up.

On the way back into Amos's room, Alec went by the kitchen and fixed himself another drink, the last light from twilight just enough to see by. He couldn't remember now, what he had wanted. Where was he? What had he set out to do today? He saw himself in the mirror again: *They say ya fucked ya son.* The defeat he felt stared at him from every direction, seemed to have no particular source, seemed like twilight to come from everywhere at once and to give every object a surreal distinction. He wanted to see no one.

Amos was asleep again. Alec was out of liquor. His car was in front of the building, and Alec determined to go to the liquor store. He wondered, fleetingly, where Gaetano and Michael were. At some point during the afternoon, they had brought the car home. Maybe Gaetano, with his money, had bought a new car. A new bike. If they had come in, they would have found Margaret with Amos. Had Horace, Arabella, told them? He considered asking Margaret, again, then decided no.

Alec drove around the road on the perimeter of the fens, swerving in and out of traffic, throwing on his brakes at one point to avoid hitting a car in front and then, by stepping on the ignition, slipping through a light before it turned red. It was warming now, and the moisture which earlier in the day had created the heavy floppy snow was now so wet it seemed to smother the scene as well as cover it.

Winter Rain

At the liquor store, he bought two bottles (Gaetano's money), and returned to the car. He felt restless and aimless. There was no more point in trying to find Stephen. That battle appeared lost. He had allies now in Horace and in Bernice (Bernice!) and presumably Alec's father, in addition to Arabella. Maybe Gaetano. And why was Michael clinging so to Gaetano today? Instead of going straight home, he drove around the district, over behind the Museum of Fine Arts and the Gardner Museum, through the hospital district (this was where all the sirens were headed), and past the colleges, where students jaywalked across the road. Street lights had just come on, and the district under its heavy wet snow no longer seemed tired.

Where would he go? He felt no compulsion now to go home to Amos. That seemed over, too. He would go home, but not now. Amos no longer needed him, could do what he had to do alone . He saw a messenger on a bike, and for an instant, he considered that it might be Stephen. But he knew it wasn't Stephen. He considered driving his car into a concrete piling, a bridge abutment. He could drive to the Tobin bridge. He was driving very fast and very recklessly. Then, along Storrow Drive, he heard a siren behind him, turned, glanced, saw the flashing lights, and saw that he was being pulled over by a cop. Maybe he would be arrested and taken to jail.

He was told to get out of the car a nd was asked for his license.

"Do you know how fast you were going?"

Alec had no idea.

"65. The speed here is 45." His eyes lingered on Alec for a moment, a moment too long, and then he said, "Have you been drinking?"

Alec tried to answer forcefully. "A drink with dinner, officer—" He thought it must be around dinner time. "—but just one." He kept his eyes steady on the cop.

At length, the officer silently considered his answer, staring at him. He started writing up a ticket. He tore it off and gave it to Alec, along with his license. "OK, you can go." He stood there in the road while Alec, indifferent to whether he went or stayed, got back in his car and drove off.

Alec didn't want to go home, but he didn't want to be with someone who might say, *They say ya fucked ya son.* He drove home and left his car on the street in front of his building. He ran in and found Amos still asleep, then he ran down the two blocks and over three to the bar. It was too early for a crowd (that didn't happen until

eleven or twelve), so he dropped himself down at the bar and gave
Donald his order.

"Whooee." Donald was laughing. "You boys ought to tie
Gaetano up until he calms down—"

"I haven't seen him since this morning—"

"He and Michael were in here this afternoon, partying. They
bought drinks for everybody here-" He went away and came back.
"Nine million dollars! A lot of money!" He brought Alec a drink.
"I met your boy—"

Alec couldn't think what he meant.

"—nice fella—"

"Michael? You know Michael—"

"Naw. Your boy. Your son—"

Stephen was with Gaetano and Michael. Cold hands around his
heart. He didn't want the bartender to know—. He didn't want to
know what the bartender knew. What was the bartender going to
say?

"—nice fella. Handsome, too—"

"Yeah. He is. Nice fella." He had to get out of here. Alec tossed
off his drink, paid, gathered his coat, and left. As he was walking out
the door, the bartender called. "Alec!"

"Yeah?"

"Do me a favor!"

"Anything."

"Tell Gaetano to cool it."

Alec thought for a minute. "Sure."

"You guys look after him!"

He was outta there, trotting uneasily over the slushy snow -
saturated sidewalks back to his house, where Amos awaited him in
his bed.

The apartment was silent. The light from the street now showed
the outlines of a chair or a picture frame. Everything seemed
transparent, and what showed through was the dark, the black dark of
the room, which seemed bottomless and impenetrable. Alec switched
on a light. It was a hideous room. He turned on the tv without
sound. The picture was another view of the desert, of long lines of
conscripts in white, their arms in the air, surrendering. Alec thought
of what they were giving up. They had homes, places to live
somewhere, families, friends. They were saying, their hands in the
air, I won't fight any more. They were saying, There is nothing at

home worth fighting for. They were up against a force of such strength, of such overwhelming power, that resistance was merely stupid. I can't defend myself. Watching the picture, which hardly changed during several minutes, Alec considered how it felt to be so powerless and so helpless, where there was no point to going on. No matter how much home might be valued, one could no longer fight. And, of course, if home were no longer value—

He fixed a drink and went in to Amos and sat on the side of the bed. Amos moved slightly. Amos and he had used to fight one another when they had sex. It had been a way of proving to themselves the importance of what it was they were doing. If you want me, fight for me. Alec held the drink in his hand, sipping it, and looking at Amos. He slipped his hand into Amos's and squeezed, gently. Amos had given no indication that he was awake or that he was aware that Alec was in the room. Now, something unexpected happened. Amos spoke.

"Hug me."

What was this? Amos hadn't asked for anything in days.

Alec leaned over Amos and slipped his arms under Amos's body, lifting him slightly, his cheek next to Amos's, and hugged him, gently. He held it for a long moment, feeling Amos's ribs, his fragile body. Then, "That OK?"

Amos's response was an unintelligible murmur. About to release him, Alec felt Amos move. His arms encircled Alec's back. Amos was hugging him. More surprisingly, Alec felt Amos's fingers, tentatively and as if they were made of spun glass, slide over his back. He was feeling Alec's back, copping a feel. It was a gesture anciently familiar to Alec—the other man's hands kneading the muscles of his back in a sensual, erotic exploration, different in aim from the way that Stephen would have returned an embrace. Amos's fingers explored his body, from his shoulders to the base of his spine, and there was in the gentle fingers a memory for Alec of all the other times the two of them had slipped into bed and turned to one another and embraced, facing one another, their hands exploring each other's backs, as they moved through the first stages toward sex.

Alec kissed him on the neck. He felt against his lips Amos's dry loose skin and felt through his lips a rattle in Amos's throat, a murmur, some communication. Alec kissed him again and then licked his skin there in the area under his ear, tasted salt. Amos's hands continued to move, lightly, tentatively, across his back, and Alec loosened his arm from under Amos and with this free hand explored Amos's body, his neck and chest, his nipples, his stomach and his cock and balls. For a few moments they touched each other in this way, making reference with their fingers to a history they shared in each other's bodies, to moments in beds in Boston and Provincetown in 1982 and 83 and 4 and 5, when they had been lovers and had found in each other the mirrored image of themselves that had let them know who they were.

Alec disengaged himself from Amos, stood up, slipped out of his clothes, kneeled on the bed naked. "Would you like me to get in bed with you?"

Amos murmured something again, some unintelligible assent.

Alec lifted the covers and got in, sliding one arm under Amos's head so that he rested on Alec's shoulder. He lifted Amos's side slightly so that he was nearly cupped in the hollow of Alec's body and was enfolded with Alec's free arm. The light from the living room, the only light in the room, was just enough for Alec to see the shapes of things. They were enfolded by the dark as much as by each other's arms.

"Amo—" Alec's voice was pitched so low it rumbled in his throat, and he felt it more than heard it. Amos didn't respond. Alec felt his body relaxing into him, melding into the curves of his torso and thighs. He didn't know what to say. He wanted to die, to be dead. He thought of the Tobin bridge. It was all over, now. For a long while, he lay there holding Amos, feeling his disappointment and grief. "—we loved one another, didn't we? Wasn't it good, while it lasted?" He was sure Amos responded. He could almost feel him smile. "We had good sex, didn't we?" It was unmistakable that Amos settled into him more closely. "Wasn't I OK?" But there was nothing there, no answer of any kind. "You were fabulous." We missed the brass ring. He settled his arms around Amos and hugged him gently. He had done this a thousand times. We had a chance at something that would have made people point at us when we went by in the street, and we blew it. We didn't know what it was we were throwing away— He stopped. "Amos, I'm sorry." He heard a siren in the street, a police car, an ambulance, some car being stolen. They said on tv an old man was murdered the other night, head bashed in. The alcohol in him fogged his brain. He wanted a drink. Amos was silent, and Alec felt his faint breathing, the expansion and contraction of his chest, within his arms. "My father—" Amos was silent. The apartment was silent. "There's something wrong. I can't find Stephen. I thought that walking across the Back Bay, I'd find

163

him, draw him to me, but it didn't happen." He wanted Amos to say something. He wanted him to say, *That's tough. You must miss him. I forgive you.* He wanted him to say, *I always loved you.* Amos was silent. Alec knew he wouldn't say anything. "You know what they say, Amos? They say I fucked Stephen. I don't know whether I did or not." He blinked to clear his eyes.

He couldn't stay here. Alec disengaged himself from Amos, who murmured something unintelligible, and went into the kitchen and fixed a drink. He stood at the window, naked, his drink in his hand, staring out into the dark. He wiped his eyes. He wanted to do something, make something happen, somehow bring things to a conclusion, find Michael and Gaetano and make them come home and help. He didn't stop to consider what he wanted them to help him with. Help in some way. He wanted to find Stephen and talk to him. His charge was like a heavy box he carried everywhere, and he was tired. Take this. He wanted him to say, no, it never happened, or yes, it did, and here's the proof. Then he could cope. Alec wanted a new apartment, wanted a job, wanted money. Alec wanted luck, the kind where the machine spits forth—your number!, where the most beautiful man in the bar comes over and says, I want you! He finished his drink and fixed another.

Alec sat on the sofa and punched in numbers on the phone. *Gaetano, call me when you get in, I need to talk,* imagining Gaetano coming in and hearing the message and calling right away, coming over immediately. He called Michael: *Hey, I need you.* Call when you get in. He thought about Michael. He hadn't wanted to deal with him last night. He hadn't done right. He punched the numbers again. *Hey, Michael, I'm sorry about last night. I'm sorry you're pissed. Give me a chance, I'll make it up to you. Things have been crazy, and I've had a lot—* He hung up without finishing, not knowing what he had wanted to say. Michael hated him. The dark was closing in on him, the light by the sofa was unable to keep it at bay. It seemed to creep out of the corners and form pools into which objects — chairs, tables, boxes of books—sank and disappeared.

He would go to prison. There would be a trial, attorneys and prosecutors and a judge and jury. He would be led into the courtroom in shackles, and people he didn't know would point at him. He fucked his son. He felt his wrists and ankles confined by the cold steel shackles, and he wanted to stand up and throw his arms out wide. He would be forced to sit in a chair and listen while men and women described in tiny detail what he had done. He would lose his freedom, be confined to a cell (cement and iron), and would have to submit. And for the rest of his life, he would be confined to jail. It hardly mattered. Alec began pacing up and down, measuring the length and width of the room with his bare feet, as if he were already caged. He marched up and down, up and down, breathing hard. Everything was lost. He had to get out of here. The apartment walls were closing in on him, and he had difficulty breathing.

He had to escape. He dressed, grabbed his coat from the back of the chair and headed for the door. On a thought, he went back to the kitchen and, in the dark, found the second unopened bottle of whiskey and slipped it into his coat pocket. Then, without checking on Amos (what the hell), he opened the door into the hall and, at the front door, stepped out into the dark night. The warming had continued, and now the moisture descended as rain. He stood on the steps for a moment. Cars went by in the street, headed for the intersection two blocks down, their brake lights large and red in the dark, reflected off the wet pavement. Alec's own car was parked in front of the building. It was raining, hard.

7

His forehead lay on something hard and rough, and for a long time he drifted in and out of consciousness, feeling the surface against half his face. Coming awake, he felt it hurt. He opened his eyes. His right eye, on the side facing down, opened directly onto the concrete. It was daylight. He was cold. He ached all over. He didn't move, closed his eyes again. After a while, when the cold concrete was waking him up more, he shifted his head a little to the side so that he could see with both his eyes. The movement sent sharp points of pain down his spine and up into his skull. The sky was fluorescent gray, and the harsh light hurt. He closed his eyes again. He was drunk. His eyes were dry, and his lids felt like they moved over grains of sand. He swallowed, but he produced no saliva. His hands were between his knees, and he shivered in the cold.

He opened his eyes again, this time more slowly, ready to close them if he saw something incomprehensible. He saw a landscape in which snow came down steadily and lay on the ground three or four inches thick. He saw an expanse of concrete and a wall of gray stone. The gray sky hurt his eyes, he closed his lids enough to shut out the glare. He opened his eyes again and raised his head to look around. There was a wall, the concrete on which he lay, giant pipes elbowing out of the wall above him and going into the concrete beside him, smoke billowing up. There was a huge square hole as big as a house cut in the wall opposite. Giant shapes (cubes, pyramids, three-dimensional rhomboids) reached up and intervened with the sky, veiled by a fall of snow. Clouds of smoke everywhere billowed up. Everything was outsized, nothing human scaled, and

169

the clouds of smoke which intermittently burst forth with a harsh hiss from the pavement suggested giant fires under the ground. Sirens screamed.

Alec observed this scene for a while with a profound wonder. Nothing in it was familiar. Nothing he saw suggested meaning. The giant shapes did not suggest a use. Their size suggested they had nothing to do with humans and he didn't belong here. The shapes and their immense size oppressed him, as if he were about to be crushed, and he stared at the place in which he found himself, concentrating on the use of the giant hole in the wall opposite or the cause of the smoke enveloping the scene.

With time, some things were becoming clear. He was in an alley behind a very tall building. The smoke which billowed up and which suggested hellfire, was steam. There was a street at the end of the alley. The whole scene was screened from him by a fall of snow. The hole in the wall opposite was a loading dock. These discoveries opened up new uncertainties, mysteries, suggesting he was in danger. He didn't know where this scene was. He didn't know how he had gotten here or why. His mind was not working. He tried to think, nothing would happen, one thought did not lead to another, and he fell back to contemplating some aspect of the scene, a door down the alley, the concrete under his head, wondering what it was.

He asked himself where he was, but he couldn't go beyond an alley behind a tall building. He had no memory of anything prior to his waking up. He might as well have been born at the moment he opened his eye. He didn't know what it was that he didn't know, and the narrow limits of his knowledge, the extremely short answers he was able to give (an alley behind a tall building), cramped him and made him afraid to move.

He watched men and women walking through the snow on the sidewalk at the end of the alley. They were dressed for business, carried briefcases and didn't notice him. Alec lay on his side, his hands between his knees, near the wall of the building and watched them. These thousands (the sidewalks were crowded with them) had places to go, but they had nothing to do with him, and they assumed the same importance as the pipes and the giant hole —they were constituents of a bizarre and threatening scene, whose meaning was hidden.

Winter Rain

Overhead, the sky was an even sheet of glare, the intensity of dark hot platinum. There was nothing to suggest morning or afternoon, and he was unable to sense by the position of the sun the time of day or even what direction he faced. He closed his eyes. H e concentrated on the sharp pain in his head, trying consciously to relax the muscles around his skull, without success, and now, waking up more, he became aware that he was trembling from the cold. He was covered with snow. He opened his eyes and stared out of the alley into the street with lidded eyes, suspicious that a joke were being played on him.

Alec tried on possibilities. If he weren't here, in this alley behind this tall building, where would he be? He couldn't think where he lived, or if he had lived here always, didn't know if he knew anybody, people like those thousands walking by on the sidewalk. Gradually, while he lay on the cold concrete under the metallic sky, under a light snow, the image of Michael, first, and then Gaetano came to him, without his knowing why. He remembered Stephen. These memories were dissociated and were not connected with his plot of concrete, nor could he think why he knew these people or what they meant to him.

He sat up and moved over to the foot of the building, leaning his back against it. The movement revived his nausea, made his brain throb. At first, he tried to draw his knees up for warmth, but couldn't, and his legs lay splayed out on the concrete, his arms hanging down by his sides. He sat there, propped against the building, looking at the people passing. He remembered looking for Stephen, who didn't want to be found. The thought troubled him. He knew he was dirty. He was hungry. On an idea, he put his hand to his chin and felt his beard. It was long, almost soft, and, feeling sick again, he knew it had been days since he had shaved. Days.

He was afraid. The world was harsh and unforgiving, the concrete cold, unyielding, the whole scene phantasmic and threatening. He had no memory that he could control, and his life, such as it was, there on the pavement in the snow, was without meaning. That is, he had no memory, and therefore no past. His nausea came up in him again, and he was sick all over himself, before he could prevent it. He opened his eyes wide so he could see the vomit on his coat. It melted the snow. He felt weak and helpless. He knew he couldn't stand. He didn't know what was to become of him, suffered in both his body and his mind, had no hope, had no strength to get up off the concrete and end it all (there would be a train, a bridge somewhere) or to prevent what was going to happen from happening.

Alec tried to stand, but his knees would not hold him. He knelt against the building, ran his hands up the wall and then pushed himself up. He fell once and tried again. Finally, he was standing. He found he could walk, if he steadied himself against the wall. The vomit on his coat was rank, and nausea crept up his throat. He crept along the wall until he approached the end of the alley into the street. Here there were the people. He was aware of being noticed, and he felt an intense and helpless anger.

He looked around. There was no building he had ever seen before. They were all anonymous shapes —immense sharp-edged glass buildings 30 and 40 floors high, giant concrete buildings on pedestals twenty floors high. The only thing familiar in this horrific landscape was the topography of the streets which curved and angled off, suggesting an old city, on a landscape that sloped. To find his way, Alec went uphill.

People glanced at him and gave him a wide berth. At some point, in his unsteady progress from wall to wall, climbing upwards, he noticed a curious weight in his coat. He put his hand in his pocket and felt—a bottle of whiskey. He hadn't known, until he touched the bottle, that he wanted a drink, and now he pulled the bottle from his coat and, putting it to his lips, swallowed twice, feeling the sharp smokey liquid course down his throat. He felt it in his head. Climbing upwards, his moved along the walls of the buildings. As more and more of his memories came back to him (he remembered now Amos in his bed, Gaetano's money), he was more aware of how vague they were, how discontinuous. The broken thread of memory left him unmoored, increased his panic, and he felt the sickening helplessness of a freefall.

He came into an area where the buildings were smaller, older, and there were shop fronts. The slope up which he had been climbing became steeper. He came into a street and was able to give it a name: State Street was ahead, the Old State House, and beyond that, Government Center. This was downtown Boston. I live in Boston.

He needed to figure things out, become moored again. A newspaper. Where was a newspaper coin box? Under the Old State House was a newstand. He approached. Men and women glanced at him, warily. He knew he was dirty and that he smelled, and he hesitated to approach close to the stand. From where he stood, he could barely see a stack of newspapers. What day was it? Hordes of men and women, their coats powdered with snow, moved rapidly in and out of the entrance into the subway, paused to buy magazines and newspapers, flowers, and moved on. Alec felt his difference from these clean self-confident people who were at home in this place.

Alec walked across the shoulder of Beacon Hill and down past the Common out Tremont Street. The names now came to him as he needed them. It was cold, and he needed his coat. There was nothing he could do about his stench. He discovered, by looking at the front page of newspapers displayed in coin boxes, that it was Wednesday. The headlines had to do with the Big Red One. He didn't know what the Big Red One was. Wednesday meant nothing to Alec . He knew enough now to know he had had another life, the bits and pieces of his memory told him that, but the connection between this and that was lost. He tried to remember the last day in his old life.

As he walked, Alec knew he shuffled, but his feet refused to move more decisively. The journey away from downtown, which he was seeing in all its alienating horror for the first time, seemed to take hours. Alec sat down on the snow in the middle of the sidewalk and drank from his bottle, unable to go on, his mind empty.

Once between Chinatown and Park Square, his bottle in his pocket and his hand limply in front of his waist, Alec leaned against a building, staring into the traffic. A woman passing very close reached toward him, their eyes met. She fumbled with her fingers. Alec instinctively put out his hand—and found himself holding a quarter. He turned it over dumbly, wondering. He looked up at her, but she was gone. He watched her back as she moved toward the intersection. She had given him money. He turned over the shiny disk of metal, turned it over and over, paid it attention, as if it could speak to him.

Alec remained against the building, and after fifteen or twenty minutes, during which he fingered the quarter, he saw a man in a down jacket approach, Alec's age, a sense of fatigue and anxiety about him. He put out his hand, his fingers cupped. What would he do? He drew near, didn't seem to see Alec, but, to Alec's surprise, he dropped a quarter into his palm. Now he had two. Alec settled himself against the pole of a street light in Park Square and began to beg. Occasionally, one of the hundreds of men and women who passed gave him a quarter or two quarters. The activity had a

173

purpose, had meaning (when he did this, they did that), was reassuring in some obscure way. The sun went down, and it grew dark. The lights came on, and the cars' headlights hurt his eyes. The falling snow muffled the dirty cityscape. He remained against his light pole, his hand out, gathering his quarters, in a timeless, brainless activity, having let go of the discordant memories from the time before he had come to live on the street. He took the bottle from his pocket and drank.

Later, he went in an alley behind a building, passed a newspaper coin box: *Iraqis Surrender by Thousands,* which reminded him unwillingly of Arabella, found a corner protected from the wind, and fell into a sleep disturbed by dreams. In the morning, he returned to his light pole in front of the cafeteria and begged from the pedestrians passing on the sidewalk, many of whom carried newspapers (*Tens of Thousands Killed on 'Highway of Death')* . The days ran into each other under a fall of snow so light it might have been a cloud of powder blown off a table. When he emptied his bottle, he bought another from a liquor store in the square. When he was hungry he bought food from a 24 -hour store.

He found grates behind the Transportation Building which produced heat. Clustered around them were men and women living on the street who made room for him, wordlessly moved over, shared blankets, papers to wrap up in, and he slept, warmed by the heat from the grate and the bodies around him and by his own uneasy drunken anxiety.

Sharp thoughts of Stephen or of Michael, Amos, Gaetano, Arabella, his father, Bernice intruded into the smooth lumpless pocketless liquidity of his days and nights. Most of the time, even when he remembered Stephen, he wasn't sure who Stephen was —or why thoughts of him brought such sharp, conflicting feelings . Other times he knew Stephen, remembered the phone number (783-5962), remembered Stephen had lived with him, had left, had told Arabella that he had sexually molested him. He remembered his anxiety, holding the phone in his hand, when he had heard the n umber (783-5962) ring and ring and ring. Alec sometimes remembered that Amos was in his bed dying of AIDS, that he had promised to look after him, had abandoned him as he was dying, and sometimes he knew the truth that he was drinking himself to death.

174

Winter Rain

Alec, standing in the snow on the sidewalk in front of an appliance store, often saw the banked tv screens showing multiple images of Iraqi soldiers surrendering. Cameras, which had focussed on the long lines in the desert, now drew in close and saw them, as their conquerors saw them or as their families saw them, up close one after the other, darkskinned, with black eyebrows, their heads wrapped in tasseled scarves which obscured everything but their black eyes, which showed suffering and bewilderment. Often the camera lingered on one face, saw it as a lover might see it, saw only the eyes, which filled the screen, pained and disbelieving, wide with raw humiliation, so close that Alec saw the liquid on the eye. There were images too of the dead, blood showing on the screen brilliant red against dark skin, drying red on harsh white robes, red stains on white sand. These images were exchanged occasionally with the images of the President, speaking of the national purpose.

"Come here, friend." A man motioned Alec to a spot by the grate. His hair stood out in a tangle from his head, his mouth missing half his teeth. He was wrapped in a blanket, the snow on his shoulders, directing each of them to their places with short stubby fingers and broken nails. "—the Dodgers going to win tonight, got a hitter can find that ball wherever it is, in the dark, and hit it so sweet down the left field fence. That boy is the prettiest boy. They gonna win tonight, and you don't believe me! I can see it in your eyes! Down in Norfolk, Virginia, they got a boy who can do exactly what he says he's going to do, hit that ball out there beyond the left field fence. Rich folks ride around in their limousines, and here I am picking up trash. Li'l baby die in the crib. Oh, that boy, can hit that ball! Police beat on young man 'till he can't stand. Li'l baby die in the crib. Down in Norfolk, Virginia they can't do no wrong! Down in Norfolk, Virginia!" He paced up and down, deep inside his head. "I could tell you things, you wouldn't believe me, make you afraid to come out on the street! Every time that boy steps up to bat, the fans hold their breath, waiting to see the miracle happen. No man born of woman can play so sweet!"

Alec listened to his ranting, crazy as a bedbug, as he drifted off to sleep ("—that boy, he's blessed, he can't do no wrong, and nothing can touch him—!"), his body curled, his clenched hands between his knees, the blanket around him exposing his nose and eyes. Alec's last memories had been of the day the war started. Gaetano had won the lottery. Sometimes now he asked how long the war had been going on as a way of finding out how long he had had this life. Some people told him a figure (5, 7), and other people told him the war was over, and Alec didn't often try to figure out how long he had been gone. He had no will to go back. When he was able to think, he was sure that he couldn't go back. When he was drifting off to sleep on the hard concrete, wrapped in his blanket showing only his eyes and nose, he accepted that something had happened that made retreat impossible.

Alec was content to see what was around him, the pulsing stream of traffic, the clotted crowds along the sidewalk, and to feel the cold or the warmth from the grate, to feel hunger, thirst for a drink, the fullness in his bladder or against his sphincter. His life was lived at the level of sensation. He accepted his quarters, drank from his bottle, slept near the grate, without thinking, answering the need for oblivion. But he felt. Sometimes, he was afraid and began to cry. He didn't know what he was afraid of or why he was crying, and once he started, he wasn't able to stop. Tears wet his cheeks. He wiped them away, leaving streaks of dirt on the skin of his cheeks, and they came again. Sometimes he cried for several hours at a time. Then the feelings would go away, and the tears would dry.

He learned enough to live. He knew how to feed himself, where to sleep, and where he could relieve himself. He came to know the others on the street. The crazy man's name was Haywood, and he knew where the best begging spots were. He was no longer disoriented as he had been in the first days. He regained some of his memory of his life on Kilmarnoch Street. He remembered his father. He saw how things fit together. He knew he had had one life, which had come to an end, and now he had another. What he didn't know was how that life connected with this life. He didn't know what had happened. And he didn't feel he was capable of going back. He would have to explain, and he didn't know what to say. He could be seen shuffling down the street, his hands clutching the blanket over his head and around his stinking coat, walking through the snow, his eyes squinted against the glare, his jaw thrust forward in rude, ignorant, angry defiance.

On the seventh day (the newspapers had gone from Wednesday to Thursday through the weekend and back to Wednesday again), Alec found himself lying on his back on the pavement, staring up into the

luminous gray sky, surrounded by a crowd of people staring down at
him.

"He's having a convulsion—"

I've never had convulsions. He had vomited again. It was on his
coat.

"He's already had it. It's over."

A policeman was there.

He was asked his name. He knew it: Alec Argento. He was
helped up and led to a spot against a building, where he was allowed
to sit. The nausea, the rage in his head, his weak body, hunger, these
left him helpless, disoriented, and he waited, unable to present
himself to the people. He didn't know these people, who stared at
him, didn't know what had happened, was unable to bring himself to
take steps to find out what had happened. He sat there, his head
beneath his shoulders like an ox's.

Two more cops arrived, roughly pulled Alec to his feet.

"Are you Alec Argento?"

Alec squinted at the man. What did he want?

"Would you come with me?"

Where are you taking me?

"You're under arrest—"

The man read him his rights. Alec was dizzy. "You're charged
with having been the driver of a car which struck and killed a man
eight days ago." The charge was manslaughter.

He was handcuffed, driven through the snow-covered streets in a
squad car ("You stink!") and taken to Area B headquarters in Roxbury,
where, in a daze and an overheated building, he was dragged briskly
through a series of procedures by men who paid little attention to him.
He was still drunk. They looked at their papers and worked their
devices, wrote things down, glanced up occasionally if he were slow
answering, talked casually among themselves about things he didn't
know, didn't understand. He was asked to identify himself,
fingerprinted, photographed and read his rights again, searched (the
bottle was long gone), and led down a hall, down stairs, through steel
doors, and put in a cell. The noise of clanging steel reverberated in
his skull.

The bars were closed on him. He sat on the bunk still in his coat.
He felt sick. He pulled himself up. The floor heaved, and he
grabbed the bars to hold on, clung to them as if they would keep him
from falling fifty floors. He lay down, and, a while after that, he
went to sleep, his rest disturbed by dreams of the man attacking him

on the sidewalk, choking him, and while he knew it was a dream, knew if he woke up the dream would end, he was not able to wake up, remained in the dream, choking, gagging, thinking he was dying.

When he did wake up, he was less drunk. The effect, however, was to increase his nightmare. The cops had charged him with a man's death. He was bewildered. This is not me, and for a while, the separation between what was happening to him and himself was so great that he felt still in a dream.

But knowing so little, he suspected. The cop had asked about his car. Alec couldn't remember when he had last been in his car. He tried to remember when he had last left his apartment. He had memories of driving, but he also had memories of being on the street on foot. He couldn't remember a last day. He remembered bits and pieces of things, and—nothing. Everything was jumbled, and he couldn't force his memories into a sequence. The cop had told him a date, but Alec didn't know what today was, and the date might as well have been ten years previous.

Everything that had happened now took on the quality of an hallucination. His life, before it ended, now seemed rational and well-ordered. The severe disjunction between his memories, a dream of peace, and jail caused him to have difficulty thinking, and repeatedly his effort to try to grasp what was happening t o him caused his nausea to return. He turned over, covered his face with his hands, and thought of something new. Stephen must not find out. But, trapped in his cell, he was powerless to prevent the discovery. He didn't know why it mattered that Stephe n not know. At this moment, he wasn't sure who Stephen was. He began to cry. He needed help, wanted someone to come and lead him to safety. Vaguely, he thought he should call, but he didn't know whom to call. Feeling abused, he expected to find that someone was looking for him, but he didn't want to be found, to have to explain. He was ashamed that he didn't know what was happening.

The cell door opened, and a policeman entered. "Get up."

Alec stood up—and felt faint and sick. He staggered. He caught himself. The policeman turned and left the cell, and Alec followed. He was aware of how docilely he was submitting to this treatment. He had no inclination to fight or resist.

The policeman led him back through steel doors, up the stairs, down a hall, down a different hall, into a room where there were several scruffy looking middle-aged men. "Go up those stairs—

Winter Rain

" The policeman was speaking to the group of them. He pointed at a door, through which Alec could see a short flight of steps. "—you will be in a long narrow room with a glass wall. Turn and face the glass wall. You won't be able to see what is on the other side of the glass. Stand there until you are told to come back here." He waited for questions. "Now go."

They did. Alec was the second man up the steps into the long narrow room. This would be the "line-up."

He stood facing the glass wall. The long walk across the city now seemed immeasurably long ago, something in the distant past. Since he woke up on the concrete in the snow enveloped in clouds of steam, everything he had done had been enveloped in clouds of ignorance. There were the people on the street, the grates, Haywood, the quarters, the cops. He was surrounded by people and doing things with no experience, that is, no memory, to guide him. Had the street been real? Was this real? Either? Neither? Both? And what about the more distant past, when he had had an apartment and Amos in his bed? He felt like a child, like a baby, and was grateful when a policeman told him what to do. He didn't have any difficulty standing in front of the glass wall until he would be told to step down. What else could he do? He had nowhere to go, other than to stand in front of this glass wall. He couldn't think why he might be here in the power of the police unless he had done what they said he had done. His memory had been so destroyed that a return to his life on Kilmarnoch Street, to any life but this one, was impossible.

At length, a policeman called from the head of the short flight of steps. "OK. Turn left." The line of men obediently turned to their left, and then waited for their next orders.

"About face." They turned around 180 degrees. They waited. He was stared at through the glass. He had been stared at ever since he woke up in the alley, by people on the street, by the police who didn't find the way he looked unusual, by these people behind the glass, and it must be usual to be dirty and to be stared at by people standing in a circle around him, by people behind a glass wall.

"Now walk this way, back down the steps." They led him back to his cell. He wanted a drink, but these calm, indifferent, efficient men would not recognize that need. He was in their hands, being led from room to room to cell to room as their mysterious needs dictated. A short while later, he was taken out of his cell again. The dialogue was the same from an impassive cop: Argento? Yes? Come with me. He was taken back to the glass-walled room, where, along with a different set of middle-aged men, he was told to turn right and then left and then was brought back to his cell. He was dizzy, nauseated, drunk and hungover, had difficulty walking, and his memory came and went.

Late in the afternoon, he was called for again, led upstairs again into a small room where there was a table with two chairs. Two policemen waited for him, one with a tape recorder.

The other had a folder with papers. "OK. Sit down."

The cop read him his rights. "What is your name?" The man who spoke was about Alec's own age, slender, even gaunt.

"Alec Argento—" He added, after a mere fraction of a second's delay, "—sir."

"Where do you live?

He gave his address.

"What kind of car do you have?"

A memory from the distant past, in another life. Alec told him.

"What is the license plate number?"

Alec gave him that, too.

"Where were you early Tuesday morning, February 26, 1991, around one a.m.?"

Alec tried to put his head together, but it was impossib le. The date meant nothing to him. "I don't know, sir."

"You don't know."

"I don't know."

"Were you in the 2400 block of Dorchester Avenue?"

Alec shrugged. "I don't know—"

"Were you in your car early Tuesday morning?"

Alec wondered what he could say to this stern, distant man. "I don't know anything about early Tuesday morning —" He paused. "—I know today's Thursday. I remember when the war started —"

The cop grimaced. "That was a Sunday. Today's Wednesday. We're talking about last week. The war's over. We're talking about Monday night, early the next morning—"

Alec was dazed. That was Sunday. He saw images of the soldiers in white giving up. Alec couldn't remember Monday—Tuesday— night. "Something happened Monday night? the night the war started?" This might be a hook to hang things on.

The policeman laughed at him. "Oh yes. Things happened that night. Were you in your car that night?"

Alec shrugged. "I don't know—"

180

"Where were you Monday night?"

"I don't know."

"Who were you with?"

"I don't know."

"What did you do Monday night?"

The nausea. "I don't know." The panic rose in him.

"Can you tell me anything that happened between Sunday noon and today?"

Alec tried, but he couldn't. *Who was the man they say I killed?*

"Shit." He asked about Alec's roommate, his friends, his lover, made an anti-gay slur. He had a great thick folder and apparently he knew a lot about Alec. He knew, for example, Michael's name. Then he left abruptly, and the other policeman took Alec back to his cell. Alec shuffled and hit up against the walls as he lurched down the halls and down the stairs, sick, his whole body trembling, afraid and confused.

Alec had been coming off alcohol for six or seven hours now. The pain in his head was harsh enough to keep him from thinking. He wanted a drink, calm the clangor in his head. He needed food, too, but he didn't think about that. They came and got him and took him back upstairs to the line-up room, put him through his paces again. All of this was becoming familiar, the police, the yellow concrete walls, the gray steel, the concrete floors, the steel stairs, the line-up room, the halls crowded with policemen. He had learned the gig, and he was beginning to sense that Alec Argento had a place here. As he came off the alcohol, his memory became sharper of that other time, when Alec Argento had a place on Kilmarnoch Street, with Amos in his bed, his jealous lover Michael, his friend Gaetano who was now suddenly rich, visits from Arabella, calls from Horace and a constant, feverish need to find Stephen as a means of salvaging his own life. Memory was fragile and easily broken, and when it was broken, nothing remained coherent.

Moreover, feeling his present life had no antecedents, beginning with his waking up in the alley behind the tall building, he lived entirely in his emotions. Without memory, he could not think, couldn't compare and establish patterns, judge, universalize, deduct, induct. He was trapped in the feelings of the moment, swept along on a crested tide. Most of all, over and over, even beyond the bewilderment and confusion which he had felt since he had been

181

arrested, he felt alone. For years he had gone from one lover to another, someone always in his bed, the phone ringing regularly. He came home to a dozen messages on his answering machine, the names and numbers of people reaching out to him. Now he was alone, surrounded by people who stared, who had large folders on him, who knew more about him than he knew about himself, and who didn't speak all they knew. He watched the other men in the line-ups. None of them made eye contact with one another. They moved through their paces cocooned in their own space, and Alec knew he was one of them.

He spent the night in the jail, hardly sleeping, having cramps and jerking awake out of nightmares. The next morning, before he had a chance to become apprehensive about the day, he was put in shackles and driven across town to the courthouse through a city lightly covered with snow. The cop escorting him told him it was a hearing to determine bail and to assign him a lawyer.

"What is this all about?"

"You still don't know?"

"No—"

"They'll tell you—"

"Hey—" He reached out to the officer.

"What?"

"What day is it?"

"Today?"

"Yeah—" Alec felt the need to apologize. "I—"

"Thursday, March 7, 1991."

He was in the courtroom, aware vaguely of people watching. A woman from the District Attorney's office read the charge against him, "that the accused, Alec Argento, on Tuesday, February 26, 1991, at 1:03 a.m., did operate his car, a 1983 Toyota sedan, license plate CDC-627, with reckless endangerment so as to cause the death of one Simon McCorkindale, at the intersection of Dorchester Avenue and Black Street, in the city of Boston, Massachusetts." There were two witnesses to the accident, signed affidavits attached to the charge. Simon McCorkindale. They might as well have said Alec had embezzled 20 million dollars in Utah.

The District said of him that he was a "hopeless alcoholic."

He knew so little about himself as he was now that almost anybody, the District Attorney, any of the policemen in the jail, Stephen, knew more about him than he knew himself. They had thick

182

folders with information. Like a child assuming the grown-ups knew how things worked, he didn't know other than to ask and accept their answers. He felt trapped and dependent.

"The accused is without funds, your honor." He was assigned a lawyer and taken back to jail where his shackles were removed and he was put in a cell with eleven other men.

He spent the weekend in that cell. He faced the fact that he wasn't going to get a drink. The anxieties which were layered on him peeled away now to expose the fundamental, immediate need for a drink. It had been twenty-four hours, and his body was beginning to rebel. Alec had often in his life gone twenty-four hours without a drink, during stays in the hospital, traveling, but he had been able to see an end to it, and what settled on him when he was placed in the cell after his court appearance was how this new condition in which he found himself was open ended. He had no power to end it. Yesterday, so much had happened so quickly, and he had been so drunk through most of it, that not having access to alcohol had hardly mattered. Now it mattered. Late in the afternoon after his court appearance, his cramps returned and stayed. His headache grew worse, and his body ached in his joints as if he had malaria.

He lay on his side on the bunk, his hands between his knees, his head down, trembling. He tried breathing deeply, tried consciously relaxing, got up every so often when the lying on the bunk was too painful and walked the cell, holding on to the wall. The men in the cell watched him warily. The immediate pain was so great that the larger fear of what was happening to him ceased to matter. He slept intermittently, each time drifting off into nightmares of being choked to death, of having his body cut up into little parts. The torment was inside him, in his own body, and even the bars on the doors did not cause in him the sense of being trapped that his own body caused him.

He went crazy. He pushed himself back up against the wall, his arms clutched across his chest and saw enemies peopling the room. Now Stephen and Michael came back to him with inescapable clarity with their charges. They came into the cell with him, sat on the bunk next to him and accused him with their eyes. He pushed himself further away, up against the wall, his arms protecting his chest. *You were supposed to be a comfort to us. Nothing bad can happen to me if Alec Argento loves me.* But his body, in such rebellion against him, instead of defeating him, made him angry. Though they came and sat down and accused, he didn't have time for them, his body in such rebellion against him. And he turned to the wall, his arms clutched around his chest, his knees up, and fought the rebellion inside him.

Then, on Sunday, it was easier. Alec realized when he woke that he had slept most of the night, the ache in his body was less intense, and his mind clearer. Michael and Stephen no longer came to him, though the concrete walls, the steel bars, the wire cages, were no less imprisoning. He felt less at war with himself. The cell in which he had been caged was lit throughout the day and night by bulbs protected by steel mesh, and they threw hard shadows. During all the day and night, the men in the cell talked and mumbled among themselves, fought, cursed one another, walked around, bumping into each other and the walls. The door, steel with a barred window, opened and shut regularly with the hard clang of steel on steel as guards came and went with prisoners and had loud violent exchanges with the prisoners and each other. The environment was harsh and violent, and Alec, the war inside him winding down, was exhausted in the middle of it. He watched it all, but he took no part in it, and the reverberating waves of noise washed over him and left him untouched. He had the sense of having fought a battle and of having survived, of having used his powers to the extremity of his ability — and of having no strength left. He lay on the bunk, his hands gripped between his knees, and accustomed himself to the fact that he might be here, in some place like this place of concrete and steel and twenty-four hour lights, for years, and that it might be years before he had a drink again.

The thought was less inconceivable than it might have been a week ago. What was also less inconceivable than it might have been, had he thought of it a week ago, was that he might not ever see any of them again, either Stephen or Michael or Amos or Gaetano or Arabella, or any of the other people who had populated his life. While he was becoming accustomed to the harsh light in this concrete and steel room, his mind was clearing and he was able to see that none of them had ever been here, didn't belong here. It was like trying to imagine animals from a temperate zone, a fawn, say, in the middle of an equatorial desert. They'd die, here.

On Sunday night, in the middle of the night, he had a fight with a man who attempted to throw him out of his bunk. He got him around his neck and beat his head on the concrete floor, until a guard came

Winter Rain

in and broke it up, and, on Monday, a young woman, completely
without emotion, identified herself as his lawyer and arranged for
bail, and, at one in the afternoon, he was released through the great
doors into the bright cold winter sun. But he was not free.

His lawyer, Mrs. Lichtenthal (she was all brown wool), drove up,
opened the door, said, "Get in," and took him to her offices where
she fixed coffee for him, found him a comfortable chair, was
solicitous of his comfort. She seated herself at her desk. Her office
was small and shabby. Like everyone else connected with him, she
had a large folder on him. She opened it, glanced down the top page,
and said, "Well, here it is, so far. Do you want to hear where you
are?"

She gave the same sense of distant authority over him as the
guards. He shrugged.

"They say you had been drinking all day Monday, February 25,
1991, two weeks ago. They've got witnesses. You left the house at
11:30 in the morning. They've got a witness to that, too. And you
went to a gay bar—is there one called 'Sporters'?—on Cambridge and
stayed there for about an hour, drinking. Apparently you talked a lot
about your friend who had won the lottery. The bartender and a
couple of other people are ready to swear you were there. About an
hour later, you had a fight with your brother in the Back Bay fens.
He swears you were drunk and attacked him. He says you tried to
kill him, actually—" She glanced up at Alec, over the tops of her
glasses, and then peered down, continued reading from her notes.
"—they're looking for an old man, who apparently witnessed the
fight. Your super, a woman named Margaret Herlihy, had been
staying with your sick friend. His name is—ah—Amos Konetzny.
She will testify that you came back about three in the afternoon.
Later, about six, they can place you at the Piston, for about forty-five
minutes, where you had four drinks. There are half-a-dozen people at
the bar who can be pretty precise about when you were there—"

Mrs. Lichtenthal, sharp-faced, scrubbed clean, subdued and
business-like, glanced at her notes and then at him.

"—about seven, you left and returned to your apartment. After
that, for four hours, there're no witnesses to what you were doing. I
assume—they assume—you were in the apartment with your sick friend
—" She looked up from her notes. "The point in all this is that they have
sworn witnesses to how much you were drinking that day. They have
witnesses to your drinking—" She ran her pencil down

the page. "—some twelve, thirteen, fourteen drinks, which, at one and a half ounces per drink adds up to 21 ounces of alcohol between eleven in the morning and seven at night." She glanced at him. "I take it you have no memory of any of this?"

Alec shook his head.

She let her eyes linger on him for a moment, above her reading glasses. Then, looking back down at her notes, she went on. "At almost exactly one in the morning, your car, witnessed by two people who were standing outside a bar, struck and killed a man —a Mr. Simon McCorkindale—on Dorchester Avenue, didn't stop, and was last seen headed South on Dorchester. Both witnesses agree on the license plate number and on the description of the car. They called the police and an ambulance. It was too late for Mr. McCorkindale, but a bulletin was put out on your car, and once your identity had been determined, a warrant was issued for your arrest."

She turned over a page of her notes, glancing at him. She smiled. "They know a lot about you!" Then she was all business again. "On Wednesday, February 27, 1991, your car was found, out of gas, the keys still in it, on Grimes Street off West 8th in South Boston."

She looked up and frowned. "You didn't show up until the cop found you on the street in Park Square, in convulsions, last Wednesday, March 6, 1991. Apparently you'd been in blackout."

She turned over her pad on the table so that it slapped the wood, put down her pen, and looked at him. "Do you do this kind of thing often?"

"What kind of thing?"

"Go off on a bender and lose ten days—"

Alec wondered how to answer. "I don't think—" He had forgotten the car, forgotten he had been at Paradise. "Sometimes. Not this long—"

She observed him. "It's a tight case—"

There were things he should ask her, say to her, but he hurt so, was so confused, he wanted only to escape. He didn't know what to say. Who was Simon McCorkindale?

She turned her pad over and turned to a fresh page. "You need an alibi. Who are your friends? Where do you usually go when you go out drinking? Who can you remember seeing that Monday?"

He told her about Michael, his lover, and about Gaetano. About Margaret, the super, and Donald, the bartender.

"The DA is going to be questioning these same people, and anybody else they can find. They're also going to be going over your car to try to establish that you were in it. I suspect they're going to search for more witnesses to the hit-and-run. What about bars?"

The straight bar in the Fenway. The Piston. Then, he saw it in his mind, the string of bars down Boylston Street from Massachusetts Avenue into Copley Square.

"Names?"

"No. I don't know their names."

She grimaced.

"What about your son. I understand you have a son. What about him? He lives with you?"

Alec hesitated, hated to tell this. "He used to—"

"And—?"

"He moved about about two months ago—"

"Where is he now?" She was poised to write down the address.

"I don't know."

She let her eyes rest on him briefly, then dropped them to the pad, where she wrote something.

"Have you seen yourself?" She slid the paper across to him. On the cover was more on the war, the end of the war, major pictures of the Kurd's suffering, women with sunken cheeks holding lifeless children in their arms. She reached across and flipped to the second section, third page. There, below the fold, was a picture of Alec.

She laughed. "Look, I've got work to do—" She glanced at the list of names Alec had given her. "Why don't you take a walk. I'll call you later." She stood up. "Here are your keys. You'll need them to get into your place. Of course, they've kept your car."

When he walked out into the bright winter sun, Alec Argento carried with him a new identity. Walking down the long steps away from the building to the street, days-old snow in the crevices against the buildings, Alec saw that nothing can be trusted, that it was dangerous to assume that what he closed his eyes on when he went to sleep would be there when he awoke. The world was reconstituting itself before his eyes. He was reconstituting himself before his eyes, and reality was like the clouds, roiling across the sky.

Alec walked down the steps. The bright cold winter day was invigorating after the fetid atmosphere of the jail, and he took deep breaths. At the foot of the steps, Alec turned right, a direction which would take him, eventually, to Amos, and to Michael and Stephen and Gaetano, and to their unanswerable questions. As he started off

toward the Fenway, Chinatown, Park Square, the street people and
the grates came back to him. It was a moment, suddenly, of intense
anxiety. Fear of what he faced when he arrived at the apartment on
Kilmarnoch Street—the impossibility of justifying himself—led him
to want to turn toward Park Square and the anonymity of the streets.
I *can disappear, toward oblivion, I can run away*. There was the
option of the bridge, the train. But he was already too sober, his
mind had cleared too much, for him to turn consciously away from
finding the answers to the questions that had now been raised. He
couldn't disappear into Park Square or off a bridge as things now
stood, thinking he had killed a man.

The city was transformed when seen through the eyes of someone
accused of manslaughter. The energy expressed on the street, in the
size of the buildings thrusting up their huge bulk against the sky, the
traffic in the streets, the thousands of people on the sidewalks
shoving and pushing, the sounds of the city, the honk and roar of the
traffic, the voices of the people, the sirens of the ambulances and the
police cars, all this immense energy now seemed directed against
Alec himself, and he felt a fugitive from it.

His eyes roamed the streets, from force of habit, for a bike
messenger with long dark curls, and when he arrived at the Piston in
the Back Bay fens, on his way home, habit gave him the words to
give the bartender. They were in his throat (give me a drink), before
he said to Donald, "Hi—"

Donald didn't respond, stood across the bar from him and stared.
"Man—" Then, "You're a mess—"

Alec was about to speak, say, tell me, do you remember —

"—get outta here. Get yourself cleaned up. Man, you got a bad
rep—"

"Donald, wait—" Do you remember Monday night, the day the
war started—

"—no!"

"—I want to ask you some things—" was I driving—

"Right. The police have been all over this place for days because
of you, and we don't need that. Get outta here. Don't come back—"

"Hey, man—" I got to know—

"Where did you go, anyway?" Then, before Alec could answer,
"No, I don't want to know. Just get outta here —"

Alec left, I need to ask, did I kill a man, went back out into the
bright sun and walked down to the end of the block, turned, walked a

block, turned, walked another block, and was home. He stood on the steps. They had said he had convulsions. Alec had never seen anyone have convulsions, and he didn't know what they were like. It was odd to have had convulsions and not know what they were like. It was odd to be standing here in front of his apartment when he had been living on the street and had been in jail. He had lived here six years, and he was afraid to go in.

He rang the bell. He waited. He rang again, and waited a long time. No one answered. He rang again. No one was at home. Amos should be there, and somebody should be with Amos. Michael, or Gaetano. No one answered, and they weren't there. Michael or Gaetano could have taken Amos to one or the other of their apartments, or something could have happened to Amos, and they could have taken him back to the hospital—or to the hospice. He gave up and sat down on the top step, his elbows on his knees, his head resting in his hands, and waited. His memory of having lived here was coming back, still in bits and pieces, pages from a manuscript picked up floating in a lake. His rent was due. Margaret. If nothing happened soon, he would ring her bell. His body ached, his head felt as if a spike were being driven up through the base of his skull by a slow force, and his hands shook. He felt frail.

People passed on the street, glancing at him, turning away quickly. Alec felt how dirty he was. He felt greasy all over, and he could smell the vomit on his coat. He was tired, he needed to go to sleep, wanted to be protected from people's eyes, and, at length, he leaned back against the building, rested his head against the wall, and closed his eyes. He had not thought that he would have to go into the apartment alone. He had been apprehensive about seeing Michael or Gaetano, but he had not imagined how it would feel to arrive home and discover no one, not even someone angry, there.

Eventually, since he had to give into this sometime, he stood up and put the key in the lock (his car key was missing from his ring) and entered the building. Margaret was coming up from downstairs with her mop.

She saw him, and her eyes widened. "Welcome home."

"Thanks, Margaret—" He hesitated, wondering if she were going to say anything.

"The police've been here—"

Right. "Yeah, I expect—"

"I made sure they had a warrant—"

189

Winter Rain

"Right, thanks." He made a little gesture with his hand, a kind of wave, and went down the hall to his apartment.

The apartment contained no living people. Amos was gone. The shades were pulled, left that way from the last time he had been here, and he set about, from force of habit (his habit was actually first to go to the kitchen and fix a drink), to raise them, let in the winter sun, but he left them the way they were. The apartment was dead. He looked around. It was as if the gang of them had grabbed their coats and walked out to a movie and never come back. Life seemed interrupted, and then killed.

Still the thought came to him of running away. What would they tell him about him when he found them? Alec sat on the sofa and brought the phone onto his lap and started dialing. First, Michael. There was no answer, and no answering machine. He called Gaetano, and got no answer there, either. There were still things all over the apartment from Amos's illness—bottles of pills, the IV apparatus, diapers. If Amos had been taken somewhere, they would have taken his pills, too. He was not at Michael's or Gaetano's. Alec was beginning to suspect an explanation. He called the hospice.

"Can you tell me about a resident, Amos Konetzny?"

There was a pause. Records were being checked. "I am very sorry, we don't have a resident by that name."

Alec's mind, strung out still, was jumping from idea to idea. He called the medical center, but they had no record of him.

Amos had no family who were interested in him or to whom he would have gone. Alec got up from the sofa (he couldn't sit still) and paced the apartment. The bed had been stripped. The sheets had been washed and folded and lay at the foot of the bed. Alec wondered who. He washed some dishes left in the sink, a glass with stale whiskey in it still, picked up magazines off the floor, put off again the decision to have a drink, threw away newspapers. The last was for Monday, the day the start of the war was reported in the papers, and Alec retrieved it from the trash where he had just thrown it and sat down and read. This was the last day before it happened. He read the entire article on the hospitals which were being set up in the desert for the wounded and the plans that had been made for their evacuation to Europe and to North America.

Beside the phone was his pocket calendar, opened to Monday. With a pen, Alec tried to sort things out. The ground war had begun on Sunday, February 24. He remembered the pictures on the tv of the

190

Winter Rain

Iraqi soldiers surrendering, remembered speaking to Arabella about them (that must have been Monday), about feeling deflated. All the pages of the calendar were crossed out, up through Sunday. Monday the twenty-fifth would have been the last day. He turned on the tv, flicked past images of the war (an agonized head wrapped in a tasselled scarf) and found a screen which gave the date. Today was Monday, March 11, 1991. He counted, putting the tip of his pen on each date. He had been gone for fourteen days.

There was a telephone number written in. Movers was written beside the number. Stephen's things. He remembered. Bernice and the phone call. Her sugared voice. Stephen's things. He walked around the apartment, noticing Stephen's things. There were books scattered about, magazines which he had bought, a picture on the wall stuck up with pushpins. Stephen had slept in the living room and kept his clothes in the hall closet—-coats, jackets, his one suit, half a dozen shirts, a pair of ski boots. There wouldn't be much to pack up and ship.

The apartment was harshly lit. The brigaaqht glare from outside showed in a line around the drawn shades. It was an ugly room. Michael's things were everywhere, too, clothes hanging in the hall closet, books lying around, a pair of boots, toilet articles in the bathroom. There was no sign that Michael had been here since— since that Monday.

It was five o'clock, and Alec didn't know what to do with himself. He had no money. Eventually, he went into the bedroom and took off the clothes he had worn for two weeks—jeans, a white tee shirt, grey sweat shirt, white socks—and dumped them all on the floor. He went into the bathroom and let the water run until it was hot. He got in and let the water run over him, soaping his body and rinsing until he felt clean. He shaved for the first time in fourteen days, dressed again in clean jeans and a clean white tee shirt, combed his hair.

He called Michael again. He had been on the street and then in jail, and Michael had not tried to reach him. He wouldn't want to talk. He allowed the phone to ring. No one answered. There was not even an answering machine. He called Gaetano again, too, but no one answered there, either.

Alec was unable to focus. The objects in his apartment spoke dumbly of another life. Each picture on the wall —the nude in the English stadium—reminded him of the feelings he had had when he tore it out of the magazine. Accused of killing a man, Alec couldn't

191

take himself back to a moment when it had been possible to think with pleasure of a man's thumbing his nose at British culture by taking off his clothes. Each object his eye lit upon —the pair of brass candlesticks on the bookcase—reminded him that something had happened to him so damaging to his sense of himself that he was not the same person who had chosen the object. *I am accused of killing a man.* He turned the idea over in his head and considered it. Inevitably, it led to the corollary notion, I am a killer. His apartment was transformed when seen through the eyes of a man who was coming to admit his ignorance about himself.

He knew what it was like to be driving fast, the sense of the car surging forward, aimed rather than driven, the increasing speed causing his body to be pressed back against the seat, the sense of being tossed about as he swerved the car around a board or a pothole, and then to feel, but not to have seen, a bump, to feel the car's motion forward hindered for a moment, the frame of the car shuddering, and the wheels, front, then back, bumping over something hard, solid, but soft, before the car regained its unhindered forward movement. Would there have been blood? Blood on the fender? The windshield? Bone?

As Alec walked about the apartment, gathering things together, a magazine on rock music Stephen had bought, a tape of a movie of Michael's, he imagined driving down Dorchester Avenue at one in the morning, careening from side to side of the road avoiding potholes (the streets used to be cared for) and feeling the car shudder when it hit something hard, solid, but soft, first the front wheel (thump) and then the rear wheel (thump), the shudder of hitting flesh different from the shudder of hitting a brick or a board or a pothole, and driving on.

He found among his own dirty clothes tee shirts belonging to Michael and to Stephen, and he began a pile for each one of them, finding underpants, a jock, a belt, sorting them, dropping them on to Stephen's or Michael's pile. Michael, who had accused him, *Nothing bad can happen if Alec Argento loves me,* on the last day had put his hands on Gaetano's shoulders and felt his arms. He felt himself in his car, careening down the road, and felt the thump of the body against the fender, the thump thump, as it went under first the front wheel and then the rear. Alec felt this with a sickening clarity. He had a tee shirt held by the tips of his fingers, about to drop it on Stephen's pile. It was oversized, faded, read Anthrax: Among the Living, and the feel of the thumpthump under the wheels of the car stopped him, caused him to go still for a moment, the tee shirt still held from the tips of his fingers, as he felt the moment of killing a man.

Among the Living. He dropped the tee shirt on the pile along with the others. He had washed the clothes of both these men. Done their dishes. Where were they now? There were two pairs of jeans of Michael's, socks of Stephen's. There were moments, reliving the thumpthump of the body under the wheels, when Alec rebelled. The thought rose up in him, *I couldn't have done that*, but it passed. He had driven drunk half his adult life. Every time he went out drinking in his car, he ran the risk (1:50,000? 1:25,000? 1:100?), and it was predictable that if he played the game often enough, his number would come up (1:10, 1:1?).

Given a provocation, when he was drinking, he would hit someone. But he didn't want it to have happened to him, didn't want his number to have come up, didn't want to say, *I killed someone*, I am a killer, and he held onto the chance that the witnesses were wrong, that someone else's car had been involved. What he wanted was good luck, or, since the odds were tremendously against that, he wanted to prove he had been somewhere else, that someone else had had his car at one in the morning on Tuesday fourteen days ago and had careened down Dorchester and felt the car shudder (thumpthump) and then right itself.

But he felt that he had killed someone. He felt murderous. Nothing in his house, now, mattered. Its dumb discourse spoke to him eloquently of his transformation. The objects in his house were like old toys—electric trains—which spoke of what one was no longer, ten years old and submersed in fantasy, capable of having faith.

The apartment was silent. In the living room, Alec was aware that he didn't hear Amos breathing from the bedroom, the harsh rasp from deep in his chest which had filled the apartment, and he found himself looking into the bedroom to check on Amos's still form —and discovering a bed stripped of its linens. Without Amos, and without Michael, who had gone off with Gaetano, and without Gaetano, the apartment had come to a full stop. Why hadn't Arabella called with a message, I need to talk. I'm coming into town tonight at eight and will pick you up?

Amos must be dead. Alec couldn't think of another explanation. Amos had died while Alec was out on a drunk, living on the street.

While he walked around the apartment picking up things left by Michael and Stephen and Amos, dirty clothes with the characteristic limpness of clothes taken off and left for days where they had fallen, he became accustomed to the sense of the apartment having belonged to another time in all their lives, a time which had now come decisively to an end.

He vacuumed. He got out a bowl and a sponge and detergent and scrubbed the kitchen counters, the sink, the fixtures in the bathroom. Then he did the kitchen floor and the bathroom floor. While he did these things, he took the bags of dirty clothes and sheets next door to the laundromat, and between the kitchen counters and the fixtures in the bathroom, he ran next door and put the clothes in the dryer. Coming back, with an armload of Michael's and Stephen's things, he determined that he had to reach Gaetano and Michael. Somehow, he had to find someone who could tell him he had not killed a man.

He dumped Michael's and Stephen's clothes on the bed beside piles of Amos's things and Stephen's things. He'd pack up Stephen's things later. He got his coat and left, ran to the subway stop and caught a train. In half an hour, he was in the district in which Michael lived, and when he stood in front of his door, he rang the bell. There was no answer. He rang again. Michael was not in. He didn't want to go in. Some sharp break had happened, and he no longer had the right to use the keys he had in his pocket, but he went in anyway, feeling like an intruder.

The apartment was empty. That is, it was filled with Michael's and his roommate's things, but Michael was not there. He found a piece of paper and wrote: I'm home. Please, I need your help. He left it on the mantelpiece. Under a picture frame, there was a clipping from the paper: South End Man Wins Lottery with a picture of Gaetano.

Having set himself in motion, he didn't s top. He caught the subway back across town to Gaetano's, in the area behind the YMCA. He rang the bell, listened to the silence, knew there was nothing to be done. He had no keys to Gaetano's place and no way to leave a message.

He remembered, then, the time (six-thirty), and ran out into the street and down the block toward the gym. This was the time both of them could normally be found at the gym. At the service desk, he blurted out, registering already, seeing the attendant's face, that it was the wrong question, "Is Gaetano Leoncello here?"

"Man!" The attendant frowned, opened his eyes wide. "You are in a peck of trouble!"

That had to be dealt with. "Yes." There was nothing else to be said. "Is Gaetano Leoncello here?"

"The police've been here asking 'bout you, man! Did you kill that man?"

Alec was about to speak (I don't know), when he reversed himself. "No. I did not kill that man." He said it decisively.

"Well, that's good, 'cause they sure think you did. They going t'send you away."

"Well, they're not, because I didn't do it—" He didn't know where this was coming from, but he found he liked saying it. "—Is Gaetano Leoncello here?"

"Gaetano? No. He ain't. That big guy ain't been working out recently. Don't know where he's been."

"That the truth?"

"That's the truth."

"Shit."

"Did you know that guy won the lottery? Won 9 million dollars?" He shook his head. "I wouldn't come 'round this place either, if I won 9 million dollars! Some people have all the luck!" He laughed, and gave Alec a leer. "He's hot, too. ain't he? Ya seen his body?"

Alec was out of there. He'd lie. He'd say, No, I didn't do it. Everybody had read the newspaper now, and he couldn't survive in this town if he said, Yeah, I did it, couldn't face the looks on people's faces that said, *You poor dumb shit*. Worse, he couldn't face himself if he ever admitted, Yeah, I did it.

There was a bar near the gym called the Hawk, where Alec stopped in before or after a workout. Gaetano and he had made it a habit. Maybe. The bar was empty. It was too early for the evening crowd, too late for the after-work people, and the bar was desolate in the way that bars are when they don't have people in them —used up, like a full ashtray.

"Andy—"

The bartender had seen him enter. Now he leaned on the bar with both his hands, his elbows bent out a little.

"Man—"

"Oooo, man—" Andy whistled. "You are in deep shit!"

"I know—"

"I thought you were in jail—"

"They released me on bail—"

"They gonna be able to pin this on you?"

"I don't know—" He sat on a stool. He stood up again, got out of his coat, threw it over a chair, and sat back down again.

"Usual?" Andy was set to go.

"Ah—" This was the first time. "No. Coffee. Please." Alec didn't want to drink now. He wasn't making any decisions about the future.

"Did I come in here that night? It was —" He pulled out his pocket calendar, now marked with crosses on significant dates. "—Monday, the twenty-fifth? That's—" He counted. "—14 days ago. Uh—" He calculated another way. "—two weeks ago, today—"

But Andy was ahead of him. He was smiling. "I know when you're talking about, my friend, 'cause you were here."

"I was!" It was like—someone saying, you have the winning ticket!

"Sure you were. I'd never seen you like that before."

"Have you spoken to the police?"

Andy frowned. "Naw. Not me. They haven't come around here."

"How was I?"

Andy shook his head. "Drunk. I guess I've seen you drunk before, but never drunk like this, my friend. You sat there —" He pointed to the end of the bar. "—and you couldn't stop crying—"

"Why was I crying?" Andy was nudging things buried under the sand, but they hadn't come to the surface, yet.

He shrugged. "Who knows? You wouldn't say. I said, *Are you all right?* And you said, I'm OK. I'm OK. Then you said, I may never be OK again. Which didn't make any sense."

Alec felt it, now, this overwhelming sadness. He could almost remember being there and crying. "Did I drink much?"

"A couple. I woulda cut you off, but you didn't have enough to give me a chance. I could tell you were drunk, but you've been in here—you and Gaetano—lots of times like that, and you weren't out of control. It was just that you were crying. And it was Monday. And both of them were unusual."

"What time—?"

"Almost twelve. Eleven thirty. You stayed about an hour."

Crying. "Did I make a scene?"

Andy smiled. "No, buddy. You were real sedate about it. You just had tears in your eyes the whole time, and you'd wipe your face."

196

Winter Rain

Half an hour before Simon McCorkindale was killed in Dorchester. Alec could have left here and made it to Dorchester in plenty of time to kill a man. He was drunk enough. He had been crying. It would be difficult to see. "You think I left about twelve-thirty?"

"Round then—"

"Do you know? They're trying to say I was in Dorchester at one. If you could place me here at one—"

Andy turned serious. He thought. Then he shook his head. "I guess I can't help you out. You left about twelve-thirty."

"Damn."

"Sorry. I guess I know how you feel. You left before last call—"

How could he know how Alec felt?

"—but I guess I want to say one thing—"

"What's that?"

"I don't think you're the kinda guy that coulda done what they say you did. I mean, life's funny. If it'd been one of you, I woulda said it would be Gaetano. He's the giddy one."

Why had he been crying? Alec went back out into the rain. Thumpthump. What kind of man kills a man? Am I that kind of man? What kind of man leaves the scene! On the street, under the protection of the buildings, were street people, men and women asking for quarters. This time, when a rheumy old man stuck out his hand and said, "Please sir—," there was no distance between them. Alec felt raw pain.

At home, there was no message on the answering machine. He found a box in the living room and emptied it of its books and took it into the bedroom, where he had laid the stack of Stephen's clothes. Now he walked around the apartment searching for anything of Stephen's. First, he searched the obvious places—table tops, bookcase tops—and found books and magazines, which he placed in the box in the bedroom. He went through drawers, next, and found a calculator, an old check book, and a calendar. He did this with a methodical thoroughness. This was something that could be carried to completion. He could search every small corner of the apartment and strip it of any evidence that Stephen had ever lived here. He sat on the floor in front of the bookcases and went down the shelves, one by one, pulling down possible books (Nobody Here Gets Out Alive) and trying to remember its history, because sometimes Stephen had bought a book and then both had read it, or the other way around, and

197

it was then difficult to remember whose book it was. When he couldn't remember, he put it in the box. There was a drawer in which Alec had kept snapshots, and he went through that, culling out the rolls of pictures which he thought Stephen had taken. There were albums: *My Bloody Valentine, Peace Through Chemistry* . He was trying to separate Stephen's history from his own, which was impossible.

Finally, he went into the bedroom and tried to fit everything into the box. He found he needed another box and emptied another box of his books. On top of the books, the pictures, a pair of bookends, a lamp, and the rest of the objects, his placed Stephen's clothes. The objects didn't speak so strongly of Stephen, but the clothes, which were old and worn, the way Stephen liked them, ratty and soft, seemed unbelievably personal. It was impossible to hold one up without remembering how it hung, draped, on Stephen's thin body.

Alec sat on the floor. He had a tee shirt in his hand (*Among the Living*), freshly washed, folded. Since it was clean, it smelled of detergent rather than Stephen, but Alec held the cotton shirt to his face, put his nose deep into it and smelled it, looking for Stephen. It was as if he, like Amos, who had left only a pile of underwear and thirty or forty vials of medications, were dead. What he was doing seemed to have the finality of disposing of belongings after a funeral and, his face in the soft cloth, felt to him as if he were closer to his son at this moment than he had ever been in life. Breathing deeply through the soft cotton seemed like a violation now (there was no one around to see) of Stephen's privacy, an act almost too intimate between them, long after it mattered. The pain he felt, raw loss, was irreparable. And for a long time, before he stood up, placed the last things in the box and sealed it, he sat on the floor with the tee shirt held against his face by both his hands.

8

"I have bad news."

It was Mrs. Lichtenthal. Alec had gone through his clothes, the closet in his bedroom and the one in the hall, and pulled out the things he didn't wear. He laid them across a chair to wait until he could bundle them up for the Good Will. He was in the midst of going through the closets a second time when the phone rang and Mrs. Lichtenthal made her announcement. She was abrupt.

"The police ran your name through the computer and discovered that you got a speeding ticket a little before six that evening. Did you remember that?"

Alec, holding an old jacket in his hand, stood by the phone. "No—"

"Storrow Drive, just at Charlesgate. That's bad. That places you in your car. They already had information which placed you at the Piston immediately after that, drinking." Mrs. Lichtenthal paused. "They're closing in on you. They've got you driving around town that night going to bars, and speeding. They've got you up to seven o'clock. They're going to keep searching until they can find someone who can place you in your car at one. You know that, don't you? And if they do, it's all over—"

She expected him to say something.

"Yes, I know that."

"Do you have anything to say?"

Winter Rain

Alec had already given her the names of everybody he knew and the bars he went to. There seemed nothing more he could do. He was trapped in a lethargy, in the deep sleep after a seizure, and he couldn't rouse himself. For the first several days after he was released from jail, he remained in his apartment, the shades pulled. The phone didn't ring, and Alec made no calls, except the second morning, to the movers to come get the two boxes of Stephen's things. Michael and Gaetano, who would have gotten his messages, didn't return them, and Alec wandered from the living room to the bedroom and back, a cup of coffee in his hand, his eyes raking across his possessions, across the silent tv screen (the Kurds), unable to take root. He lay on the sofa, his arm across his forehead, his eyes closed. He lay on the bed, the pillow clutched up against his face. The movers came (it was one man) and got the boxes and left, his connection with the time in his life when Stephen lived with him now severed. He had considered putting a message to Stephen in the boxes, but thought, What's the point?

He had seen almost as soon as he had gotten home from jail that he would move. His apartment had the feel of a closed theatre. He would look for a furnished room. After he packed up Stephen's things and made separate piles of Michael's and Amos's things, he began to throw away his own things. Suits and dress shirts were easy. Tee shirts commemorated some event —a rock concert, a march, an anniversary, a holiday. They went back ten years. But he finally put them in a green plastic garbage bag.

He rarely went out. He had no money to spend, and he had no place to go. The places he could have gone, the gym, the Hawk, the Piston, he couldn't because he didn't want to face men asking him about the hit-and-run. He stayed at home and cleaned and sorted and threw out. Occasionally, he stopped in the middle of the living room and watched the pictures of the aftermath of the war. The images were of a dry hillside crowded with dark-skinned people, a refugee camp, makeshift lean-tos, tarpaulins strung messily from low shrubs, women carrying children and men carrying rifles.

At odd moments, he found himself going to the kitchen to fix a drink, but there was no whiskey, and he didn't rouse himself enough to go out to buy some. The issue, and this surprised him, wasn't whiskey any more. The third day, because he had no money, Alec went out. He passed Margaret in the hall, and they nodded. He found a job at a loading dock in North Point Channel, the graveyard shift. It was the kind of job he wouldn't have taken before, but now it suited him. He wouldn't see anybody, and nobody there knew him. He went to work at ten at night. It had begun raining again, and he crossed the city in the dark in the rain. He got off at six a.m. and came home and slept most of the day. His work week was Wednesday through Sunday, which took care of weekends. And after two days of this schedule, he got an additional job waiting tables for the supper shift (5-8) at a diner in South Boston.

He didn't think much about Mrs. Lichtenthal or the police or the District Attorney. Whatever was going to happen was going to happen. Everything felt temporary, and, cleaning and stripping his apartment, he was aware that at least one of his goals was to prepare for going to jail for a long time. He didn't care. He was wasted by what had happened, by the silence of his telephone, by the tightness of his nerves, and it was hard to get excited by Mrs. Lichtenthal and the District Attorney, or even the idea of jail.

He asked Mrs. Lichtenthal what hit-and-run drivers got.

"Oh—" He could imagine her shrugging, turning down the corners of her mouth, considering a matter of little importance. "—it's manslaughter, second degree. You'll get ten years or so, time off, you'll serve four, four-and-a-half."

He enjoyed the night work. He enjoyed driving a fork lift. He worked largely alone, and that was good. As long as he went about his business, he was left alone. The waiting job was less good. He wasn't as quick as he needed to be, as he had been when he had last waited tables in college, and he forgot things and customers got angry. He came home angry and frustrated. He wanted to drink. He didn't make much in tips, but he made something, and it was a way to fill the time. The rain was continuous now after the weeks of snow, and every time he went out he got soaked. Alec hated the rain. It made it hard to see, the car headlights reflecting off wet pavement. The rain meant danger, now. It came down everywhere, couldn't be escaped and was indifferent to particular human concerns. Often when he was out in it, he felt powerless, helpless, and panic rose in him. Walking across the city through the rain, he felt a bone loneliness, which the rain made worse. He missed his car, but he didn't want it back.

Mrs. Lichtenthal called one morning and woke him up, his first call in days. The police wanted him for a lineup and for questioning, and the next morning, standing in the lineup, he imagined the people on the other side of the glass. There would be someone to say, "That's the man that drove the car that killed Simon McCorkindale." He tried to imagine what that person would be like, who would identify him. Since he had seen the accident, he would have been on the street at one a.m. It would be a man, someone fairly young. The bar crowd in Dorchester would not be middle-class, middle-aged. He couldn't take the thought very far, however. He imagined Stephen on the other side of the glass. Yes, that's my dad.

Alec was questioned further about the night of the 25th. The police had found out that Alec had loaned his car to Gaetano and Michael.

"Did anyone beside yourself have keys to the car?"

Alec shrugged. "Well, yes—" Then, "Stephen has a set of keys—"

"Stephen—?"

"Michael and Gaetano both had keys—"

"Keys to your car?"

"Well, keys. Keys. Key rings. I had them made up when Amos Konetzny came to stay with me—"

"Amos what?"

"Konetzny." He spelled it. "A friend. He was dying, and —"

"K O N E T Z N Y. What was he dying of?"

"AIDS. People had to be able to get in and out of the apartment. Sometimes you couldn't leave Amos to answer the door, so I had these keys made up. Each of the rings had a car key. Michael had keys anyway—"

"Who is Michael?"

"My lover—"

There was a barely noticeable shadow. "Michael what?"

"Michael Colt. He has had keys for about three years. He kind of lives at my place—" Only all that was over. While he talked, Alec drifted back to that time, the memories coming back to him effortlessly now, reminding him of his crowded, noisy apartment, reminding him of the phone ringing, of the urgent messages. "—and he drives my car a lot. Gaetano picked up a set of my keys from the drawer when he began to need to get in and out of the apartment. There was a car key on the ring. Stephen always had keys."

"Stephen?"

"My son."

"Ah—" Then, "Who else?"

Alec couldn't think of anybody. "Arabella."

He looked weary. "Who is Arabella?"

"My sister-in-law. She's married to my brother."

"Do they ask you when they use it?"

"Well, sure—"

The cop gave the sense of a person who had seen it all and didn't believe any of it.

Alec didn't care. "—unless I'm not around. They leave notes —"

The cop squinted at him, wondering if Alec were bullshitting him.

"—we're pretty relaxed about it."

Alec's memory had largely come back to him, the anxiety over having Amos living with him, the whole series of decisions that had been made to bring him home, Michael's being positive, Gaetano's ecstasy calling that Monday with news of the lottery, even his joy walking across the Back Bay looking for Stephen. He was pretty clear about much of his time on the street and some of the time in jail, but the memories remained discontinuous, and his current life had the quality of having emerged from a cloud.

When they were leaving the police station, Alec asked Mrs. Lichtenthal what she knew about Simon McCorkindale.

She shrugged. "A man, in his thirties I think. A truck driver." She stopped. "I can find out more, if you want."

"Yeah. I want."

Alec experienced all this from a distance. He wondered about Amos (he believed he was dead) but he didn't want to ask. The question, "What has happened to Amos?" exposed too much of himself to the people he would have to ask it of. He didn't think that at some point this would all be cleared up. That is, he wasn't waiting, so much as things for him had come to a pause, and he lived in the pause, the pause before he got up off the sofa to fix another drink. Stephen was in the past. That amputation was healing. He went to bed at seven in the morning, when he came home from the loading dock, and slept hard through most of the day, until three. Then he went to the diner in South Boston for his shift. He had two hours between the diner and the loading dock, to which he had to report at ten. He cooked himself food, and he no longer went to the gym. He had stopped thinking, at some point. His nerves were shot, and the process in which he was trapped was moving on without him. He gave notice to his landlord for the end of March, saw Margaret in

the hall and told her, but they didn't speak beyond the necessary
exchange of information, and when he walked past liquor stores on
his way home at six in the morning, he picked up empty boxes.
While he packed his clothes, the TV was always on, showing the
pictures of the Kurds on their hillside. They were trapped,
surrounded by Iraqis, and now they were starving.

One Monday, when he was not driving the forklift, Alec went to
the library and looked up old newspapers. He found the issue for
Monday, February 25, with the articles on the start of the ground war
and the feature on the preparations made for the wounded. He read
everything again in that paper. He found, in Wednesday's issue, an
article on Gaetano's winning the lottery. a picture of Gaetano's
handsome face grinning as if he had just had sex. To the question, "Is
nine million dollars going to change your life, Mr. Leoncello?"
Gaetano was quoted as saying, "You bet. I hope!" The interviewer
then said, "he laughed." In the same issue, he found an obituary
notice for Simon McCorkindale, 39, survived by his wife Susan
McClintock and his three children Kevin, 11, Sarah, 9, and Ian, 5.
He was, as Mrs. Lichtenthal said, a truck driver for Star Markets, for
whom he had worked for nine years. Alec had read the newspapers
regularly every day all his life, and here was a string of papers about
days he didn't remember. He found himself reading the papers all the
way through. He read about the Kurds, who had believed, wrongly,
that America would help them if they rose up against the Iraqis. In the
next issue, there was an article about the hit -and-run, this time with a
picture of Simon McCorkindale (blond, receding chin, thin). There
was also an article about Alec. He was the owner of the car which had
killed Simon McCorkindale, he lived in the fens, and was sought on a
manslaughter charge. The papers helped him fill things in, which was
good, but he wondered about Kevin and Sarah and Ian and about
Susan McClintock McCorkindale, whose lives had been so suddenly
transformed. He thought about them. There was nothing he could do,
there was no way to escape the fact that he knew their names, and
when he walked across the dark city to his job, he thought about
sudden death.
    Alec wrote Michael a card about his things, and when he came
home one day from work he found a message on the answering
machine. "I need my boots and my other possessions. Unless I hear

from you to the contrary, I will come over Sunday afternoon to pick them up. About three."

When Alec opened the door and stepped into the hall and watched Michael come down the hall toward him, he was the same man Alec had fallen in love with three years before: tall, strong, athletic, with a look of careful preparation about him. You couldn't tell that he was HIV positive. The bitterness was new. The whole set of his body was an accusation, as if his wound was so apparent it demanded an answer, some exclamation (*You're hurt*). It was as if he walked into the room bleeding from his temple.

He stepped back and let Michael enter.

"I've come for my boots." Michael didn't move toward a chair, didn't look as if he were going to sit down. He stood in the middle of the living room floor as if he didn't want to touch anything, and he didn't allow his eyes to linger. "I left some other clothes here, too."

Alec hesitated. He wanted to touch him, hold him, say, *It'll be all right.* He wanted a drink, but he resisted. "I have them in the bedroom." Alec had put all of Michael's things in a couple of liquor boxes.

"Could you get them for me?"

When he came back with them, stacked one on top of the other, he put them down on the coffee table. He sat down on the sofa. Michael would have to pick them up himself.

"What happened?"

Michael's eyes, involuntarily, moved around the room, in which packing boxes occupied most of the floor space. Lying across the tv (the starving Kurds) was a pile of posters and pictures from the walls.

Michael took a deep breath. "You killed a man. You're going to jail. You're not a part of my life any more. I want nothing to do with you." He moved toward the boxes. "You've hurt me enough for one lifetime."

Alec took that in. He was determined not to respond. To give in to him now was to be swallowed up in his demands, and Alec had no strength.

Michael picked up the boxes.

"Did you drive my car that night?"

"No." His movement toward the door stopped. "Yes."

"It could have been you, couldn't it."

Michael turned. "No. We used your car between ten and eleven. We brought it back after about an hour, before Amos died. Ask Margaret. You had your car. I've told the police all this."

Before Amos died. Alec followed him to the door. Michael, with both his boxes, was unable to open the door, and Alec opened it for him. "I didn't kill anyone, Michael."

Michael was headed down the steps.

"Hey Michael!"

Michael turned.

"I loved you."

"Yeah, right." And then he was gone.

Mrs. Lichtenthal called. "The lab reports are back on your car. The blood on the grille and fender match Simon McCorkingdale's. They can prove that your car was the one that killed him. Lab reports, plus the lab analysis of the damage to your car suggests you were going sixty or seventy miles an hour when you hit him. You didn't stop. That's going to look bad to the jury. You're in deep shit, Mr. Argento."

"Mrs. Lichtenthal?"

"Yes?"

"I want you to know I didn't kill that man."

"Well, I'm glad to hear that." Mrs. Lichtenthal had grown angry with him. If she were to prepare an adequate defense for him, he must take a more active part. He had to make an effort to prove that he was innocent. "Don't you care?"

vSomeone, they said Alec, had killed Simon McCorkindale, husband of Susan, and father of Kevin, Sarah, and Ian. He resisted seeing them too clearly in his mind. The damage had already been done. Simon McCorkindale (blond, receding chin, thin) was dead, and all the life in his apartment was dead too, and even if he could escape conviction on the legal charge, escape jail for the res t of his life, it hardly mattered. Everyone that he loved was now lost. His legal predicament often seemed to him to be merely an afterthought, the tying up of laces after the boot was put on. He couldn't be bothered.

And yet. And yet. Whatever had happened that night had brought all their lives together to an end, and if the damage could not be repaired, he still wanted to protest, to say to Michael, *I didn't do this thing.* When Mrs. Lichtenthal brought it up the third time, increasingly insistent, he set the alarm the next day for eleven.

Winter Rain

The rains drenched the city, and he walked in on Boylston and started with the first bar nearest the fens. It was just noon, opening time, and the bar was empty except for the bartender.

"I'm in some trouble."

"What's up?" The bartender was familiar, although Alec didn't know his name.

"My name is Alec Argento." He noticed the bottles, but he couldn't remember how it felt to be drunk, and he turned his attention away.

"Yeah. I know you."

"One night a while back—" He reached down into his memory to dredge it all up again. "—it was the twenty-fifth of last month, a Monday night—"

The bartender laughed. "The twenty-fifth! That's—" He calculated. "—a month ago."

They talked a bit, trying to fix the night, talked about the weather that night (snow, turning to rain) and that it was the second night of the ground war. They couldn't fix the date. Alec asked about the bartender's shifts. Did he work on Mondays? Who else worked on Mondays?

"It would have been me, buddy."

"Do you remember me?"

"Oh, sure. You come in here."

"Do you remember the last time?"

The bartender thought and then shook his head. "Days are pretty much the same."

They talked about when he might have last seen Alec.

"What's so important?"

"Oh—" This was the question. "—I'm trying to find out what I did."

The bartender laughed. "Right. And you fucked somebody you weren't supposed to."

"Right."

Then Alec was out of there, back out into the rain. He went into other bars and asked the same questions. The people he talked with took it lightly. You total somebody's car? You lost your wallet? People remembered Alec, but they weren't able to place him or place the last time they had seen him. The police had talked to some of these people, and some said they had talked to his lawyer, "a real tough chick." He hated asking these questions. And, he admitted to himself, he was afraid to get the answers. Sure, you were here. You

209

were driving, too, because we talked about that. And when you left, you were going to Dorchester. He would have found the answer he didn't want.

He checked out all the bars on Boylston, getting names of bartenders, barbacks, doormen who worked that night and who might know, making a list on a yellow pad. He felt now the speed of the car going sixty or seventy miles an hour down a city street and hitting (thumpthump) something alive (hard but soft), a moment of extraordinary bad luck which would have brought a drunken driver together with a pedestrian walking into the street at a moment of extremest danger. He imagined the city from some high vantage (fifty floors up), seeing the headlights of a car driven by a drunken driver moving across the grid of streets, seeing through a heavy rain, coming from the opposite end of the grid, a pedestrian, and watching these two make their turns, right or left on this or that intersection, each time coming closer, at every intersection making the choice to turn toward or away, not realizing that a sufficient number of these choices, each almost irrelevantly inconsequential, would bring them to an eclipse of both their lives. He imagined the growing sense of suspense, as the person fifty floors up watched these two make a whole succession of choices which increased their danger, until, finally, of all the intersections in the city, in the whole of the eastern part of the state, in the whole grid of streets in the nation, from coast to coast, they met there in the rain on Dorchester Avenue, at 1:03 a.m., and everything was destroyed for both of them.

Bad fortune. He resisted the notion that luck could be so bad, that life could be so weighted, wanted still to believe that what he was meant he didn't kill people, was furiously angry. He wanted to be able to say, even if the damage could not be repaired, even sodden with alcohol, his instincts, his sense of concern for another human being, were strong enough to fight, to overcome the deadening of his senses, of his judgement, and to make him careful of other people on the grid of streets. And even if the accident actually happened, if it were he driving, he wanted to believe that his instincts, his concern for another person who loved and was loved (by Kevin, Sarah, and Ian and Susan McClintock McCorkindale), would overcome the fear and the alcohol and make him stop the car—to prevent the accident, which any one could have on a dark rainy night, from turning into a hit-and-run, which was something that only shits committed. He had to believe that, feeling the thumpthump, he would have thrown on the brakes and stopped. What did I hit? Only a shit wouldn't care.

But there was no one around to tell him he wasn't a shit. Alec had lost all contact. He spent his days in the apartment with the shades down, his nerves hanging quiveringly on the rack, and went to work when the rest of the city was asleep. He worked alone, came home as the city was waking up, slept all day. When he woke, he turned on the TV with the sound off, and the pictures, news of life around the world, formed a solitary moving silent connection with life outside his apartment. Without the sound, the impact of the pictures was carried entirely in the faces of the people on the screen, Alec's closest human contact, these faces strained with the attempt to explain and justify, to set forth their need. As he walked through the four rooms (living room, bedroom, kitchen, bath), he felt abandoned, but, like an oil slick, his take on what had happened to him changed colors in an instant: he had abandoned his old life in a careless moment. Hating Michael for his demands, he could change to hating himself for asking so much of him. The constant during these days was his sense that he was alone, an observer of, rather than a participant in, the life represented by the moving silent pictures on the screen.

Every day Alec phoned men who worked the bars on Boylston, trying to establish some contact, find out something to prove he wasn't a shit. He became known as that guy. Oh, are you that guy trying to find out about that night in February? It was now near the end of March, and he began to look for a place to live. It was cheap in South Boston, and no one knew him there. He found a furnished room in a rooming house on an anonymous street and made plans for a garage sale of his things.

He got a card. *I've heard your tragedy. My heart goes out to you, my friend. You were so wonderful for me for so long. Thank you Thank you Thank you. Arabella* He kept it on the coffee table and picked it up whenever he sat down on the sofa and read it. It was postmarked Maui. *You were so wonderful for me for so long.* She would be there with Gaetano, it was where she belonged. He imagined her lying on the beach of some new and luxurious resort, her body sleek with oil, her tiny white bikini setting off her deep tan. She would order a margarita (cloudy, rich, tart) from the beach boy and would light a cigarette and watch the men from behind her dark glasses, her memories of urgent phone calls and messages (*I need to talk to you. I'm coming into town tonight. Meet me at Paradise at nine. What's happening to me?*) growing dimmer with each tide until it would be as if they happened in another incarnation entirely. The image on the front of the card was of a tropical sunset on the water, the sun already behind the curve of the globe, turning all of nature — the sky and the sea, which is all there was—blood red and gold. Alec contemplated that sunset and imagined being on that sea, sailing toward the sun. And when he lay on the bed, his head down in the pillow, he dreamed of sailing into a sunset in which every element had become red and gold.

But he was wrong in thinking that she was lying on that beach with Gaetano. One day he picked up a gay magazine on his way home from work. In the gossip columns (New York social scene), there was Gaetano, his beautiful, tanned face grinning into the camera. He was wearing jeans and a tank top, and one deeply tanned, muscular arm was draped over the shoulders of a blond man. The columnist called Gaetano a "piece of major buff beefcake" from Boston, in town for the party.

Alec had thrown away, in the last week, clippings of himself and Michael at other parties here and in New York. He had thrown away the tee shirts and the clippings, there not being enough room in his furnished room in South Boston for shit from other lives. *Will you remember when you were poor?* Memory was a poor instrument. A man's entire sense of himself hangs on it, and it betrays him at every turn, betrays him into thinking that things are permanent, that he knows how things are, that he knows what he does, that life isn't an iridescent oil slick, reflecting back a red and gold sky.

He threw away the postcard and the magazine too. He wouldn't have room for them, for anything but himself and his clothes, reduced severely to jeans, a few tee shirts, a leather jacket. His furnished room in South Boston contained a single bed, a chest of drawers, a straight chair, white walls. There was hardly room for more than one person. He had thought he would have time, a chance, to talk. *What happened, Arabella?* and she would tell him, and even if she were wrong, they could talk about it, find where they had seen things differently, discuss, analyse, find some common memory. *Oh shit, of course, that's why you did what you did.* Or, coming upon it differently, *What did we do wrong? What did we do with our hands?* But Alec could tell from the tone of her postcard, it spoke of things in the distant past from one who had moved on, moved on to Maui, who had forgotten the urgent fear, *Am I an alcoholic?* and there wouldn't be a "talk." The most he could hope for was, *Oh, Alec, I don't remember. That was such a long time ago. I really don't remember. Don't make me go back.*

The best of Alec's life was walking across the city after work before the city was up, before the sun had risen above the curve of the earth, and things were held in suspension, the colors muted. The storefronts were dark, and yesterday's trash blew down empty streets. The traffic lights turned from green to yellow to red, controlling yesterday's cars, and, walking up Summer Street, past the financial district and his tall building and alley, into Winter Street, he heard his footsteps reverberate off the walls of buildings. The city was so quiet, still in that deep sleep just before waking, that Alec could hear his own thoughts, which rattled around in his head like empty beer cans blown by the wind down Winter Street. His thoughts clanged and clattered. It was the time before the city rose and went back down the hill to its rock.

He wasn't lonely. That is, there was no person he wanted to be with. It was over with every person who had ever been important to him. He had no desire to pick up a man, though men came onto him regularly, not knowing they were cruising a man who had returned from the dead and who knew therefore that sex was a poor way to reach transcendence. But he was as alone as the Kurds on their hill, encircled and watched, and there seemed to be nothing he could do about it.

Alec returned to the Hawk.

"Can you remember whether I was driving?"

"Naw. You were flying, but I don't know whether you were driving."

Alec made a list of the bars he had gone to even once in his life, looked at a ma p, placed the Hawk in the center of it, and marked the bars in successive concentric circles out from the center. He visited them all, running through the rain. He knocked on the doors of other people in the building, asking them if they remembered that night, and if they had seen his car in front of the building. "1983 Toyota." He explained carefully who he was, described the night he was investigating, said, "I need to find where I was —exactly where I was —at one a.m." He no longer cared how odd, weird the question

213

seemed. The people he was talking to looked at him with a blank stare. By now, that night was five weeks in the past.

"But wait, don't leave me—"

He would begin again. "It was snowing that day, do you remember? And late in the day the snow got heavier —"

"Look, buddy. I don't know nothing about that day."

"Wait. It was the second night of the ground war. It began to rain—"

"Look, buddy. Fuck off."

"You can't—"

"Fuck off, buddy."

Someone had to be found who could tell him what had happened. The idea of not knowing was inconceivable, a piece of his life permanently lost. He obsessed on the moment just after impact, thumpthump, on his sensation in his leg, his right leg, on the accelerator. He relived the moment over and over and found himself waking up in the night feeling the thumpthump. It was as if his whole right leg had been stripped of its skin, and he felt every nerve ending. He waited for the reflex in his leg, the jerk upwards, off the accelerator and toward the brake. It would have happened so fast from the thumpthump to the brake that he wouldn't have had time to think. Had it happened? Had the leg jumped off the accelerator and moved toward the brake? Over and over, drifting off to sleep, he experienced the moment, and in his mind, walking home up Summer street into Winter street, he felt the moment and waited for the lurch of his leg. But he couldn't tell, now, whether his leg had actually jumped, whether his instincts, which were nothing else but himself, with every other extraneous piece of meat cut away, had made him react so, lurch, ask, throw on the brake, and while he had become a stranger to everybody in the city, he was also now a stranger to himself, for the urgency behind the questions he was asking at the bars all over town arose from this new urgent need to find what he was at his core.

Then one day, he had asked everybody he knew to ask. There were no more bars he had ever been to that he had not now been to and asked *What did I do that night?* He came to a full stop, and, while there was the possibility that he had left the Hawk and gone to a bar he had never been to before, that possibility left him with the prospect of asking, since he didn't know where this bar might have been in the city, random strangers on the street, *Did I kill a man?*

Winter Rain

Michael had said, *Ask Margaret.* He had avoided her, because he didn't want to know what she knew. Often, when he came in and out of his apartment going to work or returning, he would pass her, and they would nod. Now every other avenue of escape blocked, he went in search of her and found her on the stairs.

"Tell me what happened the night Amos died."

She was standing on the landing, and she carefully, heavily, put down the mop. She lowered herself onto a step and spread her knees, relieving herself of the weight of ages. Alec sat down, too.

"You don't remember."

"No."

She grimaced. *I might have known.* "Well, dear. It was about ten. You were standing on the front stoop, and I asked you how you were. You don't remember this?"

"No."

"My husband used to never remember what he did either." She closed her mouth in a satisfied frown. "You were acting crazy. I could tell you had had too much to drink. You said you were going out, but I knew that was not the thing to do. I said, 'Dear, don't you think you should go in and lie down?' And you told me Amos was dying. So we went back in together and sat with him while he died." She opened her eyes wide. "That's what happened."

While he died. "How did he die?"

"Well, dear, it was hard. He had convulsions, and he threw up all over everything, and he was screaming. He was in a lot of pain, I would say." She shook her head. "It was not an easy death. I think he suffered terribly right there at the end. You always pray that your loved ones will have an easy death, don't you?" She looked at him. "I thought, from the look on his face he must have been very afraid. I worried about you, too."

Why?

"Oh, dear, you took it so hard. I was as worried about you as I was about Amos. Men don't know how to take these things. It hits you so hard. You're not used to suffering. You're always outraged by it, as if you didn't deserve it. You!" She resettled herself. "You, you acted like God was doing this to you personally."

She had learned this from the priests. Then, "Did he know me?"

Margaret didn't understand.

"Amos. Did he know I was there?"

"Oh, yes, dear! Did he know you were there! Of course he knew you were there! He was calling out to you every minute. You held onto each other as if you could keep him alive. I thought it would break my heart." She looked at him as if he had done something particularly stupid. "You held him all through his suffering until he was dead. It's always wrong to hang on to someone. Let 'em go, I always say. Let 'em go into God's bosom."

She put her hands on her knees and pushed herself up. "I don't understand why people fight so hard against God. But you were drunk and you wouldn't listen. You were sobbing like I've never seen a man before. I knew you wouldn't remember any of this."

"Why?" He could hardly listen to her.

"You were suffering so. God is merciful. When it's too bad, God always steps in to share the load."

God. "When was this?"

"Well, we told the ambulance people that he died at 11:30. But I don't rightly know the exact time. And you were no help."

"I guess not." Then, the question. "Do you think I killed that man, Margaret?"

She picked up her mop and pail. "Oh, dear, I don't know about that. You were certainly upset enough."

What died with Amos (youth, love, forgiveness, trust, faith) had gilded his life. "What'd we do?"

"Dear, I called the ambulance. You were no help. They came and got him, and I took the sheets and washed them. I don't know where you went." As she went back up the stairs, she said, over her shoulder, "You found the sheets, I guess. I don't usually do that kind of thing for tenants, but this one time —"

Amos was truly dead. His only memories came from a little old Irish cleaning lady who went to Mass every morning. He could hear Amos now, the only memories of my death are from a little old lady who believes in God! What a joke. Why weren't you sober, so you could tell it like it was! They were all going to die, and each one would be funny in its own way. Instead of being surrounded by his friends Amos had only the cleaning lady and a man too drunk to remember. There had been no one to hold Simon McCorkindale, either, when he died, who was survived by his wife and three children. The universal comic predicament: To be confronted, in the end, by the thing we least expect.

"I know—" It was Mrs. Lichtenthal. "—they've got you, now. They're going to use this as a motive. Your friend dies in your arms, and you are so distraught you get in your car, drunk, go to a bar (they've put you at the Hawk until 12:30), drinking yourself even more silly, sobbing in your beer that you'll never be ok again, and then get in your car again and drive to Dorchester where you kill a man. But if it comes to that, I'll have the jury so sympathetic with you for sticking with your friend dying of AIDS that they'll forgive you anything—"

Alec wanted purity, wanted to be exonerated, to know that this particular manifestation of an absurd world, this moment when two people had made a hundred choices which had resulted in both of them dying, had not proceeded from him. In the midst of all this, the soldiers came home victorious, and the picture on the screen of the starving Kurds, the fat leached from under the skin until only the universal skull remained, were replaced with pictures of the fat sleek boys disembarking from planes, tanned, handsome faces grinning, waving. Alec came home at seven in the morning after his walk across the city, sat on the sofa and watched the tv morning news, the image of the President, grinning, waving, everywhere, proclaiming triumph. Alec turned the pages of the paper and read about preparations for parades down Fifth Avenue. What Margaret had told him gave him no room to maneuver. It seemed, despite everything he wanted to believe about himself, fitting, even understandable now, that after Amos's death he had gone crazy.

Alec's mind now was drawn to images of Kevin and Sarah and Ian, to construct for them (he had never seen them) an appearance, hair, skin color, height, weight, an attitude. Since he read the obit and knew their names and ages, they had moved in on him, occupied his mind in the way that Stephen lived inside his head. Alec brooded on them, couldn't escape them and their charge, couldn't escape the hurt they were feeling that he had caused.

Anger and fear settled on Alec, and the question was no longer whether he could defend himself against the charge. It was *Tell me what I did. Don't get me off.* He prowled the museums on the other side of the fens, passed by paintings of saints suffering, a crucifix on a wall, and stared for a long time at a huge canvas whose title was *Time Revealing Truth.* He stood in the rain in front of the museum and stared at the bronze Indian on his horse, his head thrown back and his shoulders extended, his arms straight and lifted out to the side in an attitude of openness and trust, taking the rain full in the face, his arms embracing it.

Winter Rain

He imagined himself talking to Kevin and Sarah and Ian, telling them how it happened, that he had had more to drink than he had thought, that it had affected him more than he had known, and that he had killed their father, in an accident, that he hadn't meant it but that it had happened anyway, that he was an addict, that he didn't know how he had become an addict. *I killed your father.* He put his hands on Kevin's shoulder, on Sarah's shoulder, and said, I regret what I've done. The image came back to him, was persistent, the core of it, though it took different forms, sometimes it was happening now, before the trial, sometimes it was happening when the children were grown. Sometimes he imagined writing a short letter after the trial.

He was prepared now to go to jail. His stay in the furnished room would be a short one, would, in fact prepare him. He had been shackled enough now to know how that would feel (cold steel on his wrists), and he saw ahead of him years of confinement, unable to walk about the city, Summer Street into Winter Street, imprisoned in a cell, trapped inside his mind with Kevin and Sarah and Ian.

Bundled up against the cold, wrapped in his heaviest coat and sitting under a poncho against the rain, Alec sat for hours on the granite plinth of the War Memorial in the middle of the fens and played his flute. His music was composed of notes held until they became part of the landscape, part of the sounds of the city—the sirens of police cars and of ambulances, the screams of car alarms, of phones ringing at the corner—held until they were part even of the leafless trees and the frozen ground, until they seemed to cause even the cold granite to resonate.

On the weekend, he held a sale of his things, of everything he owned but the tv, his flute and four boxes of clothes. People, responding to sheets of paper he had tacked up to trees, came by and inspected what he had, picking among the books and the kitchen things and the furniture (the bed, the sofa and chairs), choosing and offering money, taking away what they wanted. He made enough to pay rent for a month, and what was left (half the books, half the kitchen things), he took down the street to a junk shop. His apartment was now empty, and for the next two nights he slept on the floor.

On the first of the month, two days away, he would take a taxi across town with his four boxes of clothes and his tv to his furnished room in South Boston. The consequence of his killing Simon McCorkindale was a permanent strangerhood. Sitting on the granite

218

plinth under his poncho, he felt it all around him. Were he to leave his perch and walk up to that man walking by, he would have to say, eventually, at some moment when the necessity was not expected, *I killed a man.* Alec watched the shoulders of this man as he went by over toward the bridge and the museums and knew that if that were one of the things he might say, it would be the only thing that mattered.

These other humans he passed on the street, or who passed his granite plinth in the fens, were innocent. Now, as he walked about the city, even the people in the black stretch limousines seemed innocent, the white middle-class men in the financial district in their dark suits, the soldiers disembarking from their airplanes to the joyous noise of bands and cheerleaders, even the President, speaking of the national triumph, seemed innocent in comparison to him, who had to say, *I killed a man.* Men commit crimes, and eventually even a man who has to say, *I killed a man,* will find the company of other men who committed crimes and form a brotherhood of criminals. There would be a brotherhood in jail. Instead of Stephen and Arabella and Gaetano and Michael coming and going from his apartment, his friends would be Alec and Richard and Gerald and Ronald and George, murderers all. He played his flute under his poncho in the rain on his plinth at the War Memorial. Was there a company of child molesters? of men who betrayed? of men who were simply careless with their lives? who turned left instead of right at the intersection for no good reason and because of that destroyed everything? From under his poncho, Alec could see crossing the fens the real dispossessed, the homeless men who stopped at trash barrels to look for empties, who were sick or crazy or drunk, who couldn't help themselves. What was ahead of him was an aloneness so profound it would be like deep space: When you scream, no one hears.

He played his flute from under his poncho, a figure so still that he might have been a part of the sculpture group on the War Memorial. Even his wet poncho had the color and sheen of bronze. For long hours on his last Sunday in the fens, he played his flute as if the long single line of notes could get at the heart of the feeling, could reach down and touch the core of his condition and cause it to vibrate. The dark notes could be heard by some person leaving the museum and walking to her car across the fens, leaving an afternoon of study, looking for meaning in seventeenth-century painting, or by a homeless man gathering empties from the trash barrels, looking for something, anything, that could be redeemed. These notes were as close as he could come to reaching himself, and their sound, though pure and soft as a mountain stream in spring, was the unclear sound of someone lost in the woods, who didn't know where he had taken a wrong turn, and didn't know the way out.

On the Monday morning, the last day in his old apartment (he would take a taxi across town this afternoon with his four boxes), suddenly, everything changed. Mrs. Lichtenthal called and said there had been a break in the case, and Alec got a letter from his father. He was reading it, standing in the middle of the floor, when the phone rang, and he was listening to her while his eyes still lingered on the page.

"Something has happened. I don't know quite what. But there is to be a hearing this morning. First there is to be another lineup. That's at 10:45. The hearing is to be at 11:30."

"What is this about?"

"I think they've found a witness who'll place you in the car. We're in trouble—"

An hour later, Alec was standing in the lineup behind the glass wall experiencing the sensation to which he had become accustomed since he had waked up on the street, of being watched by people he couldn't see. The letter had come in the expensive envelope his father affected and was recognizable even before he saw the handwriting. He had slit it open, walking back from the mailbox into the apartment, and had begun to read. *March 25, 1991 Dear Alec, You will understand by my using the term "dear" that I have some sympathy for you. I love you, in fact, as a father should. And it has grieved me to see the difficulties you have put yourself in since you reached adulthood. You have been careless with the good things given you—your education, the honored place in society provided for you, etc.—but you have hardly wanted to listen to advice. Nevertheless, I still sympathize with you. It will perhaps surprise you to know that I have long since known that you were unable to handle your liquor. But Time has a way of punishing these transgressions, of showing our faults to ourselves, giving us an opportunity to correct them. If you would see a psychiatrist, you might be able to straighten yourself out. In the meantime, it is perhaps best if we keep a certain distance between us. You will understand if time and distance prevent my comments from being more pertinent at this moment. You have often blamed me, I know, for your difficulties. But perhaps you will be willing to admit now that I am blameless, and that you have brought these things on yourself. Horace's recent difficulties are now resolved. All charges have been dropped. I have been able to aid that process by advancing Horace some small portion of the inheritance he is to come into. I wish there were something I could do for you. Sincerely, Your Father.* Alec turned left on command, and then made an about-face, watched all the while. While he stood in the lineup and felt, even if he could not see, the persons on the other side of the glass inspecting him, he thought that his father was right. It seemed so easy, what he said. Why had it been so hard? The men in the line-up were asked to step down, and Alec was taken to a small consulting room.

Half an hour later, she burst in.

Alec rose, prepared.

"Something new. There's something new!"

He was accustomed to this now, held onto the back of the chair he had just risen from to steady himself, no longer believing that things were stable. He steeled himself against what she was about to say. She threw her arms around him, then pulled back. "Be happy, Mr. Argento! You're not going to jail! They're going to drop the charges!"

The sound he made was the bleat of an ox just hit.

"None of the witnesses has been able to identify you."

"Did they—" He was trying to formulate an idea. "—exonerate me?"

"No—"

"Did they say I was innocent?"

"Well, no—"

Alec couldn't assimilate what she was saying. She had to repeat herself: The state's case collapsed when no witness could be found to place Alec at the scene of the accident. Already prepared for another outcome entirely, ready at last to know the truth, he asked dumb, faltering questions, and she answered him, becoming increasingly irritated with him for not being joyful, grateful to her for having pulled it off, for not looking already toward the future.

It was as she said. Ten minutes later, they were in the courtroom for the hearing. Alec listened to the proceedings in a daze.

221

Winter Rain

Afterwards, the only phrase he took away with him was one used by Mrs. Lichtenthal when she moved dismissal of the charges: There is no evidence to place Mr. Argento at the scene of any crime. Alec remembered this because the judge repeated it, when he dismissed the charges. *There is no evidence to place Mr. Argento at the scene of any crime.*

9

The witnesses to the hit-and-run—it turned out there were three of them—had each been unable to identify Alec as the driver of the car. No other witnesses could be found. With no identification, the state had no case. While evidence was overwhelming that the car involved in the hit-and-run was Alec's, at least four other people had keys, three of whom had been driving it on the day in question, with or without permission. Mrs. Lichtenthal had further been able to demonstrate that while prints from three people who had keys were found in the car, there was a fourth, unidentified, set. It was a distinct, an unexplored, possibility, that the car had been stolen after 11:30, the last hour anyone was able to certify that the car had been in front of Alec's apartment. In short, the evidence was hopelessly muddied and incomplete.

"Who was driving, then?" They had talked while they waited for the hearing to begin.

She laughed at him. "No one knows. The judge will agree with me that the state has no case. While you own the car, the others had almost equal access to it, and absent an identification of the driver, there is no reason to bring charges against one of you any more than one of the others. Oddly—and this muddies things even more—the state has been unable to place any of you at one o'clock. None of you, I speak here of your friend Gaetano Leoncello and Michael Colt and your son, have been able to establish alibis. Apparently, all of you were too drunk to remember what happened, and no witnesses

225

have been found. The case is a non-starter." She put her hand on his arm. "Are you happy?"

Mrs. Lichtenthal had a look of triumph. She appeared to have defeated all her enemies.

"I'm not innocent."

"You're considered innocent until proven guilty. You get that only after a trial—"

"I'm not guilty either."

"Well—you may be, but the criminal justice system has not been able to prove it."

Now they were walking down the steps of the court house into the rain. "It's a question of evidence, which in this case is inconclusive —" She dropped papers into her briefcase, fished for her keys, fumbled with her umbrella. "I'll try to get your car back. I'll call you tomorrow about that—" She found her keys. She checked her watch. She was thinking of her next appointment, her next client. "Although I'm not sure you want it back. They say the accident was very messy. The body, I'm told, was dismembered. There was an horrendous amount of blood. Perhaps it's a good thing you don't remember—" Then she was gone, down the steps and into her car, leaving Alec on the stone landing in front of the court house, uncertain what to do or where to go.

He sat down on the wet granite steps and let the rain come down on him. *I'll die in the rain.* At one point he had wanted to live in the Southwest, where it was hot and dry, and now he couldn't remember why that had never happened. A decision he had thought was still in the future was in the past. One day he knew that he would live here always. The rain was coming down on him in big, hard drops, and there was no sign that it would pass. It was after one, and he had nothing to do. Sometime today he had to go home, get his boxes, take his taxi. After that, he would have nothing to do. Today was Monday, and he didn't have to go to work until Wednesday.

The people passing by on the sidewalk were hurrying to their appointments. They passed the shops, walked under the signs, weaved in and out past each other along the pavement, their faces closed against the cold and the rain—and each other. He sat on a step, his legs spread, an elbow resting on each knee, held his hands together, and watched the scene. The rain came down on the building fronts, on the signs, on the glass windows and the coin boxes. It soaked the pavement and the people walking on the pavement. It fell on metal and glass and stone and asphalt, through the air, on cloth and skin. It fell, wetting everything, and then ran off through the downspouts and drains and sewers, back into the earth.

Alec waited on the steps. Then he stood up and walked down to the sidewalk, hesitated, then turned right and walked through the rain, the thing coming down on his head and wetting his hair and his scalp, running down his face into his eyes and down his cheeks. It ran down his neck under his coat and wet his skin on his shoulders and chest and back. He walked down the street. At an intersection, he turned right again, and, after several blocks, turned left. For an hour, he walked across the city, moving slowly through the crowds of people on the sidewalk, feeling them moving around him, past him, breaking on
him like water in a stream over a rock. He shuffled, and he bumped into pedestrians. When he turned, at an intersection, right or left, it might as well have been left or right. All ways were the same.

In the coin boxes, the papers carried a large photograph showing yesterday's victory march down Fifth Avenue for the returning troops. Storefronts were decorated with yellow ribbons, and, in the store windows, TV screens showed images of the President, grinning crookedly, giving a thumbs-up signal. Alec passed through shopping districts, subway stations, business districts, warehouse districts, through more shopping districts and business districts, through the financial district and the downtown crossing, up Summer street into Winter street.

Everywhere, he passed the homeless, men and women whose faces showed continuous pain. They clustered around the subway entrances and on corners, a dirty, hopeless gang, the needy preying on those who were not needy, on those who have been needy, or are not needy at this moment, or not yet needy. They left Alec alone. As he moved through district after district, the people were the same, the ones getting into their limousines and carrying their briefcases and shopping and the ones on the street.

Alec's father had been rich, poor, was rich again. A mysterious investment. He explained that he held steadfast to his principles. Alec's father's letter, which Alec had, folded in his jacket pocket, carried the tone of all of his communications, caused the same rage in Alec that his life had caused him. His father, in his certainties, knew nothing of it. Alec floated through a city, through the rain, in which everything was in flux, nothing clear or certain, unable to find a mooring.

Alec's anger at being adrift made it difficult to think. *I have to decide what to do*, but he could not get beyond—go back to the fens, get my things, get a taxi—before his mind floated free again. He would turn another corner, take himself off to the right, pass the coin boxes with the newspaper picture of the parade. He saw older newspapers in the trash along the streets with other pictures —of the Kurds on their hillside, in the process of being forgotten.

Alec was tired. It was just before two. He had gotten two hours sleep. Kevin and Sarah and Ian would be perplexed, unable to understand what had happened, and, when they were older, they would be angry. Susan McClintock McCorkindale had already arrived at that feeling. Alec was angry too, and confused, and his feelings expressed themselves in his wanting to hit someone. He wanted to hit Mrs. Lichtenthal.

Alec was on Beacon Hill. He stood in front of the State House for a few minutes taking in the certainties of Federal architecture. He turned left on Bowdoin street through the district of state and federal office buildings. His aimless wandering about the city, unable to be still, unable to conceive of a goal, brought him past all the centers of government, and through gangs of the homeless. From near the top of the hill, through the gray torn curtain of the rain, he could see the Tobin Bridge, the expressways along the waterfront, the train tracks.

All streets lead to the bottom of the hill, and Alec ended up on the Esplanade, going upstream on the Charles river. The ground was slushy, the walkways puddled, and the rain came across the river from Cambridge in heavy waves, causing the water to look like brushed steel.

Alec passed the Hatch Shell and crossed one of the small ornamental bridges across the lagoon, then followed the path along the water's edge, going west. He left a grove of trees, looked ahead to an expanse of lawn along the water and another grove of trees which contained a giant willow, now blown in the wind. In the rain at this time of year, the Esplanade was deserted. He had become accustomed to being alone with his thoughts and no longer had the impulse to get to a phone. The people who hadn't moved asked pointed questions.

Occasionally, Alec was passed by a runner or by someone on a bike, wrapped in a poncho against the rain, showing bare legs

228

pumping furiously. From this vantage, he could see the whole of the back side of the row of buildings on Beacon street. He imagined the life beyond a particular window. Then, because he was walking west, his attention was drawn to a new window in a new building. The pressure of the movement of both their lives had caused Michael and him to separate: they had been together for a time, and then their separate movements forward at different speeds had disconnected them.

The helplessness he felt—and his anger—settled on him. Not to know. It was this which separated him from his father, his father's blind certainty. He knew what he felt for him: contempt. The view on the world was opaque, like windows in a john.

Then, he knew the voice before he saw the face.

Stephen. It was behind him.

"Dad?"

Stephen straddled his bike, his feet now on the ground, wearing a nylon running suit with a hood. His face and hands were the only parts of him that showed.

"I almost ran you down—"

Alec, holding his breath, bit his lip.

"—then I saw it was you."

Alec didn't know what to say. He smiled. He knew it wasn't a clear smile, but it was all he could do.

Stephen pushed his bike forward a few feet, swinging his legs. They were going in the same direction. Alec turned and walked beside him. Stephen's face was wet with the rain. It formed in drops on his eyelashes and on the tip of his nose. He carried a satchel over his shoulder.

"You're working?"

"Yeah. I'm on till four."

"You're taking the scenic route."

He laughed. "Yeah. It's a slow day."

"Are you making enough?"

"I get by." Then he said, "Yeah, it's enough."

Their conversation, these questions and answers, was slow and quiet and contained long pauses. At the willow tree, Stephen stopped, and Alec stopped with him. They stared at the water for a while, this great gulf between them.

"How's it going with the police?"

"I've just come from there—" Alec wished he had something else to say.

"What happened?"

"The charges were dropped." He looked at, but he didn't want to see, Stephen's face. "They didn't have enough evidence." He looked away.

They both surveyed the other side of the river, the heavy, solid, graceless domes of MIT, and the hotels. Far ahead of them, crossing the river to Cambridge, was the Mass Avenue bridge. Seen through the rain, its edges were blurred. It seemed to be fading away in the rain.

Finally Stephen spoke. "I don't know what to say."

Alec grimaced. "I don't either." He didn't have anything to say. There was no evidence. They watched the rain, silently. He wanted this to be over. Finally, he gestured toward the path, and they started off again, moving out from under the willow's drooping branches into the rain again. He looked ahead, not at Stephen, at the next stretch of open lawn, and, far ahead. He saw the water and the rain roughing it up, turning it dull gray. Finally, he spoke out of a need to be explicit, to tie something down, to express something which was true. "I don't know if I did it."

Stephen was silent beside him.

They passed one of the footbridges across Storrow Drive and measured their progress by the distance to the Prudential building.

He elaborated. "I could have. I was drunk enough. I was in blackout for three or four days, before I was arrested."

It didn't matter that Stephen was not saying anything. It was ok, just if he had a chance to talk.

"I had the time. It was my car." He was saying things that were true and didn't require Arabella's explanation or a jury's agreement.

The gears in the bike's wheels made soft clicks.

"But I don't know." They stepped around a puddle, one to each side, and then rejoined. "My lawyer said it was conceivable the car was stolen." He settled his coat up around his shoulders. "That's possible." He looked ahead. "Barely conceivable."

Stephen had put one foot on a pedal and was swinging his other leg, pushing himself forward.

"I think about his children all the time. He had three. They're small. Two boys and a little girl."

The wind blew the branches of the trees above them, causing a secondary rainfall, "Someday—" He didn't complete the thought. He didn't know what he would do someday. As they walked, they listened to the click and hiss of the branches and the rain.

"I think about Michael, too." He dug his hands in his pockets and hunched his shoulders. "Do you know how he is?"

"Last time I heard he was ok." Stephen swung his leg. "He and Gaetano are going out now, I think."

He fingered his change. "I thought they
would." "They're enjoying Gaetano's money."

"Right."

He had hurt Michael. He had gotten so wrapped up in Amos that Michael had gotten lost.

"I heard about Amos."

They had fondled one another in the dark room.

"I'm sorry."

He had been in love with Amos, even after he was in love with Michael.

They came to a place where a small lagoon was formed by protective arms of lawn. Here there were ornamental gateposts of stone and stone steps down to the water, much weathered and worn. It was a place where a ceremonial barge carrying an important personage might land.

"Arabella told me what you told her, about me molesting you."
They had stopped and were looking down the steps to the water.
Trash, paper and empty cans floating in the water had blown up against them.

"What did I do?" What did I do with my hands? He felt the hot, stinging blows on his buttocks—the memory was as fresh as this morning—but he couldn't recall whose hand had administered the slaps, Michael's or his father's or Amos's. He could feel the stinging in the palm of his hand, too, the buttocks raised to receive them.

The water, blown by the wind against the stone steps, splashed and gurgled.

"I don't know."
A person the city wanted to honor might come ashore here,
from a riverboat, having received the cheers of the people from
the banks.

"I don't remember."

They walked on. The Esplanade in this district was planted thick with trees, which afforded no protection from the rain and poured it on Alec and Stephen.

"I think it happened. My therapist says it must have happened because of the way I am now. He's trying to help me find the memories—"

"Do you remember anything?"

"Uh-uh."

They were even, now, with the Prudential Building. The trees hid the buildings in the Back Bay from them, and from here, in addition to the sound of the water, the hiss of the rain on the surface of the river and the soft click of Stephen's bike, they heard the traffic in Storrow Drive, the high whine of low pressure rubber on wet asphalt.

"I don't remember, either. I've thought about it, but I don't remember anything. I've tried to remember how it was when you were small—" An ambulance, something with a siren, went by and drowned out his thoughts. "I used to think I couldn't do such a thing." It changes your view, when you think I could have done such a thing. "Do you want to talk about it?"

"No."

They passed a wooden dock and saw, out in the river, a lone sculler. He watched the city, fading. "Are you ok?"

"I'm ok."

Alec wanted to say something else. "Did you get your things?"

"Yeah."

Alec was ready for this to be over.

"How's your granddad?"

Stephen smiled. "Ok. Getting old—"

"He is old—"

"I guess. He's been all wrapped up in Horace's shit—"

"What?"

"Well, you know." He laughed. "I think they bought off the prosecutor." He paused. "Bernice is horrible."

The Mass Avenue bridge was ahead of them. As they came up to it, it began to shut out the sky. From down by the water, it brooded over the river and the path like a giant bird. Here, under the bridge, the path and Storrow Drive were squeezed together, and the noise echoed off the concrete pilings.

"Are you drinking?" Stephen had to shout.

Alec shook his head.

Stephen looked at him and smiled, tentatively.

They stood under the bridge for a while, hearing the thump of the traffic over their heads and the pneumatic whine of the traffic on Storrow, and underneath it the slaps of the wavelets against the bridge pilings.

"Look, Stephen—" He had to do it. There was no way around it.

Stephen looked at him, almost smiling, waiting, almost apprehensive.

"I'm sorry."

Stephen grimaced, frowned, looked a little impatient, turned his head away, as if *Oh, that, that's nothing*.

Alec had to say it even if none of the things that had to be known were known. This had to be said even if nothing else were said or known.

"I'm sorry. I didn't mean to. I regret it now. I wish it hadn't happened." He said the things, one after the other, like hitting a nail with a hammer.

Stephen pushed his chin up and smiled—or it could have been a frown, it was so twisted, it was hard to tell—and looked at his watch.

Then he was gone. He had said something—Alec thought it was, *I've got to go*—but he couldn't hear. He gave a kind of nod and pushed off his bike and pedaled up the ramp to the bridge, not looking back. Alec leaned on the railing and watched him go up, watched his back and his furiously pedaling legs, until he turned and was gone. He wanted to shout to him to come back, there was more to say, but there wasn't more to say, and Stephen was gone.

Alec considered going up on the bridge. From there he would be able to lean on the railing and watch the water, feel the rain at his back and see it sweeping across the basin toward Beacon Hill, across the rough water. The view would be only partial. The rain obscured the city. The tops of the Hancock building and the Prudential building were in the clouds, and nothing could be seen of the buildings in the financial district behind Beacon Hill. The city was fading from view.

I'm OK. Stephen was his blood. He was his own flesh and blood. Looking at him, Alec saw himself thirty years before, the set of the shoulders, the swing of the hips, the same resentment. He had wanted to touch Stephen, his arm, the nylon cloth on his arm, even just to shake his hand before he left. But he had left quickly, and Alec had not thought it was OK to ask. He leaned on the railing, the

233

huge bridge above him, the darkened sky over all, everything fading into nothingness. It was hard to know what to do, how to be. Things were hard, and at the same time insubstantial. The cars overhead made thumping noises crossing the bridge. Stephen's bike. In the whole grid of the city.

Alec's heart beat in his chest. He was tired. He felt old. He considered going up on the bridge. It had grown dark, and after a while, he took a deep breath, felt his lungs, and walked on up the path. He felt immensely older, with a distant view of things, a view from across the river, or even from the top of a building, a view obscured, even impeded, by the rain. Stephen had taken something of him with him when he left. Like the greatest events —the explosion of stars and all things spiritual—his transformation was happening in silence. On the way to the fens, he bought a paper. The latest figures were in: ninety thousand Kurds had died in the aftermath of the Gulf War while they waited for us to help them, and, under the headline, Accidental Death, was a story about a small boy waiting for a school bus, killed by a stray bullet from a shootout down the street.

Boston, Massachusetts
September 1990—July 1992

www.ingramcontent.com/pod-product-compliance
Lightning Source LLC
Chambersburg PA
CBHW030537030726
47495CB00004B/1026

* 9 7 8 0 9 7 6 4 0 4 3 6 1 *